This Broken World

Also by Eric R. Asher

Keep track of Eric's new releases by receiving an email on release day. It's fast and easy to sign up for Eric's mailing list, and you'll also get an ebook copy of the subscriber exclusive anthology, *Whispers of War.*
Go here to get started: www.ericrasher.com

The Steamborn Trilogy:

Steamborn
Steamforged
Steamsworn

The Vesik Series:
(Recommended for Ages 17+)

Days Gone Bad
Wolves and the River of Stone
Winter's Demon
This Broken World
Destroyer Rising
Rattle the Bones
Witch Queen's War – coming fall 2017*

*Want to receive an email on the day this book releases? Sign up for Eric's mailing list.
www.ericrasher.com

Mason Dixon – Monster Hunter:

Episode One
Episode Two – coming summer 2017*

*Want to receive an email on the day this book releases? Sign up for Eric's mailing list.

This Broken World

Eric R. Asher

Edited by Laura Matheson
Cover typography by Indie Solutions by Murphy Rae
Cover design ©Phatpuppyart.com – Claudia McKinney

Deep, meaningful dedication goes here. Don't forget to update this. Seriously, or you'll look like an idiot.

~

Acknowledgements

Book four? As in the number four? How in the world did that happen? As always, thank you to all of Damian's fans. Without you, I'd just be talking to myself. It wouldn't be all that unusual I suppose, but thank you all very much for making me look a little less crazy.

An enthusiastic thank you goes to my beta readers: Amy Cameron, Jason Cameron, Angela Shafer, Vicki Rose Stewart, and Ron Asher.

Thanks to the Critters.org workshop and their superb critiques.

Thank you to The Patrons of Death's Door.

Thank you to my editor, Laura Matheson, who kindly—and occasionally with great sarcasm—saved me from that oh-so-treacherous sea of grammar.

CHAPTER ONE

I STARED AT the man sitting across the table from me. Shiawase. Happy. He sipped from his cast iron teacup and settled into the overstuffed leather chair. The old samurai armor he wore was surprisingly quiet. Shelves of old books stretched across the room behind him, scraping the ceiling and accumulating dust from the floor up. Philip Pinkerton's black journal thumped as I dropped it onto the walnut table between us. Its brittle pages were swollen with a thousand dark things I wished I could scrub from my eyes.

"There are things you do not know," Happy said. He glanced down at the journal.

"Why did Zola tell me you'd know about this?"

"It is a long story. We do not have the time."

"Shorten it."

He took another sip and his lips curled up in a smile. "I was one of you, before I became a Guardian. I was a necromancer, one of Anubis's sons."

I picked up the journal and flipped to the last yellowed page. A musty scent pungent enough to tingle my nose over the roomful of old books rolled out of the journal. A translation was written there, a translation of the runes on Philip's hand of glory.

To the youngest brother.

I set the journal back on the table with the words facing Happy.

He simply nodded. "And so it came to you."

"Explain to me how that is possible," I said, and though my voice was quiet, I couldn't prevent the violence behind the words.

Happy set his teacup down and rested his hands on his lap. "I am sorry my friend, but you are one of the Sons of Anubis."

"Ezekiel," I said, digging my fingernails into my palms.

"In this time, yes, but he bore the name Anubis for many more years."

"Why didn't Zola tell me?"

"She did not know. I only told her when the war began."

I rubbed my face and blew out a breath. "It's not a war yet."

"It is," Happy said. "The first salvo, the first sword, the first death have borne fruit."

"What the hell does that even mean?" I muttered. "At least you made sense when you were just a damn bear."

Happy laughed. "I am still a bear, and a man, and I am neither."

I groaned. "Scratching you behind the ears is going to seem very wrong."

"I rather enjoy a good scratching. I must confess, Vicky has the scratching down better than any of you mortals."

I stared at the man who was a bear, is a bear. Whatever.

"She is safe with us," Happy said. "Aeros and I would both die to protect her."

"Gurges could have killed Aeros," I said, remembering that

titan of wind and debris. The fight left Aeros wounded, an Old God bleeding molten rock. "He killed Cassie."

Happy's smile faded and he ran his hand over his topknot. "She was a good friend. I spoke to her most nights in the park." He frowned and drained his teacup. "She was a friend of Gwynn ap Nudd." His dark eyes met my own. "This is war."

I caught a flicker of motion in the corner of my vision. At the far end of the aisle, Bubbles and Peanut had their heads resting on the top step, bristly green ears pricked forward like they were listening to every word we spoke. I saw Foster land on the low shelf to my left, slowly shifting his black-and-white atlas moth wings, but I didn't acknowledge him. There was a question I still had to ask, a question that was trying to eat its way out of my brain, and I dreaded the answer.

"Who are my parents?"

"Dimitry and Andi are your parents," Happy said.

"Damn straight," Foster said. He plopped down on the edge of the bookshelf, sword across his lap.

"Think of it as …" Happy paused and frowned a little. "Think of it as an adoption. You have to understand, the bloodline of Anubis is complicated. Every so often, with hundreds of years in between, his descendants have a child. A son. That child is born with the gifts of the dead, and is as much a son of Anubis as a son of the parents who birthed him."

"So my mom," I said, "is my mom?"

"Yes."

"There is more you do not know." Happy leaned forward. "I knew your great grandfather, Hinrik."

Foster let out a low whistle.

"Where?" I asked. Hinrik was my great, great, several times over, grandfather. "When?"

"I have been dead, or not alive in the traditional sense, for centuries. I was at Stones River when he defeated Prosperine. The Watchers speak of him as a dark necromancer. Let me tell you, it is a thin line between you and the dark. Seeing the things Hinrik did, the good he did, the people he saved. I wonder … how much of that moniker is merely a stigma?"

I thought about Happy's words. What he was saying, and what he really meant.

"Most of the Fae believe Zola walks in the dark," Happy said. "You've met the Old Man. He is a demon among men who has slaughtered thousands. I would argue no one has died at his hand, outside of a war, that did not deserve it."

Happy refilled his teacup.

"It is a thin line."

I finished off my own tea—the sweet taste of chai lost in the bitterness of my thoughts—and set the cup down on the table with a heavy thud. "Koda, from the Society of Flame, said the same thing to me once."

Happy nodded. "He is a wise old ghost."

I heard raised voices echoing up the staircase. A growl shook the floor, and then Bubbles and Peanut vanished down the stairs. Someone began shouting, and it took me a moment to realize it was Frank, his voice muted by the shelves of books around us.

"I said to leave. We don't have anything to say to you!"

A woman's voice grew equally loud. "It is our right to ask you about that video. Now, I could clearly see your store in the video's background, so tell me what happened."

"You're the press, not the police, now leave."

I glanced up at Foster and we both said "Shit" at the same time.

CHAPTER TWO

T HE LEAKED VIDEO had gotten completely out of hand. Not even the Watchers had been able to stop it once it went viral. Ezekiel killing off their strongest Mage Machina didn't help. At least once per day, some brave reporter would come barging through our front door. They thought they'd either be the ones to expose the hoax, or they'd be the ones to prove magic was real.

Who would have thought the world would be so interested in the fight between a necromancer and a blood mage? Then there was Ashley's little display with the cloud of doom. Most magic didn't show up on film, but I'll be damned if the camera didn't catch every second of that cloud exploding from her shattered runes. Metal and stone had vanished in a crack of thunder, and the dirt beneath the cobblestone street had been laid bare.

"Get. Out." Frank's voice was eerily calm. I could see Bubbles and Peanut beneath the door, sitting at his feet.

"Those dogs are huge," she said, and I knew she was staring at the cu siths. The reporter had no idea she was one bad move away from being lunch. She turned her attention back to Frank. "You can't just—" the reporter began.

I slammed the saloon-style doors open and glared at the woman. She was short, maybe five foot two, and her dark eyes

ERIC R. ASHER

met my gaze without flinching.

"You!" she said, her mouth twisting into a wild grin. "You were in the video!" She ran at me, holding her phone out with what I guessed was a microphone sticking out of one of the ports.

"I'm with Channel Six. Can we get a quote? Tell us what you saw. What do you think really happened? Do you think people are right when they say magic is real? Wizards have been among us since the beginning? Hiding in plain sight?"

I was somewhat surprised at how much she had right. I guess video evidence is enough to persuade some folks.

Then she started with the craziness.

"How do you feel about the government task force that's rumored to be investigating the incident?"

"A government what?" I said as the sheer horror of that possibility dawned on me.

"Or the suspicion that we witnessed a failed terrorist strike? Right here in Saint Charles? Did you know the terrorists? Are you involved? Are you a terrorist?"

The fire left me and I just stared at the woman.

"Well?"

"Miss … what is your name?"

"Emily Beckers."

"Can you please turn that off?" I asked, gesturing to the microphone.

"No, it's my right to …" she trailed off and stared at what was left of her microphone. Its foam top lay on the floor, cleanly severed by a fairy sword strike she couldn't have seen.

"You need to get her out of here," Foster said before sheathing his sword.

"Call Edgar," I said to Frank. He was on the phone in a heartbeat. "Emily, walk with me." I picked up the severed microphone and placed it in her hand.

She looked up at me and blinked. "Did you do that?"

"Break your microphone? No."

I started toward the front door, up an aisle filled with feathers and mortar and pestles. She followed.

"Now, I think it's pretty obvious that video was a hoax, don't you?"

"I …" she said, tucking the phone back into her purse. "No, I've seen too much. The video is just the evidence I need to prove it. To prove I'm not crazy."

The bell on the front door jingled as a man in a bowler and a three-piece suit crossed the threshold. Emily glanced at him and he smiled.

"Emily!" Edgar said, as bright and cheery as I'd ever heard him. "How are you, my old friend?"

She looked at him, confusion obvious on her face.

"Let me help you remember," he said. I couldn't turn away as the Watcher's hands latched on to either side of Emily's head. I didn't hear the incantation, but his hands glowed. The tail of some tattooed beast snaked its way out from the edge of Emily's collar as Edgar permanently rearranged her brain.

His face fell. "No. That can't be." He looked up at me. "Did she tell you about the task force?"

I nodded.

"Gods, she heard it from her brother. He's a Homeland Security agent."

Another Watcher trailed in behind Edgar after he finished speaking to someone outside the front door. Edgar lifted Emily and set her into the other Watcher's arms.

"That's her van outside. Get her home."

The other Watcher nodded and carried the reporter out of the shop.

Happy pushed the doors open from the back room and nodded at Edgar. The samurai walked slowly around the counters. He stopped to scratch the cu siths behind the ears when they came running over to him from their post beside Frank.

"Shiawase," Edgar said. "You are truly here."

"Ra," Happy said. He traded grips with Edgar. "Surely you knew it was me all these years."

Edgar shook his head. "I didn't. We will have to get reacquainted another time."

Happy caressed the sword sheathed at his side and smiled slowly. "That would be most welcome. You spar like no other."

"Uh, guys?" I said. "Reporter, government death squad, impending Fae exposure?"

"That sounds dirty," Foster said.

Edgar actually smiled. We really were doomed.

"Though it pains me to say it," Edgar said, "Vesik is right. Our community can't ignore the threat of war. Damian, we'll need you to talk to the wolves. Of all of us, they trust you the most."

Happy and I both nodded in silent agreement.

"Cara and Aideen are already in Falias," Foster said. "They're helping with the cleanup as much as they can. It's only a matter of time before the King calls for the Concilium Belli."

"Gwynn ap Nudd will go to war with Ezekiel," Edgar said. "I don't know if he realizes we may soon be at war with humanity."

I shuddered. "It can't come to that."

"It might," Edgar said.

"It can't," I said. "We can't let that happen."

"What humanity fears, it exterminates," Happy said. "This has been true for as many years as I can recall."

"There are a lot of people that think the video is proof of our world," Foster said. "What happens when something else gets captured on film? When the wrong person receives the Sight?"

"I would be more concerned about Ezekiel exposing us unintentionally," Edgar said. "He intends to kill the world. He doesn't need to keep secrets from a people he expects to kill."

"You have to stop him," Frank said.

We all turned to look at him as he sat on the stool behind the register. I'd have expected him to shrink away from the gaze of the samurai and the sun-god. Instead, he leaned forward.

"No one else can stop Ezekiel," he said. "Even Zola says so. You have to stop him. For Sam," he said as he looked at me, "and for Vicky." He locked his gaze onto Happy as he said Vicky's name.

Happy's hand tightened around his sword and he gave Frank a small nod.

"Frank is right," Edgar said. He drummed his fingers on a shelf and glanced up at me. "It's a simple concept, but we are outmatched."

"Outmatched?" I said. "We have the Watchers on our side. How can we lose?"

Edgar took his bowler off and I saw the bags under his eyes

for the first time. His sandy skin was pale, and sweat stained the collar of his shirt. "The Watchers are falling apart, Damian. The damage Ezekiel did to us was more than I realized. Some of our most powerful members have fled to Faerie. Others have vanished to God knows where."

"What?"

"There has been a rift for many years. Centuries, in fact. The Watchers have always been formed from the strongest practitioners of every art you can imagine. Some of us have been called gods, some devils."

"And?" I asked.

His fingers circled the brim of his bowler and he stared at the hat as he spoke. "I wonder if the wrong Watchers were sent to secure the video."

"The wrong Watchers?" Happy asked.

Edgar nodded. "You remember James. He would have killed us all to please Ezekiel and Philip had Zola not …" He glanced between the three of us. "Had she not taken care of him. He could have worked his way back through his chain of command. Secrecy has been so paramount, we might not have realized what was happening." He looked up at me again. "Some of us no longer wish to hide in the shadows."

CHAPTER THREE

I CLOSED THE door to my '32 Ford Victoria. I'd always called the car Vicky, but Happy's little ghost was calling herself Vicky, so it felt strange to call the car by its nickname. I started the car and the engine roared to life.

"Howell Island," Foster said from his perch on the dashboard.

I sighed and nodded as we rattled off the cobblestones of Main Street, Saint Charles, leaving Happy and Edgar behind before zipping up the modern asphalt.

I felt a tug on my senses a moment before I realized we had a stowaway. Foster's hand jumped to his sword. I glanced behind me as my Sight came into focus.

"Eavesdropping?" I asked casually.

"Not at all," Carter said from the backseat.

Foster blew out a breath and relaxed as soon as he realized it was Carter.

"You've never been to a pack council before," Carter said.

"This isn't an invitation I could say no to, even if I wanted."

"No, it is not."

"You'll tell me if I use the wrong fork, right?"

I glanced over my shoulder. Carter's disapproving look was the same as it had in life, but his body was all warm, golden light. He had the same scruffy beard, strong chin, and brilliant sunburst irises.

"Hugh is a strong wolf," Carter said, "but the night is still likely to be violent. Wolves don't do well with change, especially rapid change."

"Good to see you too," I said. I changed lanes and asked, "How's Vicky?"

The kid was running with a group of wolves that called themselves the Ghost Pack. They harrowed the Burning Lands, rescuing some, and destroying anything in their way.

"She's good," Carter said. "Her strength grows more every day."

"You're looking pretty solid yourself," Foster said. "I can barely even see through you right now."

Carter held his hand up to his eyes and nodded slowly. "We seem to become more solid as new members join the Ghost Pack."

I nodded. "I can feel it when you rescue a new wolf. Not like I can hear your voices or anything, I just know there's a new member in your merry band of misfits."

Carter grinned, revealing a row of teeth slightly too sharp to be human. "Pack magic."

I still wasn't sure what the pack magic would let us do. I could guide ley line energy into Carter and his wife Maggie, and they would become visible to the other pack members, but that was really the most useful thing we'd found so far. Werewolves adopting a necromancer wasn't exactly standard operating procedure.

"I still can't speak to Hugh without your help," Carter said.

"You want to make an appearance tonight?" I asked.

I caught Carter's nod in my peripheral vision.

I knew he didn't just want to talk to Hugh. He wanted to speak to the entire council. There were going to be other packs there. Hugh had told me there were still some wolves who wanted to devour me whole. I avoided the topic for the time being. "How's Maggie?"

He let out a slow laugh. "Vicious, loving, destructive. She's quite well."

I grinned and swung onto Highway 40 for a few minutes. "Is she coming tonight?"

"Can you bring another over?" Carter asked, his voice rising in pitch with the curiosity in his voice.

"I have help."

"What?"

"Don't worry about it," I said.

"Oh, sure," Foster said. "Damian's the last guy you should listen to when he says 'Don't worry about it.' "

"I've noticed," Carter said.

"Be nice, or no one gets a pretzel," I said.

"I can't eat pretzels anymore."

"No problem." I shot a smirk over my shoulder. "I'll eat yours."

✦   ✦   ✦

I PULLED ONTO the grass outside the entrance to Howell Island. The small parking lot was overflowing with vehicles. Motorcycles and vans sat between sports cars that cost more than I'd make in a lifetime.

I grabbed the focus and slid it into the loop on my belt. It was the hilt of an old Scottish claymore. No blade protruded between the sloping arms that ended in quatrefoils. Small holes spiraled up the grip, channels for an aura, and power beyond anything a mere aural blade could conjure.

"Illinois, Iowa, Kentucky, Ohio, Maryland," Carter said as we walked by the closest cars. He stopped and grabbed my arm. "Damian, Hugh would not have invited so many packs."

"He made it an open invitation," I said.

"Yep," Foster said. He hovered above Carter's shoulder. "Bring your friends. It's gonna be a party."

"Or a death march," Carter muttered.

"Maybe you'll be adding to the ranks of the Ghost Pack tonight, eh?" I said. I slapped him on the shoulder hard enough to cause him to stumble.

"Sometimes I forget you can still hit me."

"Don't feel too bad. You can still hit me a lot harder."

Snarls echoed through the night, rolling over the levee that separated us from the island.

"Let's move," Foster said. He zipped out in front of us.

Carter and I broke into a slight jog. We moved quickly through the trail. I swung right at the old tree I could now recognize blindfolded. Hugh had given me some explanation about the spirit of the island living within the old oak. All I knew was that ley line energy pooled around it in electric blue arcs, which I could follow straight to the pack.

I could hear the rush of the river and smell the wet earth surrounding us. I deliberately stomped on some thick twigs and branches as we closed on the gathering ground. Surprising werewolves was a good way to get dead fast.

"Holy. Shit." Foster hovered at the edge of the gathered crowd. There may have been over a hundred wolves, some separated into small groups, the largest being the River Pack. I was sure the others were out-of-town packs. I recognized no one outside of the River Pack.

Hugh stood near the edge of the earthen platform with Haka, his son. Below them, an alpha had another wolf pinned beneath his right foot. I knew he was an alpha because the shifted wolf couldn't budge him, despite his snarls and muscles and claws.

The alpha leaned forward, moonlight glinting off his Spanish features, and captured the gaze of the downed wolf. "You will be silent. This is beyond any meaningless grudge you have with their dead alpha."

My eyebrows rose and I glanced at Carter.

"Jackson." He said nothing more, only stared at the pinned wolf.

"He fought for Philip," Foster said, "against us at Cromlech Glen."

"I killed his brother," Carter said without emotion.

I rubbed my right hand across my stubble and inhaled loudly through my nose. Half the wolves turned toward us at that exaggerated breath.

"Welcome, Damian," Hugh said. "Guardian of the Piasa Bird. You honor us." He gave a slight bow to Foster as the fairy glided over the heads of the gathered wolves.

Whispers crawled through the gathering.

Necromancer ...

Devil ...

Murderer ...

They left out sarcastic bastard. Some people can be so inconsiderate.

"You expect us to ally with a monster," the other alpha said.

Jackson was no longer under his foot, but restrained by two larger wolves behind the alpha.

Hugh shook his head slowly. "I expect you to ally with the River Pack, with all of the gathered packs. There is a war coming. A war we cannot survive alone."

"We have been hunted for centuries," said a strong female voice off to my right. "There is no reason to ally ourselves with evil due to some new, undefined threat."

"Not so undefined, Caroline," Hugh said.

Carter filled me in as they continued speaking. "Caroline is the alpha of the Irish Brigade."

I eyed him. "That's an odd name for a pack."

Carter nodded. "It's exactly what you're thinking. They've been around since the Civil War."

"Christ," I muttered. "Antietam?"

"Yes."

Caroline. A new name on my list of people with whom we do not fuck.

"If we meet Ezekiel at Gettysburg—"

"We'll be close to her home turf," I said.

Hugh laid out the entire problem for Caroline and the gathered wolves. Ezekiel would not stop until our world was ash, ravaged and sown into oblivion by the eldritch things and the Old Gods.

"The death of Ezekiel will break one of the Seals and mark the return of the dark-touched," Hugh said.

The Spaniard exhaled. "Please. Children's stories. There are no such creatures."

Hugh turned to the wolf slowly. "No such creatures? You have not ridden beside the might of Camazotz on the blackest night and seen him cower before the touch of the noonday sun."

"Even if that were true," Caroline said, "what reason would we have to ally ourselves with a necromancer? A necromancer!" Her voice rose, violence crackling along the edge of her words. Her hands formed fists at her sides.

"He is a direct contact with the Ghost Pack."

"More stories," the Spaniard said. "Lies to keep your wolves submissive."

Hugh gestured for me to join him on the slightly raised earth that acted as a small stage.

"Brothers," Hugh said. "Believe what you will. Allow me to make this abundantly clear. An attack on Damian Valdis Vesik is a strike against us all. A strike against everything we are." He reached out, tore the left sleeve off my shirt, and held up my arm.

"Another shirt?" I said under my breath.

The shiny, hooked line of scars that marked me as pack glinted in the moonlight.

Cries of outrage and awe mixed into a riot of sound. I didn't think the wolves would even hear what came next, but Hugh projected his voice with a volume and authority I'd never heard him use.

"Damian Valdis Vesik is pack! He is our brother! He is under our protection, and any move against him will be met with force." His words fell like an anvil.

Silence smothered the clearing. Whispers competed with the hoot of an owl and the rush of the river behind us.

"We must fight as one," Hugh said. His arms stretched toward the gathering and he held his palms out. "Without each other, we cannot survive."

"You grow weak, Hugh," the Spaniard said. "Alpha of the River Pack. You allow a lowly necromancer to lead you around by the nose. You should be devoured by your own kind."

A quiet rumbling started on the left side of gathering. Snarls erupted down the center between the River Pack and their closest adversaries. A small flurry of light fighting broke out across the line.

"You know nothing of what you speak," Hugh said. His voice quieted the gallery of wolves. "Damian is an instrument of change. He may be the only instrument that helps us survive the coming war."

The Spaniard barked. "We are the wolves of war. War is our home." He smashed his fist into his chest with enough force to shatter a human ribcage.

"We are not gorillas," Hugh said, a hint of a frown crossing his face. "I would like you to hear our old alpha's thoughts on the matter."

"Your old alpha is dead. Carter was just as weak as you. I should have ripped his sniveling head from his shoulders and devoured his body."

"Gross, man," I said. "Just gross."

The wolf turned his head to me slowly. There was nothing human left in his face. His eyes were completely lost in their swollen irises. His teeth were elongated, and his face was drawn out far past human proportions.

"Damian," Hugh said. It was both a warning, and my cue.

I nodded as I slid the focus from my belt. "Play time's over, pup." The wolf knew what it was. Some stories travelled faster than others. The story of how I killed a demon had travelled very fast. The Spaniard stepped away. I flashed him the most psychotic smile I could muster. I flipped the focus into the air, and before it could land, I channeled.

My aura leapt to the old claymore hilt and spiraled through the focus. A deep red blade shot into the ground, occasional bursts of yellow and blue light firing around it as it suspended the hilt in the air. I slowly curled my right hand into a fist. Each finger felt like it was battling against a rigid spring as I drew on the lines. My scream was quiet at first, as I slowly pulled more energy from the ley line beneath me. It grew primal as my arm began to shake, and some of the wolves backed further away from me.

I let my scream go. It tore at my throat, piercing the night as I closed my hand into a fist and slammed it into the ground beside the sword. The electric blue ley line energy spiked from my fist and hit the focus. Lightning bolts of power cascaded around us, lighting up the Ghost Pack like a blue sun.

Shock, screams, and terror ran through the gathering of wolves. It was a calculated risk. Hugh knew what to expect. He'd choreographed this entire event.

Vicky appeared in a crack of thunder, the earth smoldering beneath her feet. Blinding, golden soulswords hummed from each of her hands. "This pack is under my protection."

Happy the ghost panda strolled out of the shadows and leaned against the child. Only she wasn't a child any longer. She was taller, thinner. Lean musculature had replaced the softness of her youth. She was aging, changing, becoming … something else.

She scratched the ruff of his furry neck and spoke again. "To cross the River Pack is to cross the Destroyer. And for that, you will not survive."

If I wasn't already on my knees, I would have collapsed in realization of what was happening. I didn't want to see it, but what else could it be? The girl who had become a demon, and the demon who had become the Destroyer. Belphegor had said it when he'd fought Vicky. I'd heard him say it. He'd called her the Destroyer. It hadn't registered.

What did it mean? How could I stop it? Would she become the monster we all fought against? My breath came slowly. I fought the stinging in my eyes. This was not a time to show weakness. This was a time to show the domination of the River Pack. Oh, and we had done that. The Spaniard was cowering at the edge of the woods. Terror was written across his face, even as Vicky let her soulswords evaporate into the ether.

Carter was staring at Caroline, a small smile etched onto his face. His entire body rippled and blazed with the power I channeled through the focus.

Caroline's hand was over her mouth. It took me a moment to realize she was crying, whispering Carter's name over and over.

"There is nothing left to discuss," Carter said. He spoke quietly, but his words were carried across the ley lines as though the flood of power was a quiet wind. As if he was whispering into each of our ears. "This war will change the world."

The Ghost Pack shifted, the flood of ley line energy spiking through my focus until the ground burned beneath it. I wrapped my hand around the hilt and held the scorching blade to the heavens. Carter howled, and the Ghost Pack joined him. It shook the ground, even before the River Pack added their voices to the chorus. Caroline shifted and joined the calamity, her body expanding into a hulking form covered in pale brown fur. Three more, then ten, then twenty. Hugh met my gaze. A sadness hung on his face before he shifted, his howl carving a swath through the echoing howls in the field of werewolves.

Vicky laughed. She threw her leg over Happy's back and flashed me a huge grin. I returned the grin. But all I could think was, *You won't become the Destroyer. I won't let that happen.*

CHAPTER FOUR

I T WAS A good thing everyone was parked close to Howell Island. Shreds of clothing were scattered around the woods where the mass werewolf shift had occurred. As they slowly shifted back and began to leave the area, mountains of fur piled up along the ground. By the end of the night, it looked like someone had shaved a hundred wolves and left the fur behind.

Caroline, mostly naked, had her arms wrapped around Carter. I wanted to know how they knew each other, wanted to know the story behind her reaction to his appearance.

Hugh laid a hand on my shoulder. "Thank you, brother."

I met his deep brown eyes and nodded. "Much better to have a tenuous ally than an ancient enemy."

He laughed in slow, quiet pulses. "I would not argue that." He squeezed my shoulder again and walked toward the entrance to the wolves' underground lair.

Vicky was at the bottom of the stairs that led into the lair, a huge smile stretched across her face. "How'd I do?"

"Better than I could have asked, little one." Hugh ruffled her hair as he reached the bottom and stepped into the large circle lined with dark leather couches.

"Hey kiddo—" I started to say.

She bounced on her heels once and then jumped onto me. She giggled and hung from my neck before letting go and landing lightly on her feet. "Happy said you'd be here."

"Well, he's pretty smart," I said. I hugged her back. "For a *bear*."

The bear trundled out of the kitchen area behind us and chuffed at me.

Vicky let out a high-pitched giggle that made me smile.

"That could have been worse," Hugh said as I sank into the leather couch across the low, circular coffee table.

"You understate things as badly as Carter," Alan said, walking out of the kitchen.

I hopped up and traded grips with the mountain of a man. His dark skin vanished beneath the camouflage suit he was wearing. Alan had been a sniper in Vietnam. I didn't know how old he was, but he looked like he was in his mid-thirties. If I had to guess, he was much, much older.

"It's good to see you, Damian." His smile was as warm as his deep voice, and belied the hard edges of his face and his close-cropped Mohawk. He tossed me a bottle of water, which I bobbled and caught before he cracked open his own.

I nodded to him. "Taking up the Vik hairstyle, I see."

He ran a hand over his hair. "The old fang does have style. How's he been? I haven't spoken to him in a couple months."

"Better," Foster said. He glided down the stairs and made a walking landing on the coffee table. "I think the time he spends in the archives with Zola has really helped him get over Devon's betrayal."

Carter came down the stairs after Foster, a quiet whisper. Carter glanced around the room before moving past the table and lowering himself onto the couch.

I stared at the golden werewolf and said, "You look like

you've seen a ghost."

Alan snorted and spat his water across the table. "Oh, oh shit." He erupted into laughter.

Hugh let out a slow breath and raised an eyebrow at me.

"Boundless wit," Carter said, his voice flat, but he didn't completely hide his smile.

I bit my lip and took a deep drink of water.

Alan poked his thumb at the ceiling. "What's with you and the vixen up there?"

"Caroline," Carter said. He was silent for a moment. "I failed her brother once. A very long time ago."

"Antietam," Hugh said.

The golden wolf nodded.

"She never blamed you for his death."

"I should have been there," Carter said.

"You had your orders," Hugh said. "We all did."

Carter crossed his arms. "A convenient excuse for letting our brothers die."

"We did not let them die. No one *let* them die."

"Antietam?" I said. "You were alive and fighting at *Antietam?*"

"Some of us," Carter said, his voice unusually quiet and even. "Some of us fought at Antietam. The rest of us died there."

Happy flopped his head across Carter's lap. Carter frowned at the bear until Happy began shaking his head back and forth. "Okay, okay." Carter unfolded his arms and began scratching the bear.

"Where's Maggie?" Alan asked. "I didn't see her with the rest of the Ghost Pack."

"She's with Zola and the fairies, in Falias."

"Really?" I asked.

Carter nodded. "Glenn invited us. It's probably what Hugh brought you down here to discuss."

I raised my eyebrows and slowly turned my head to Hugh. "Really?"

Hugh formed a steeple with his fingers and nodded once. "He has granted us passage through the Warded Ways, into the heart of Falias."

"Really?" Foster said before I could say it.

"Tonight was no mere scare tactic. War is upon us. No one has seen Ezekiel in three months. It has been six months since he issued his challenge."

"Meet me on the field of battle in Gettysburg." A challenge I would not soon forget.

"He will not stay quiet for long," Hugh said. "It has been a month since the building collapses in Hagerstown."

"We have no proof that was him," Carter said.

"It wasn't natural," Alan said. "The local packs said there was a huge spike in ley line energy." He pointed with one finger while he held his water bottle. "Caroline was one of them."

Vicky pulled her legs up onto the couch and curled up at my side. I put my arm around her, smiled, and looked back to Hugh.

"We have to be ready. The packs are staying here for another day. We're going to section off territory. The packs that can tolerate each other will be coordinating searches for Ezekiel."

"More likely they'll be coordinating reaction parties," Carter said, a small frown on his face.

"If we don't find him," Hugh said, "he will find us. In either case, we will fall without allies."

"Shouldn't we be focusing a search around Gettysburg?" I asked.

Hugh shook his head slowly. "That would be far too predictable for Ezekiel. He will not set foot on that battlefield until we do." He turned to me. "Zola left orders for you."

"Orders?" I said.

"Yes, that is what she called them," Hugh said. A small smile quirked his lips. "Would you prefer to hear them privately?"

I immediately shook my head. "I have no secrets from the pack."

"Well, you certainly know how to make yourself more likable than the average necromancer," Alan said.

"Considering the necromancers I've known, I'm not sure if that was a compliment, or a … something else."

Alan toasted me with his water bottle.

Hugh sighed, a slight look of exasperation on his face as he rubbed his forehead. "Yes, well, Zola would like you to finish your training with the Old Man."

"Where?" I asked, before realizing I probably knew where. "At the cabin?"

"She did not specify. I would imagine it is safe to say the location has not changed."

"That is one scary son of a bitch," Alan said.

Vicky giggled and scooted up on the couch to grab one of the water bottles. I stared, fascinated, as she cracked the bottle open and drank deeply. She flopped back onto the couch beside me.

"I do not imagine the Old Man will hold back," Hugh said.

His gaze lingered on Vicky and her water. "There are not many grudges that last two thousand years."

"Do you think he could be as much a threat to us as Ezekiel in battle?" Alan asked.

Hugh shook his head slowly. "I don't believe so. He hasn't had a catastrophe since the destruction of Roanoke."

"The lost colony?" I asked.

"Before my time," Carter said.

"Almost five hundred years is before most everyone's time," Hugh said. "Only a handful of men outside of the immortals have lived so long."

"What happened at Roanoke?" I asked.

Hugh studied me for a moment before his eyes moved to the old table between us. "It is not my place to tell you. If the Old Man wishes to tell you that story, it is his burden to bear."

"Not even a hint?"

A small smile lifted Hugh's lips before he expertly changed the subject. "Glenn had a request for you, too, Damian."

"Super."

"He does not wish you to walk the Warded Ways for this council. You are to take Philip's hand of glory." He paused. "I suppose it is now your hand of glory."

"Why would Damian need to use that thing?" Foster asked.

"I honestly don't know," Hugh said. "I doubt Glenn would intend to harm you by way of the hand. He is not so subtle where violence is concerned."

Foster barked out a sharp laugh. "No shit."

"How do I even use it?" I asked.

"Oh, they're easy to use." Foster wiggled his fingers. "Just lace your fingers together with the hand's fingers, like you're holding hands. That will forge a bond."

Hugh's face was drawn as he frowned.

"I'm with Hugh," I said. "Nasty."

"Nasty?" Alan said. "You're a necromancer, aren't you?"

"Hey, that doesn't mean I like to pick up severed arms to go dancing through fields of wildflowers."

Alan blinked before his face broke into a smile. "That does make quite a visual."

"Purple wildflowers," I said. "In Kentucky."

Carter groaned and dropped his forehead onto his hand with an audible smack.

Vicky giggled as she jumped up, took a step across the coffee table, and pounced on Happy's back. "Maybe not with a severed arm, but I bet he'd go dancing with dead people."

Alan's mouth quirked to one side as Vicky settled in beside him.

"Besides, I'm dead and he still likes me."

Alan's face fell slightly. A darkness slid into the room. In silence, I mourned the loss of what Vicky had been, and I nurtured a blind rage for the monsters who had hurt her. It didn't matter that they were both dead now. Some things can never be forgiven.

I took in a deep breath and closed my eyes briefly. I could still smell the river within the musky lair of the wolves. "You got me, kiddo. I'd go dancing with you anytime."

"See?" Vicky said, bouncing her legs.

Alan studied me for a moment before he nodded his head. Whether he meant "Hey, you're an okay necromancer," or "Hey, I'm glad you killed those fuckers," I don't know, but I returned the gesture.

"I think it would be best if we all retired for the evening," Hugh said. "Alan and I have much traveling to do, and little time to accomplish it."

"Where to?" I asked.

"Some of the packs are not so open to the idea of working together. I intend to visit the more powerful alphas in the eastern states who did not attend this evening. We have made contact with each Voice. They will let their alphas know we are coming." He took a drink of water and wiped his mouth slowly. "I hope to convince them of the fact working together is their only option. Then we will join you at the war council in Faerie." He was quiet for a moment while he watched Vicky scratch Happy's chin as the bear raised his head, leaned into the scratching, and practically smiled.

"No matter how long," Hugh said, "or how well we may come to know the Fae, they are different from us. As different as a raven from a man." He looked at Alan as he said this, and then turned to me. "They are different from you as well. In some ways, even from Foster."

Foster nodded his head and rested his hand on the sword pommel at his side. "Every race of Fae has its own … quirks." He gave us a lopsided smile.

Hugh dipped his chin briefly as he said, "While we may never truly know the Fae, we can come to understand them. We can accept them for what they are, much as they accept us." He leaned forward slightly. "All of you must remember that a slight insult among friends here could be considered a grave insult in Faerie. I do not know who, or what, will be involved in this council. We must be on our guard. We must keep Glenn on our side at all costs. Then we will learn of our fate."

One week before I would travel with the hand of glory. One day before my training resumed with the Old Man. One night before lunch with Sam and my parents. I wasn't sure which I was dreading the most.

CHAPTER FIVE

"**Y**OU READY FOR this?" Sam asked.

"Fuck no," I said.

"Me either." She smiled and ruffled my hair from the passenger seat as we bounced into my parents' driveway.

Briefly, I flashed back to the previous year, to Sam's scream as she warned me our parents' home was under attack. The horrific scene as I pulled in to discover dozens of exploded zombies in our childhood home. The realization Philip had kidnapped our mother and injured my sister.

My fingers strangled the steering wheel for a moment before I turned the car off. "Let's do this."

We walked to the front door slowly. It was just a conversation, only a little story of genealogy. So what was the weight hanging over me as the door cracked open before I could even knock? The weak smile on my Dad's face as he gave Sam and me a hug in turn told me he was dreading the conversation too.

We followed him through the hall and into the kitchen. The Watchers had restored everything after the attack that tore our home apart. Mom was already sitting at the table. A glass of wine rested in her hand, and three more sat at each of the place settings. I smiled as we all took our childhood seats. Sam sat in the chair right in front of the stove, and I sat next to her with my back to the other counter, across from Mom.

"Are you sure you want to know?" Mom asked as her eyes flickered up to mine and then back to her glass.

"Yes," I said. Sam took my hand and nodded her own agreement.

"We told everyone you were premature," Dad said. He'd never been one to delay a conversation he didn't want to have. "It was almost a month before you started to look … normal."

"What do you mean?" Sam said. "He didn't look normal? I mean, less normal than now?"

I jabbed Sam in the ribs with my elbow.

"Oh, you two," Mom said before she took a deep breath. "The doctors thought you were stillborn." Her voice cracked when she said that last word. "You were so white. We thought you might be albino, but you weren't. I held you and you weren't breathing. You had no heartbeat."

Mom tried to say more, but she couldn't speak when she started sobbing. Tears trickled down her cheeks, and then I really felt like shit. "Something … something came into that room," she said. "It came out of the walls, and the ceiling …" Mom hiccuped and buried her face in her hands.

My dad looked at the ground. "The lights. "They … they dripped black. That's the only way I can describe it. There were eyes, and a voice, but no body. Unless shadows count as a body. It didn't say much. 'Beware the Watchers. His master will reveal the path. Raise him well.' "

Mom looked up at me for a moment before the words start-ing pouring out. "And then it … it just … that darkness reached out and touched the doctor. There was a flash of light. Golden light so blinding, you can't imagine. I heard a scream, and at first I think it was just the doctor, but then a tiny cry started as the doctor collapsed onto the floor." Mom looked up at me. "And then you breathed. You opened those beautiful gray eyes. And you were mine."

Sam's hug crushed me, but I barely felt it. Warmth ran from my eyes and cooled before it reached my chin as the revelation hit me. Ezekiel had killed a man to bring me over, and that fact hit me like a cannon shot. I should have been dead. I had been dead. What the hell did that make the seventh son of Anubis?

"No one suspected," Mom said with a stutter before she broke into a half-laugh. "What would they even suspect? It was simply the doctor's time to go." Her fingernail clicked as she scratched at her thumbnail. "I didn't know what you were. I just knew I loved you."

"He had no right," I said. "To take the life of a man who helps bring life into this world?"

"Don't say that," Dad said. "You've done great things for this world."

"I've killed … many things," I said, my voice not much more than a whisper. The old clock on the wall ticked in the silence.

"You've saved many more," Sam said with her face buried in my shoulder. "You saved me."

My breath came faster. I threw my arm around Sam and squeezed her tight.

"Without you, I'd be gone," she said. "Without you, Vicky's murderers would have gone free. Azzazoth would be walking the earth. Prosperine would be free to destroy the world. Ezekiel would have already won." She lifted my head and kissed my cheek. "Make him pay." She kissed my other cheek. "Make.

Him. Pay."

"Samantha is right," Dad said. "You can be his greatest mistake. The salvation for a world that doesn't even know it needs you."

I smiled and closed my eyes, thumping my forehead against Sam's. "I'm not that strong."

No one spoke for a time, and I tried to savor that moment of normalcy.

"It wasn't long before we realized your imaginary friends weren't make believe," Dad said, and the moment was gone.

I looked up slowly as I considered that. "Jasper."

"And Koda, and Grant," Dad said. "You'd tell us you'd talked to them, and then you would know things. Things about history that we had to look up online, for fuck's sake. Terrible things about wars and demons and magic. You knew more about the Civil War by the time you were four than I'd learned in four years of college." He squeezed Mom's shoulder as she shuddered. "I still didn't really believe it until I saw the dust bunny move."

I almost growled. "Jasper. He revealed himself to you? When we were kids?"

Dad nodded as Mom took a deep drink. "We saw the parrot once too," he said, "though we never mentioned it to you. I think it was best for your mother not to speak of it."

"Graybeard?" I asked.

"We could see its bones, but it spoke like a man," Mom said. "It was awful."

I'd never thought of Graybeard as awful. Other than his knack for telling Zola every little thing I did, and landing me on the chopping block on occasion. I'd stitched that bird back together and used a soul to do it. Later, before Zola took him away to god knows where, he'd developed a disturbingly large vocabulary and a penchant for rum. I may have been a slightly odd child.

"I loved Jasper," Sam said. "He was our own little guardian. He chased the ghosts away from Damian when they started to overwhelm him."

I smiled. "He did, didn't he? He also bit the crap out of me."

Sam wrapped her hands around my forearm. "I may have taught him some bad manners."

I eyed my sister. "I think he may have taught *you* some bad manners."

My dad grinned and actually laughed.

"Where is Jasper?" Sam asked, her eyes trailing toward the living room and the stairs.

"I don't know," I said with a smile. "I've never really looked for him since we moved out. He liked to bite me, in case you forgot."

"How could I forget? It's one of my fondest memories."

"How do you two do this?" Mom asked, her voice rising in pitch. "How can you make jokes after learning such things?"

You learn to laugh, or you paint the walls with your brains. But what I said was, "It's how we cope."

"The kids are strong, Andi," Dad said. "They can take care of themselves better than we ever could."

"We wouldn't be who we are without you," Sam said.

Dad's hand paused halfway to his mouth. He grimaced and slammed his glass onto the floor. The bits of shattered glass reflected light through the dark wine. "I'm so sorry, Sammy." He moved around me and pulled her out of her chair. He cried as he wrapped his arms around her. "We didn't know what to think. You were so different, but you're still our little girl. I never should have pushed you away."

"Daddy," Sam said, her voice almost a whimper. I could tell she was being careful not to crush him in one of her vampy hugs.

"You didn't need to break the glass," Mom said in between sobs.

We all burst into laughter. Teary, hugging, glorious laughter.

Sam and Dad settled onto the couch after a few minutes. She curled up beside him, almost like Vicky had curled up beside me with the pack. I took a seat on the hideous, yet remarkably comfortable, leather recliner and Mom sat on the other side of Sam. All we were missing was a game of Solarquest, a bad movie, and Dad's godforsaken "pizza popcorn"—which was simply popcorn drowned in seasoned salt—and I could have fallen backwards into my childhood.

"There is one other bit of unpleasantness," I said.

"What?" Mom asked. Her voice was steady and confident. She could deal with some craziness when she had to.

"What can you tell me about Hinrik Vesik?"

"Your great …" Dad paused and reconsidered. "Great great great? However many greats, grandfather?"

I nodded.

"Well, I know he was a magician of some sort. He was supposed to be a psychic or something along those lines."

"No …" Mom said. She looked up at me. "He was supposed to be a medium. Was he like you?"

I nodded. "Yes." Yes was the easy answer. It wouldn't give

my parents any sort of comfort to know the debate about Hinrik being either a dark necromancer or a hero. Or both.

"You used to talk to Koda about him, when you were very small." Mom wrung her hands together. "I don't think I've heard you mention him since then."

"Koda?" I said, unable to keep the surprise from edging into my voice.

"That's right," Dad said. "You used to say Koda talked about the dark manwich."

I laughed. "The what?"

Dad shrugged. "Who knows?

As soon as I thought about it, I knew what I'd meant when I was a kid. Koda didn't talk about a dark, delicious sloppy joe. Koda talked about a dark necromancer. Hinrik. Koda had avoided talking about my great grandfather when we last met. I was going to have to track Koda down.

✦　　✦　　✦

"OH MY GOD, Damian," Sam said as we pulled out of the driveway. "Dad apologized *again*. I did not see that coming."

"I didn't either," I said. "Stubborn old bastard."

"That was an amazing, horrible, amazing afternoon."

"Yeah," I said, "that pretty much sums it up."

"You're going to find Koda, aren't you?"

I nodded. "How'd you guess?" I gave Sam a sideways glance.

"When the mood changed from family bonding awfulness, I was pretty sure. Hell, Demon, I don't think you spoke another sentence longer than two words before we made it out of the house."

I laughed. "You're not wrong. I haven't talked to him in a while. Since he gave me that manuscript."

"That wasn't long after Cassie …" Sam grew quiet and her gaze wandered to the passenger window.

We'd lost Cassie in a fight with an Old God. Gurges, god of steam and wind.

"You really think Glenn is going to start a war over Cassie?"

"Maybe he would," I said. "Cassie was a very old friend to him. She was a loss to us all, but don't forget Ezekiel killed nearly an entire city of Fae. Almost ten thousand dead, all told. There aren't many people who wouldn't go to war after that."

"They are *gods,* Damian." Her gaze swung back to me. "What's going to happen?"

I glanced at Sam and took a deep breath. "I don't know, but I'm guessing it's going to suck."

"It scares me. The world at large isn't ready to see two gods tearing each other apart. If they're freaking out about that crappy video, what's going to happen when they get some real footage? A witch hunt with nuclear arms?" She crossed her arms and her head thumped against the window. "Ow."

I normally would have laughed, but my brain was following Sam's train of thought. Commoners weren't known for their compassion for and understanding of things that go bump in the night. They were already assembling a task force. If they had a task force, they probably had a strike force. What would they do when the things that haunt their nightmares came at them, guns blazing?

We drove the rest of the way to the Pit in silence.

CHAPTER SIX

M Y QUIET STEPS on the wooden stairs fell away to nothing as I reached the carpet on the second floor of Death's Door. I took a deep breath, letting the smell of the old books settle around me like a mantle of security. I knew I probably wouldn't be back for a while, so I might as well drink my fill.

I didn't waste any time, but I savored the walk between the floor-to-ceiling bookshelves. Ancient grimoires, interspersed with manuscripts and books on the history of more magical creatures than I could ever hope to memorize, stretched to the ceiling far above.

My reading sanctuary waited for me at the end of the aisle. A small shelf of my randomly stacked, current reading material was above the chairs. Yellowed manuscript pages and leather-bound tomes debating the innocuousness—or undiluted evil—of soularts were the flavor of the week. Koda, one of the wisest men ever to lead the Society of Flame, had me questioning what was right and wrong. He'd lived and died in times when dark necromancers were one of the worst plagues upon the world, but still he debated their alignments. Whatever I believed, it was a dangerous road either way.

I slid the old trunk out from its nook in the wall behind the leather chair. Wards were carved deeply into the dark wood, concealing the trunk from most of the world. Zola said they could prevent anything contained within it from being tracked. It had been a gift from the man known only as Ward, a celebration of Zola gaining the right to vote. My hand trailed along the gouges in the wood and the old iron that formed the metalwork along the corners.

Zola had dealt with the worst humanity had to offer in her lifetime … slavery, war, betrayal, oppression. My thoughts shifted to Hugh. The loss his people had incurred was immeasurable. Would his involvement with me drag the entire pack into a fool's war? I ground my teeth together. There was nothing I could do about the past, but I might have a chance to help the future. My hand curled into a fist and I closed my eyes briefly.

The lid opened smoothly, the hinges whisper quiet. I had an assortment of my most dangerous manuscripts and a few artifacts tucked away in the trunk. The Key of the Dead glinted in the dim lamplight. On top of it all sat a tube of black linen.

I grumbled as I reached in and picked it up. The hand of glory was heavier than one might suspect. The old flesh hadn't decayed, but it certainly hadn't stayed fresh either.

I started to close the lid, and then reached in to grab Philip's journal before heading downstairs to search for my backpack. It was only then that I realized there'd been a distinct lack of claws, tongues, and bristly green fur. I tapped my foot at the base of the now-enormous hole in the wall where Bubbles and Peanut liked to sleep.

Nothing.

"Huh," I said, raising my eyebrows. I shrugged it off and turned my attention to the junk shelves. They were … organized. "What have you done, Frank? What have you done?" I slid the backpack off the top shelf and nothing else rained down on my head. It was just ... wrong.

I tucked everything into the backpack as I walked through the saloon-style doors and out into the front of the shop. I was rearranging the hand of glory when someone spoke.

"Whatcha got?" Her voice was lighter, more like she used to be. It made me smile as I turned around to find Ashley standing behind me. Her piercing green eyes smiled up at me just as much as her lips. A basket with the Double D logo printed on the side was filled with clear packets of herbs and an extraordinary amount of scrap amber.

I did a double take at the basket as I leaned down to look more closely. "That's cool," I said. "When did we get those?"

"Damian!" Frank jumped out of the chair behind the register. "When did you get here?"

"Hey, Frank! Just a couple minutes ago. I think you were in the bathroom. When did you get these?" I asked, pointing at Ashley's basket.

"Just yesterday," he said. He came close enough to reach out and shake my hand. His gray hair was cut short, almost military. His face looked even thinner than when I'd seen him last week. He'd hardened in many ways since he started working with me at Death's Door.

Ashley pointed at him. "You're fading away, Frank."

"Not likely," I said. Frank was scary ripped. I could see a few leftover stretch marks on his upper arms from when he'd weighed a hell of a lot more, but his workout regimen was turning him into rock.

"You might be wrapped up in that cloak now," I said, "but we've seen you leather clad and fighting a blood mage. In fact, I think I might have seen a video of it."

Ashley's blush was damn near instantaneous.

"How'd the coven take your ascension to being a Power?" I asked.

"Some of them are okay with it," Ashley said. She tried to keep her voice steady, but instead spoke in a near-whisper. "A few left."

"The people who stayed are your real friends," Frank said. "Anyone who leaves because you change one small piece of yourself was never a friend in the first place."

This time Ashley did reach out and squeeze his forearm.

"Truer words," I said. "Truer words."

"Thank you." She walked over to the counter and set her basket down. Frank followed her and started unpacking everything. "Do you really think it's going to be a war?"

"I have it on good information it's already a war," I said. "We just don't know it yet, although we kind of do know it."

"I worry about the people that left," Ashley said as she looked up at me. "They have no one Damian. What if there's a new witch hunt? Most of us have no true power. It's one of the reasons I took up the Blade of the Stone."

"Speaking of which," I said, "Koda's book had some vague references to it. I think that is some seriously dangerous shit."

Frank chuckled. "You think? I was pretty sure it was dangerous after it dissolved a car and ate away half the street."

"Point to Frank." I pointed at him. "Where are the pooches?" I glanced at the back room.

"Pooches?" Frank raised his caterpillar-like eyebrows at the word.

I held my hand out at my waist. "You know, about so high.

Eat everything? Like to bite?"

Frank nodded and continued ringing up Ashley's goods. "They left with Foster and Aideen."

"Really?" I said with the surprise plain in my voice. "Cara said to bring them to the Concilium Belli. I kind of thought she was joking."

"The *what?*" Ashley said, her voice rising sharply.

I took a deep breath and met her eyes. Her focus shifted from my left eye to my right and back. "Ashley," I said. "Faerie is going to open war against Ezekiel and those who would support him."

"No, they can't." She looked through me, and I could almost see the thoughts churning in her mind. "Look at the damage that video is doing. An open war will reveal even more of our world, or confirm its existence to everyone who witnesses it."

"I know."

"Can't you stop it?" she asked.

"No one can stop it," Frank said. "War is war. Human, werewolf, Fae … there will always be war."

I looked at Frank as he scanned the items in from Ashley's basket. Something dark crept within his words. I had a feeling I knew what it was. He'd not had an easy life. The family gunrunning business hadn't panned out so well in the end. At some level, I knew he spoke from experience.

He took a deep breath and closed his eyes.

"Are you okay?" Ashley asked.

He finished scanning the last few pieces of amber. "I'm good, thanks."

Ashley nodded and paid before she turned back to me.

I watched Frank start bagging her items in some Double D branded shopping bags. Nice reusable cloth ones. I was impressed with us.

"Damian," Ashley said.

My gaze shifted to the priestess.

"You'll tell me when things start to happen, won't you?"

"Yes." I slid the sleek black phone out of my pocket. "Sam made sure I had your number loaded up. And about fifty others." I swiped the screen to unlock it and pulled up my texts. "We have an emergency group set up and you're on it. If something really bad happens, you'll know right away."

"Thank you," she said, picking up her bags. She turned to leave, and then paused. She took a couple steps and hugged me instead. "Thank you."

"Saving the Wiccans," I said. "It's what we do."

She laughed and smiled before heading out.

"You okay?"

Frank blew out a breath. "I was just thinking there's a lot of ways to die in a war."

I nodded. He didn't need to say more. His dad had been gunned down in an arms deal gone south. Frank had a unique, and terrible, perspective on war.

"Keep an eye on Sam for me," I said.

"I will, Damian. Have a safe trip. Try not to let the Old Man kill you."

"Yeah," I said with a laugh. "No shit."

CHAPTER SEVEN

FRANKLY, I ASSUMED training with the Old Man was going to be nothing short of absolute brutality. To postpone things a bit, I stopped off for some comfort food on the way south. Fried catfish at the Catfish Kettle in Farmington … words escape me.

I practically inhaled a hushpuppy and took a big drink of water. Slightly crunchy, slightly greasy, deep-fried cornbread. I smiled and thought of the time Zola had brought me to this place so many years ago.

The server dropped off a water refill. I nodded and continued chewing. An older, petite server near the hostess stand pointed at me. I didn't think much of it until she started walking toward me.

"You're him, aren't you?"

I swallowed and looked up at her. "Umm, maybe?"

"You're the all-you-can-eat kid. I just know it."

"I'm the who?"

"Come with me," she said before walking away.

I grabbed the last two pieces of catfish, shrugged, and followed her toward the front of the restaurant.

"You're him!" She motioned to the black and white, eight by ten photo on the wall.

I squinted and leaned down to get a better look. "Oh. My.

God."

"I knew it!"

The photo showed me, with Zola, and a tower of empty baskets on the table. I looked absolutely sick, my hands folded over my stomach. It had to be at least ten years old. Maybe even fifteen?

I nodded and took a bite of catfish and smiled. "It was some damn good food."

She pulled a phone out of her pocket. "I waited on you two back then. Never seen anything like it since. Can I take your picture?"

I raised my eyebrows and demolished my last piece of fish. "Sure. Why not?"

She handed her phone to the hostess behind the register. We stood to either side of the photo and smiled as the hostess snapped a new picture.

"Thank you so much," the older server said. She flashed a wide smile.

"No problem." I paid my bill, left an excessively large tip, and continued on to Coldwater, amused and somehow content after revisiting that little piece of my past.

✦ ✦ ✦

I FOLLOWED THE highway south as it narrowed into two lanes on either side and finally turned into a curvy, one lane death trap. The setting sun slowly lit the sky on fire as my tires crunched onto a narrow gravel drive. I didn't like taking my old '32 Ford onto gravel roads, but I didn't give it too much thought, nervous as I was about training with the Old Man. I bounced up and down a few miles of hills before I was hit by the presence of unusually active ghosts.

I saw several in the fields where the slab town once stood. Some performed repetitive tasks at a shimmering, ghostly sawmill, and others casually strolled along the old road. A concentration of ghosts that large was unheard of for the area. Most of the ghosts here didn't move around. I wondered if the Old Man had stirred them up. A long curve eventually crossed into an open field surrounded by an old deciduous forest.

At the top of a gentle hill stood the old cabin. The ancient oak tree out front cut into the starry night sky. Zola had told me the cabin had been around in one form or another since before the Civil War. I didn't doubt it. Hell, so had Zola.

Smoke curled from the edge of the front porch. Moonlight shadows kept me from seeing into the darkness clearly, but I was quite sure it was the Old Man seated before the orange glow around the old steel shutters.

A bright light flashed out behind the cabin like a lightning strike. There were no clouds in the sky and I could clearly see the Milky Way slowly churning by above us.

"You're not going to ask me to chop firewood, are you?"

A gruff laugh echoed out from the porch. "If you don't know how to cut firewood, we're both in the wrong place."

Another flash of light briefly lit the surrounding woods, followed by a quiet hiss and a sharp pop.

"What was that light?" I asked.

"Dell! Damian's here. Come around, kid."

I couldn't see the face beneath his dark blond hair until he got closer, but the grumbling was unmistakable. I took a few steps toward Dell and shook his hand. He nodded as he took a bite out of a chocolate bar. Zola had told me he used sugar to cope with the side effects of necromancy. I'd never really had side effects quite that severe. Dell's affinity for sugar had earned him the wonderful nickname of Roach.

He looked up and the moonlight caught his features. His eyes were silver in the dim glow, but I knew they were the cool gray of a born necromancer.

"Dell will only be with us through tomorrow night. He has some friends in the packs outside of the Irish Brigade. I'm sending him out with Hugh."

"Out of the frying pan and into the doggie bowl," Dell muttered.

I grinned, and as my eyes adjusted to the moonlight, I could see the Old Man's gaze sweep between me and Dell. A pipe hung from the left side of the Old Man's mouth. A steady streamer of smoke rose from the light ivory bowl.

"Adannaya trained you to be soft," he said. The Old Man stood up and stepped down the short staircase. "You've been trained to walk in the light. You have no idea what you're capable of. No idea what necromancers are capable of."

He inhaled and slowly let a cloud of smoke escape through his nose. His beard was still full. It covered many of the scars etched into his face, but not all of them. His arms were a mass of deep scars that formed a roadmap of mountains and valleys. "I'm here to teach you some hard truths. We are humanity's dark side, and we walk a path no one else can. Necromancers use the dark to keep the shadows at bay, so others can walk in the light. We are the gatekeepers, and the gravemakers."

I narrowed my eyes. "What are you talking about? Gravemakers?"

"All that stand before us face death."

"What about the gravemakers?" I asked again. "What do you mean?"

"When a necromancer falls, he becomes one of them. The weak and ignorant find their fate much sooner. They are us, as much as we are them."

"No. I would have known …"

"It's true," Dell said. "I've seen someone lose it. Fucking nasty way to go."

My mind raced back to the gravemaker I'd seen in that doomed city, Pilot Knob. As much as I didn't want to remember, I thought of the gravemakers I'd touched with my necromancy at Stones River. Was there something human hidden among the atrocities? Something hidden within that pure, undiluted force of destruction? Were there men and women within those creatures? I closed my eyes and couldn't stifle the shiver running from my neck down my arms.

The Old Man nodded. He tapped his pipe out in the fire pit off to his left. "Let's see you fight—"

To call his attack fast would be a grotesque understatement. He'd set the pipe down on the edge of the fire pit and then he was on me. His first strike connected with my stomach and the wind left me. I barely got my left arm up to parry his next blow. He moved smoothly into a spinning back fist.

"Impadda!" I said.

His face twisted into a death's head grin as he pulled his punch. *"Impadda!"* he said, echoing my own incantation.

"Bummer," Dell said.

My eyes widened as the Old Man's shield slipped beneath my own, forcing it up, and in turn forcing my arm up. I was completely exposed. He landed a sharp jab on my chest and the air left me again. I collapsed into a coughing fit.

"I could have killed you twice, boy."

I stared at his white beard and the smile he wore. He was a fighter. He was born to do this insanity. He had two thousand years of training under his belt. It was going to be rough.

"Put your bags in the cabin. When you're settled, meet me in the back. We'll train among the stones that Aeros raised." He didn't wait for a response. He picked up his pipe and headed around the cabin to the west, past the old stone well.

I blew out a breath and turned my attention back to Dell. "So, how've you been?"

He smirked as he finished off his chocolate bar. "Beat down. I imagine you'll be feeling the same pretty quick."

"No shit." I pulled two bags out of my car's trunk and took two quick steps up onto the porch. The screen door squealed a bit as I opened it. It was familiar, yet the cabin felt different with so much activity around it. The dead were restless.

I glanced out into the fields before I went inside. Pale, misty forms flickered in and out of sight in the woods. I frowned slightly, ducked through the doorway, and let the screen door fall closed with a loud crack.

There was a note sitting on the rounded, bar-height counter. It was in Zola's handwriting.

Old Man, if you smoke in my cabin, I will remove your reproductive organs with a blunt rock.

I laughed a little. The old orange chair coated in little pilled puffballs was calling my name, but I resisted. A low fire in the wood stove cast an orange warmth around the room. The Old Man or Dell must have been cooking earlier, because it sure as hell wasn't cold enough for a fire. I turned away from the living room and the seductive comfort of a well-known couch.

I ducked into the bedroom and paused. A few backpacks were already thrown into the room. The decorative iron-framed bed sat against the wall to my left and the bunks were on the right. It looked like we'd be a bit cramped, at least for the night.

After dropping my bags, staff, and pepperbox, I took the few steps back to the kitchen. The focus was still tucked into my belt. I didn't like walking around without some kind of weapon on me. I opened the refrigerator and found it stocked with steaks, vegetables, some small, skinned, unidentifiable critters, and a couple bottles of Duvel. I shut the door and grabbed a quick glass of water before heading toward the back.

The screen door squealed behind me and I turned to find Dell walking in through the front.

"You really train here with Zola back in the day?"

I nodded as Dell rubbed his arms.

"How did you handle the dead? There are so many. It's so loud here."

"Loud?" I asked.

"Yeah, man. They won't shut up, it's like I'm standing in the middle of a goddamned mall at Christmas."

"I don't hear anything," I said.

"You have got to be kidding. How the hell do you shut them out?"

"I've never really had to shut them out before," I said. "It's more like I have to tune in to hear them speak. The stronger ones, sure. I get a whisper every now and then, and I can see them without focusing my Sight."

"You're different alright." He shook his head. "Damn."

I opened the back door. "What do you mean?"

Dell walked out ahead of me. "The Old Man told me you were different than I was. Said you can even use some Fae magic."

"We can all use line arts to some degree. Every shield I've ever seen was a line art."

"Yeah, but making pigeons explode at the ex's wedding? That's not like calling a shield, man. That is some intricate shit. It would take years for most mages to master that. How long did it take you?"

I pulled the door closed behind me and glanced at Dell. "A couple hours, but Sam inspires motivation."

He belted out a staccato laugh. "Yeah, different." Dell bit into another chocolate bar and stepped off the back porch.

"I thought *I* ate a lot of crap." I followed him out into the circle of stones. Each was large enough to sit on comfortably.

"I'll be into anything with sugar until I'm dead. It takes the edge off after grabbing onto some random dead bastard's aura."

"That won't be long if you keep yapping," the Old Man said from the edge of the stone circle. He stood beside a deep furrow that ran beside a melted stone and cut through the forest beyond. It was here Zola had ended the insane march of Philip's army. Philip Pinkerton. Now I knew he'd been my brother of a sort, one of the sons of Anubis. Good riddance.

"We have one day until Dell leaves to join the wolves. To-night, you spar. Tomorrow morning, the real training begins."

Dell cursed, finished his candy, and stuffed the wrapper in his pocket. "I've been training under this crusty old bastard for years. No offense, but I'm going bury you."

I smiled and stood up. "It'll be hard to bury me while you're hunting for your teeth." We slowly began to circle each other.

Dell blew out a puff of air. "Amateur. The only way you'll survive this is if your sister comes to save you."

"I only pull out the big guns for a serious threat. I'll let my cu siths have you."

"Aww … gross, man."

"The things I've seen …" I said as seriously as I could.

Dell's kept his eyes on me before he stumbled over a rough spot of earth and I burst into laughter.

"You're good," he said with a smile.

"For fuck's sake," the Old Man said, "shut up and fight."

I knew Dell was good with a gun, but damn he was fast on his feet too. He started to throw a punch, but it was his foot that came up, seeking my face. I barely got my left arm up to block. The impact hurt. He moved to strike again.

"Impadda!"

Dell cursed, moving too fast to stop his kick. His shin bounced off the flowing, glassy barrier and put him off balance. I lashed out with an awkward kick of my own, which he easily deflected.

"*Pulsatto!*" he said as he recovered.

The wave of force caught my shoulder and knocked me off balance. Dell was not so clumsy as to waste an opportunity. He hopped toward me and landed a quick forward kick to my chest, right where the Old Man had hit me earlier.

I started questioning my choice of dinner. I slid back onto one knee and called up a shield. Dell grinned and called up his own.

"Sucker," I said.

As soon as he went to scoop my shield up, I let the shield

fall. He was expecting resistance, but there was none. His arm swept high above his head, leaving his midsection exposed. He tried to strike with an off-balance kick.

"Minas Pulsatto!"

The restrained incantation hit him hard enough to take his feet out from under him and he hit the ground with a thump.

"Fuck," he said. "That's cheating."

"That's strategy," the Old Man said after a moment. "Come, let us eat, and then we will train."

CHAPTER EIGHT

MY STOMACH WAS halfway to exploding after eating the Old Man's squirrel stew. One thing he'd learned to do in two thousand years? Cook. Good. Squirrel. I regretted indulging so much as I picked my face up out of the grass for the seventh or eighth time.

"You haven't vomited yet," he said. I looked up and could see his mustache and white beard raised slightly. The bastard was smiling.

Dell curled up on one of the stone seats. He had a nasty gash running down his right cheek where the Old Man had scored a hit.

"You sure he's okay?" I asked.

"He'll be fine. A healer will be here later."

"Healer?" I asked as I dragged myself back up onto my feet.

"Yes, for some reason Zola and the *Sanatio* of the Sidhe thought the two of you might need one."

Sanatio of the Sidhe? That was Cara's title in Glenn's court. It seemed awfully formal for getting a beat down from the Old Man. I mean getting a thorough training session, of course. I stood up and brushed the brittle clump of dry grass off my sleeve.

"Make ready."

That's how he was, orders and commands. Even his questions were commands, at some level. He'd been a leader for so long I was pretty sure he'd forgotten how the little people thought.

The Old Man had connected with the same attack three times in a row. I was pretty sure it would be the same move again.

He moved his fist forward. The wave of force came off it like a *pulsatto* incantation, but he hadn't uttered a word.

I drew the focus from my belt and the sword exploded into life, blade toward the ground. My vision dimmed as the solid red blade split the Old Man's attack, diverting it to either side of my body. I stumbled slightly. Instead of knocking my ass on the ground, I was surprised when the Old Man reached out and steadied me.

"A solid strategy," he said, "but not if you're going to ram your own soul through that focus."

I blinked a few times as my vision returned to normal. "That was mostly my aura, but what else can I do without the staff?"

"You do not need the staff." He held out his hand.

I looked between it and the focus, then handed the hilt over.

"Zola tells me you can make an aural blade without the focus or your staff."

"It's not as strong without the focus," I said.

"Show me."

I nodded and shifted my fingers into the same shape they'd be in if I'd been holding the focus. It didn't take much effort to force my aura into the thin cylinder of space within my palm. I flexed my fingers and a deep red aural blade ignited in my hand. It flickered, and shimmered, but it was at least twice as long as the last time I'd formed a blade unassisted. I opened my hand and it snapped out of existence.

The Old Man eyed the focus in his hand before flipping it back to me. "I'm fairly certain Glenn gave you this to hone your skills without you knowing it."

"What? Why?"

"I'm not sure. I do have a test for you. Form that same aural blade while you're holding the focus. Don't use a soulart."

I had enough bruises and cuts across my body, I didn't even argue. Maybe that was the whole point of kicking our asses in the first place.

Once again, I forced my aura to thicken and pool in my hand. I could sense the power of the focus as my aura flirted with the small holes spiraling along the grip. I flexed my hand.

A stable, blood red aural blade erupted from the hilt. Power snapped and surged from the blade. My vision didn't dim. My balance didn't waver. I stared slack jawed at the glowing blade.

"Hold the blade," The Old Man said. "I would advise against letting it drop."

"Okay, why do—"

"Minas Ignatto!"

I wanted to run as the streamer of flame roared from his hand. Burning death was a handbreadth away as I dropped to a knee and held the sword out. The flames parted around the blade, just as if it had been a soulsword. Two streamers of flame hit the earth to either side of me and ignited the dry grass.

I didn't hesitate when the incantation died. *"Glaciatto!"* I hit both patches of flame and they died away.

The Old Man laughed, full and rich as he slapped his knee.

Dell bolted upright on the rock and held a hand to his head. "Holy shit."

"When did you learn to scale an incantation without a modifier?" the Old Man asked. His tone was full of humor. He wasn't expecting an actual answer. He already knew the damned answer.

"I …" I stared at the frozen earth, speechless.

"You didn't use a modifier, and yet you clearly used a *minas* art."

I looked up at him with wide eyes. "I could have turned this entire field into an ice rink."

"And yet, here we are."

"Crazy old bastard," Dell muttered as he stretched out on the rock again. "He could have killed us all."

"Have you ever seen your master do that?" the Old Man asked.

"No," I said. "You and Ezekiel and Edgar are the only people I've seen use non-verbal incantations."

"You still spoke, but you internalized the modifier. Even that could be enough to give you an advantage in a close contest. And the sword." He nodded at the blade.

I let it collapse in on itself and stared at the old hilt.

"Admittedly," the Old Man said, "that is not likely to damage a demon to a significant degree. There are still times where a soulsword is your best bet. I would suggest using someone else's soul for that."

"That's the path of a dark necromancer," I said.

"That is the path of a man who survives."

There was a surge of power through the area's ley lines. None of us flinched. There were very few things in this world stupid enough to start a fight with the Old Man.

"Look at this wretched mass of bruises."

I blinked as my brain registered the voice I was hearing. I turned toward Dell. "Aideen?" I asked.

She glanced up briefly, her bright eyes peering out from the golden coif falling around her face. She turned her attention back to Dell, shifting gray and white wings that stood taller than me. "Damian, I've seen Bubbles do more damage to you than that. The Old Man must be losing his touch."

There was a gruff laugh as the man in question walked over to the fairy. "You didn't come through the Ways."

She shook her head and a bright tinkle of metal filled the stillness. "No, Glenn sent me here directly. One of the older paths. Before the days of the king."

"Not many of us remember those days," the Old Man said.

Aideen lifted Dell's hand and leaned closer to look at his swollen pinky. "Does this hurt?"

He squealed before he belted out, "Holy fuck!"

"I think it's broken," she said in a level voice.

"Oh fucking fuck." His voice shook.

"This is going to hurt." She held her hand above the damage and whispered *"Socius Sanation."* A bright, misty light flashed between her hand and Dell's. He stiffened and stifled a scream, and then the light faded.

Dell flexed his hand and stared at it. "Never get used to that. Thanks."

"I remember when a fairy had to patch Philip's leg back together in the war. I don't think he screamed as bad as you, Roach."

Aideen glanced at the Old Man and looked back to Dell.

"Never dreamed that boy would go so bad. What's the worst you ever had to patch up, Aideen?"

"I am *not* here to talk about old war stories." She traced some shallow cuts on Dell's arm. He let out a half grunt, half scream, as she closed the largest cut.

The anger on Aideen's face surprised me.

"How are you?" I asked in a lame attempt to change the subject.

"Great," Dell said, biting off the word.

"I meant Aideen."

Dell muttered under his breath and Aideen smiled, cracking her angry façade.

"I am well, thank you. I think Foster misses you. Despite all the drama in Faerie, he often talks of you, and Sam, and Frank."

"Really?"

She nodded and then paused. "Don't tell him I told you that." She leaned forward and held her hand out. A dim light flowed through another cut on Dell's arm.

The Old Man leaned against the rock beside Dell. "How is Faerie?"

"Faerie is in upheaval." She fell silent and walked behind Dell before pulling his shirt up.

"Glenn intends to start the war?"

"He did not start the war." Aideen's voice fell in pitch, and a deadly undertone crept in. "We will finish it."

"How many died?" Dell asked.

"Thousands," Aideen said, her hands falling away from Dell. "We still don't know for certain. Falias is in ruins, and so few survived." She buried her face in her hands and started to shake. "I had family in Falias."

I stepped toward her and she launched herself at me, bending over slightly and wrapping her arms around my chest. "You can't imagine the devastation," she said. Her voice was as shaky as she was, and it scared the crap out of me. "Ezekiel, he managed to break some of the ley lines. It's not supposed to be possible, but where they broke ..." Now she broke down in tears. "Oh gods. Where they broke, it was horrific. The power that was released just *erased* the city. Do you know how anyone survived?

The Old Man shook his head. The rage on his face was unnerving.

"The Warded Man, cast out by Glenn after the war with the water witches." She disentangled herself from me, took a deep breath, and returned to working on Dell's back.

"Ward ..." the Old Man nodded slowly. "He's a good man."

"He harnessed one of the broken lines and turned it against Ezekiel. It could have killed Ward to touch that line. The attack didn't kill Ezekiel, but it forced his retreat. Glenn restored the barriers after that."

"Do you know what Ezekiel unleashed in the square?" She looked at each of us in turn.

All three of us were shaking our heads. I dreaded the answer, but at the same time, I couldn't wait to digest another reason to destroy Ezekiel.

"He summoned an ancient beast into Faerie. A basilisk."

"Fucking hell," I said. Basilisks lived in the Burning Lands. There shouldn't have been a way for Ezekiel to get one into Faerie. The Warded Ways weren't compatible with creatures like that.

"Ward killed it with the help of a reaper, but not before it captured one of Camazotz's children in its gaze."

"One of the bat creatures?" the Old Man asked. "One of *his* bats?"

Aideen nodded.

"That will break the truce with Camazotz," the Old Man said.

All of the horrible little puzzle pieces began to snap together in my mind. I was beginning to understand why Aideen had seemed so morose the past couple months, and why Foster wanted to talk about anything but what had happened in Falias. He was far more interested in discussing how we were going to remove Ezekiel's balls and feed them to him. "Camazotz is one of the few beings left walking the Earth that knows how to fight the dark-touched. If we break the Seals, and Camazotz turns against us ... fuck."

"I have seen terrible things," Aideen said, "but that possibility is beyond them all." She tugged Dell's shirt down. "He's done. Damian, take off your shirt. Let me see those bruises."

I did. We fell silent for a bit as she healed the worst of them. I only winced once or twice. I think Dell was jealous. I pulled my shirt back on as she finished.

"Glenn will not start an open war with Ezekiel until the council convenes. Zola has asked me to tell you not to abandon your training. One of us will return in a few days. No mortal wounds until then."

"Tell everyone I said 'Hi.' Let Bubbles and Peanut lick you half to death for me." I winked at Aideen and she actually gave me a smile.

She ruffled Dell's hair, which seemed to annoy him a great

deal, before giving the Old Man a hug. "I'm glad you're all with us. Soon we will be joined in honor and death once more."

The Old Man stood at attention, his legs separated by the width of his shoulders as he extended his right hand, palm up. "My oath is not forgotten. In honor, nor in death."

Aideen bowed to the Old Man before she walked down the furrow carved into the earth and slowly vanished into the forest.

He slowly relaxed and picked up his pipe before turning back to me. "She's a firecracker, that one."

"She's usually the most reasonable of the bunch," I said.

The Old Man shook his head and stroked his beard. "You've obviously not seen her angry."

"Ah, but I've seen her naked."

The Old Man choked on the smoke he was inhaling and burst into a coughing fit.

CHAPTER NINE

"**I**N BATTLE, YOU defend," the Old Man said, curling his hand into a fist. "You react. To survive what's coming, you need to be more aggressive."

"You believe that?" I picked myself up off the dry grass once again. Dell had landed a ridiculously fast kick and knocked my feet out from under me.

"War has not changed so much in two thousand years. Especially war within the magical realm."

Dell laughed, rotated his shoulder, and winced from the pain where it had been slammed into the ground. "That's because the Fae are more set in their stubborn-ass ways than you are, Old Man."

He ignored Dell and turned to one of the enormous stone seats Aeros had summoned in the final battle against Philip Pinkerton. He stepped forward as he said, "One move is followed by two. Flow through your attacks. Shield to break an opponent's strike. Get inside their guard. They'll be dead before they can react."

I ran at the nearest rock and struck it with my shield. A spiral of fire leapt from my right hand as I dropped the shield, and then immediately brought it up again.

"No," the Old Man said. "You have the basic idea, but an experienced fighter will see the deception. Attack me with the same incantation."

Dell leaned back against the cabin. "You're going to be sore in the morning."

I cast a sideways grin at Dell, and then moved on the Old Man. *"Impadda!"*

He called up his own shield to deflect mine. I expected it, and dropped my shield as soon as he thrust his arm forward to make an impact. His left side was open.

"Minas Ignatto!" The spiral of flame should have scorched his ass.

Instead his shield flickered from his right arm to his left. The flames bounced off harmlessly and, in the explosion of electric blue sparks, he spun.

My eyes widened as I realized how close he'd come in that spin. I didn't get my shield up before his switched arms again and smashed me into the ground.

"Oh. Fuck." I said into the dirt.

"Still easy to read." He reached down and grabbed my hand, helping me to my feet. "You leave openings. You don't commit to the kill. Every attack should bring death. Every death should be legendary."

"Again," I said. It was more a growl than speech. I was tired of being kicked around by the Old Man.

"Stubborn bastard," Dell said. "You're going to be stuck with broken bones for days if you keep pushing it."

"Again!" I pulled the focus from my belt and set it on the stone closest to me.

"You will not soon forget this lesson." The Old Man was fast. His beard shifted in the wind as he launched himself at me.

I swung my left arm at him and called a shield, exactly like I had before.

He called his own. He expected me to drop it. Instead our shields met in an explosion of electric blue lightning. His shield flickered to his other arm and he spun. I dropped to a knee.

"Impadda!"

The smile that stretched across his scarred face was terrifying. He angled his shield down, attempting to scoop mine up. He hadn't noticed my shield was half buried in the ground. He met with a wall of force. The field lit up with the explosion of energy. His shield rebounded from mine and flung his left arm out to his side.

His grin died, and I knew he'd realized what had happened.

"Pulsatto!" I said.

The wave of force took him in the chest. Already off balance from the shield impact, he went down hard and cursed.

I scooped up the focus from the stone beside me.

"Yield to me," I said.

"He'll recover too fast to close on him with that," Dell was saying as I threw the focus at the Old Man.

I growled as I gestured at the focus, slowly closing my fingers into a fist. It was as though a heavy spring was trying to prevent each finger from forming into a fist. It was a familiar feeling. A powerful feeling, and the Old Man actually winced away from the golden blade as it exploded from the spinning hilt. The blade sank into the earth a foot from his shoulder, leaving the focus a couple feet in the air.

"I yield," the Old Man said with a shallow laugh. "Well done."

I released the soulart and the focus fell silently to the earth.

I walked over to him and held out my hand. He picked the

focus up and handed it to me before taking my hand.

"I generally don't like to hit old people," I said.

He laughed again and brushed the dried grass off his legs. "You better get used to it."

Dell punched my arm. "That was brilliant, Damian! Burying the shield in the ground? I couldn't even see it through the grass."

"Neither could I," the Old Man said. "Alright, one more round of sparring, then we rest."

✦　✦　✦

DELL WAS QUITE a bit worse for wear when we finished late that night. He collapsed into the bottom bunk with a grunt. The Old Man stayed outside. I wasn't sure what he was doing, but I was worn out enough I didn't particularly care.

I wasn't in any shape to jump up to the top bunk, so I dragged the old oak night stand a bit closer and pulled myself up off that.

My bed was occupied.

Whiskers twitched and the mouse squeaked before scurrying to the edge of the bed and flinging itself at the faded curtains.

"The hell was that?" Dell asked.

"Mice. Well, one mouse anyway."

"Ugh, am I sleeping on mouse crap?"

"Quite possibly," I said, pulling the sheets back.

"Fuck it. Don't care. Must sleep."

I rolled over and stared at the ceiling, dimly lit by the fire flickering in the stove in the living room. Deep orange shadows danced and fought across my vision.

"He's pretty intense," I said.

"That's one word for it." Dell's voice was muffled, and I was pretty sure he was face down in a pillow.

"He's pretty damn good, too," I said.

I heard Dell shift and his voice became clearer. "Yeah, until he loses it. The shit he's done over the last two thousand years." Dell's voice grew quiet. "Do you know about his family?"

"Zola told me a little bit." I knew Ezekiel had given the order to have his family raped and murdered.

"They tied his family down on top of him and did that," Dell said, as if he knew exactly what I was thinking. "What would you do to the man responsible for that? Where would you stop?"

I remembered all too well what had happened to his family. I'd seen glimpses of it when I'd touched his power with my necromancy. The night I slayed Prosperine. The night we lost Carter and Maggie to that monster. What would I do to someone who did that to Sam, or my parents, or my friends? "I imagine I would tear little pieces off of him, starting with his toes. Skin him alive. Drop him in a barrel of salt. Something dramatic."

Dell let out a quiet laugh. "Way I understand it, you'd cram their souls into a dark bottle."

"That *is* fairly satisfying," I said, remembering what we'd done to Vicky's murderers.

"Doesn't it make you wonder where the line is?" Dell asked. "Where's the line? Or is there one?"

I laced my fingers together and rested them on my stomach. There was a time I wouldn't go near a soulart. I thought it would damn me as a dark necromancer. Now I wasn't even sure dark necromancers were necessarily evil. Things were simpler when it was all black and white, when Zola told me how things were, and that's how they were. No debate. No curiosity. What was, was.

Then I read Koda's book.

"Did the Old Man tell you about the book?" I asked, dancing along a dangerous line.

Dell was silent for a moment, and I wondered if he'd already dozed off.

"What book?" he asked in a voice that told me he knew exactly what I was asking.

"What do you think of soularts?"

Dell exhaled and shifted on the bunk below me. "*That* book. I think they're dangerous. I think an unwary man could kill himself with his own incantations. Or worse."

"I was surprised that soularts weren't forbidden because they could consume your soul."

"They still can, you know? It's a risk with the most powerful incantations. Is it true what the Old Man says? They were really forbidden because of their sheer power?"

"You didn't read the whole thing?" I asked.

"No, just a few pages."

I wondered why the Old Man kept some of it from Dell. "Did you read Koda's account of the Nameless King? No written history is thought to exist with that much detail."

"No. It's probably not important if the Old Man left it out."

He trusted the Old Man to some degree. I suppose I did too, but he still scared me. I fell silent for a bit, focusing on the shadows parading across the ceiling. Many centuries ago, before the Fae hid themselves away from the world, the

Nameless King altered his own hand with a soulart, binding it to some primal power no one could identify. He used it to carve out the Warded Ways. In the early days, they'd been a boon, but it didn't take long for the courts to realize what kind of damage the Warded Ways would eventually create. The Nameless King refused to stop, even as the world's ley lines began to collapse into the voids. Then the voids started bringing forth Old Gods and the rumblings of the Eldritch Gods.

"You know it was Glenn, Gwynn Ap Nudd, who rose up against the Nameless King and began the Wandering War?"

"Yes," Dell said. His voice was quieter. Sleep was overtaking him. He was going to need rest before running with the wolves.

"Journey well," I said. I wasn't sure where I'd heard the phrase, but it seemed right for the time.

Dell mumbled something and started snoring a moment later.

I stared at the ceiling, jealous of Dell's easy sleep. Darker thoughts had been keeping me from rest. Thoughts of my friends wounded in battle, of Nixie and her Queen, and the latest nightmare, the awful story of my birth.

Beware the Watchers. His master will reveal the path. Raise him well.

What did that mean? What are the sons of Anubis? And what does that make me?

CHAPTER TEN

"**A**GAIN."

"Again he says, always again," I muttered as I picked my aching body up out of the grass again. Bloody hell, I hadn't been so beaten down by training or practice since I was a kid with Zola. I wiped the blood off my lip and spat onto the ground.

"I'm eating lunch," I said. "If you'd care to join me, super." I stomped off toward the cabin, crossing the patch of ground where Zola and the fairies had helped me bury the various pieces of the demon, Azzazoth.

Dell had been gone when I'd woken up that morning. The Old Man told me he'd said goodbye. I'd miss him. That was for damn sure. The Old Man was like Zola without a sense of humor.

I let the front door smack closed behind me as I stomped into the cabin and angled straight for the old fridge. I opened the freezer. The Old Man had said Dell had left me a present in the ice chest. I figured he meant the freezer. There was an oblong pack wrapped in butcher paper and twine. I pulled it out and slammed the freezer. The twine came off easily and I tore the butcher paper off.

A blue bag of frozen chimichangas greeted me. I stared at them for a moment and blinked.

The front door opened and squeaked as it closed behind the Old Man.

"How the hell did he know?"

"Zola told us."

I looked at him, at the scars that turned his face into a roadmap of pain and history. It was easy to forget what he'd been through. That he'd lost family and friends. Friends who might have lived if they'd just trained a little harder.

I blew out a slow breath and laughed quietly. "You want one?" I asked as I tore open the bag.

He nodded.

I slapped two down on a plate that was probably not microwave safe, pushed the handle down on the ancient microwave to open the door, and fired it up.

"Thanks," I said without looking at him.

He didn't respond, but he really didn't need to.

I dug around the fridge and turned up some sour cream. It was extra sour, being slightly expired, but I figured we'd survive. "Sour cream?"

"I ... suppose," the Old Man said.

The microwave dinged. I pulled the plate out, then cursed and juggled it briefly before sliding it onto the counter. It was definitely not microwave safe. I wrapped my hands around the cold tub of sour cream for a moment before I started slathering the chimichangas. I tucked some paper towels under the hot plate, tossed one of the chimichangas onto a separate plate, and then balanced both with a couple sodas and a handful of silverware.

The Old Man had a TV tray set up in front of the couch and I snorted a laugh as I set his lunch down on it. "Old Man indeed."

He narrowed his eyes at me.

"I heard you talking to Roach about Koda's manuscript."

I nodded as I sat down in the old orange chair.

"You left out many things."

"I didn't know what you'd told him. I figured he was safer not knowing some of the things in that book."

"There is truth to that," he before taking a bite. He frowned slightly, chewed, and then swallowed. "Not bad."

"You mean awesome," I said around a mouthful of food.

He laughed quietly, and I saw some echo of the man he might have been a long time ago. "What I truly wonder about," he said, "is whether Dell is safer not knowing everything, or if it puts him in more danger."

"Why didn't you tell him about the Nameless King?" I asked.

The Old Man's soda opened with a crack and a hiss. He took a long drink before he looked back at me. "Dell is not strong enough to face an Old God on his own. I don't want him to read of the Eldritch Gods and the dark-touched. He is stronger than he realizes, but for him to be effective in battle, it would be best if he did not realize just how outmatched he is."

I looked at the Old Man for a moment, but I didn't speak. I wasn't quite sure what to say to that.

"Does that seem cold to you?" he asked as he looked back to his plate.

"A bit, but I think I understand."

"You have not seen war, Damian. There is a reason that training soldiers has not changed much in the past two thousand years."

"I would think it's changed quite a bit."

He nodded. "In some ways, in regards to technology, yes. At its core? How you train a man to move forward and keeping fighting as his friends and family are dying at his side? That will never change." He took another bite of his lunch and set his silverware down. "I sent hundreds of men to their deaths believing in the lies of courage, honor, and glory. It was my job. And I was damned good at it."

"Rome," I said.

"All over the empire," he said. "After I … changed. It was only after that I came to understand what I was. Or at least came to understand part of what I was. For centuries I wandered. Hunting Ezekiel, yes, but joining any fight where I could get someone else's blood on my hands too. I called Nixie an ally in some of those battles."

"She told me a little bit."

He nodded again. "That's enough reminiscing. Finish your lunch and meet me out front."

I finished my chimichanga and looked at his plate as he left the cabin. Every last scrap was gone. I smiled as I gathered up the dishes and washed them in the sink. The well water was cold, but I barely noticed. I'd spent more than my share of time washing dishes in that sink over the years.

Nixie hadn't told me too much about the Old Man, but I did know he had fought in the war between the water witches. The war where Nixie's queen rose to power. That was around the time the Roman Empire finally collapsed. Next time I saw Nixie, I was going to have to persuade a bit more information out of her.

The sun was lower in the sky than I expected when I joined

the Old Man beneath the oak tree. We'd eaten a much later lunch than I had realized. More like dinner. A cool, gentle breeze was a welcome respite from the heat of the midday sun we'd been training in before. He was throwing dirt on the smoldering ashes of the fire pit. They hissed as the last ashes disappeared, but I could still smell the burning wood.

"I think I could have been a pyro in another life." I took a deep breath. "That is just an awesome smell."

The Old Man gave me a sideways smile. I was pretty sure he appreciated the change of topic.

"Come. Tonight we train on the rocks."

"What?" I said.

"We are going to train with Aeros."

"Umm, what?"

"You're driving."

"I'm … we're … how does one train with a rock?"

"If I didn't know better I'd think you were nervous," he said, wiping his hands off on his jeans.

I cleared my throat. "Nervous might be a slightly strong word." I fished around in my pocket and found my keys. I started spinning them on my index finger. "I hope you're ready for a bouncy ride."

"I used to ride chariots through roads with ruts deep enough to swallow the wheels."

I stopped spinning my keys. "You just don't intimidate easy, do you?"

"No. Your staff and your backpack are already in the car. Let's get moving."

✦ ✦ ✦

IT WAS ABOUT an hour drive. Once we finished bouncing our heads off the ceiling of my '32 Ford on the uneven gravel road, the steady hiss of asphalt was a sweet relief.

The Old Man hadn't complained once as we hit the ruts and rocks. I'd cursed the entire time.

"That's better," he said. We headed north on highway 67.

"So you *did* notice the bumps."

"Noticing something does not require me to complain about it."

I cocked an eyebrow and shot him a sideways glance. "Did you just take a shot at me? I could have sworn you just took a shot at me."

"It's probably a sign I've been around you and Zola too much in the past year. I'm normally quite respectful."

"Uh huh," I said.

The Old Man chuckled quietly as I turned on the radio. I frowned and scanned the stations. Everything was static.

"Storm's moving in," he said.

"We'll get a better signal closer to Fredericktown," I said. I glanced up at the evening sky. "Looks pretty clear."

"Not the kind of storm I was referring to."

"Oh. You think the gathering powers are interfering?"

We both fell silent. I was pretty damn sure we were both thinking about just how bad a storm was heading our way.

I hit the accelerator a bit more than I needed to on the narrow turns and hills of highway 72. The Old Man braced his hands against the dashboard and laughed as I took a turn that would have been suicidal without the wide tires the old girl was wearing.

It wasn't much longer before we reached 21 and slowly

turned off into the huge, oval-shaped parking lot of Elephant Rocks State Park. The last car was leaving as we pulled in. I'd never run into a ranger when I came to visit Aeros, so I wasn't surprised when silence and emptiness greeted us.

I threw my backpack over one shoulder. The Old Man grabbed another backpack and let the straps dangle from his hand. He tossed my staff to me and it smacked into my palm.

We started up the parking lot, loose gravel and bits of torn up pavement crunching beneath our feet as we made our way to the short pavilion.

My eyes wandered over the brown wood. "They painted it."

"And?" the Old Man asked.

"The green was terrible."

We followed the path past the little pavilion. The woods closed over our heads and every sound became suspect in the dying light. I began striking the path in front of us with my staff. The ferrule clunked against the asphalt and made a satisfying echo.

The granite boulders still drew my attention as we walked past. I'd never been anywhere else and seen anything quite like it. They weren't as large or majestic as mountains, but seeing boulders the size of cars strewn through the woods was jarring.

We rounded the large, central hill of the park and the trail began to ascend. We crested the rise a minute later and could see enormous granite boulders the size of houses sitting on a red granite plain.

I'd come to think of Aeros as a friend, and it still threw me a bit, as we climbed, to see the names of his victims carved into the boulders beside the short wooden staircase. Most of the names were over a hundred years old.

We turned left, passed the string of boulders for which I was fairly certain the park had been named, and weaved between a few standing pools of water. One pool in particular would never go dry. Smooth pebbles lined the bottom of the water.

I smacked my staff on the granite surface beside the pool.

"Hey, Aeros! You awake?"

The Old Man actually laughed.

I pounded my staff on the ground a few more times. "Come on. Do you really want me to make with the glowy lights?"

Nothing happened. I sighed and kneeled down beside the pool.

"I hope you know what you're doing," the Old Man said.

"Don't I always?"

Judging by his expression, he didn't think so.

CHAPTER ELEVEN

A S SOON AS my hand neared the surface of the water, a dull, yellow-green glow rose between the pebbles. Gentle wisps of power brightened and waved from each stone, reaching out to the other wisps. The tiny fronds of light intertwined until a pattern emerged.

"Ehwaz," I said.

The fronds twisted and shimmered until a glyph appeared within the pool—a rune, shaped like a jagged capital M and made of light. The glyph dissolved.

"Uruz."

The light shifted as the fronds began to undulate and another rune rose between the pebbles. It looked like a lowercase n with the left edge higher than the right. A sharp line joined the top of each side.

"Oh, good. You didn't get us killed today," the Old Man said.

I'd seen Aeros step through the pool before, but I still jumped back as the water boiled without heat. Bubbles of light flowed from the fronds and broke the surface of the water. Dozens at first, and then hundreds spilled out into the air. The bubbling mass expanded and the bubbles merged before they dulled into a red granite body. Two lights kindled in the black pits of the highest granite boulder. A moment later, two glowing eyes rolled down to meet mine. A wiry crack in the surface turned into the Old God's smile.

"I heard you knocking," the earth said as he pulled his boulder-like legs out of the fading pool of light.

"You just wanted to see if I remembered," I said.

"It has been a while since I crushed someone here."

"Let's try to keep that streak alive," I said.

"Alive … yes. Zola would likely prefer that."

"Uh, I would likely prefer that too."

Aeros's face fractured into a grin as he turned to the Old Man. "It is good to see you again."

"And you," he said.

"How would you like to proceed?"

The Old Man ran his fingers over the white beard on his chin. "He's never faced an Old God directly."

"He did defeat Azzazoth and the Destroyer."

The Old Man nodded. "Yes, but he had help with Azzazoth. He nearly lost himself killing the Destroyer."

I took a deep breath. He was right on both counts.

"A brief demonstration, perhaps?" Aeros said, his voice rumbling through the stone beneath my feet.

"Like old times."

"Yes," Aeros said, agreeing with the Old Man. "I am glad to see your realization of what I am has not destroyed our old alliance."

The Old Man's hands began to emit a soft, yellow glow. Streamers of power floated away from his forearms like smoke. "I admit, I thought we'd have to kill you when I learned you were an Old God. You look different than you did in the war with the witches. I didn't expect a rock to age. How long has it been? A century? Two?"

"More time has passed us by than a mere century. We met in the Civil War once more, but when last we sparred, you still wore the name Levi." Aeros took a step away from the pool, leading the Old Man onto the wider plain of granite. Every footfall thundered as granite met granite.

"I still answer to that name."

"How long since you answered to Leviticus?"

The Old Man slammed his fists together and a waterfall of power poured from his hands. "You will not anger me so easily any more, old friend."

Aeros's smile widened. "I am glad of it."

I backed away, closer to the edge of the staircase.

"Prepare yourself!" It was all the warning Aeros gave.

He threw a hook like a wrecking ball. The Old Man's shield flashed up as he took half a step backwards. Aeros's fist glanced off the shield in a shower of sparks.

"Pulsatto!"

The wave of force didn't even phase Aeros as he lunged at the Old Man. The Old Man's showed actual surprise as the wall of rock turned at an impossible angle, aiming a strike at his legs.

"*Modus Ignatto!*" A pinwheel of fire erupted across the rocks. It wouldn't hurt Aeros, but the god couldn't see the Old Man maneuver to the side behind the tower of flame. "Too slow."

Aeros's eyes brightened as he crossed through the fire. The Old Man's hand blackened as he swung a punch at the Old God's head.

My jaw hung open as he connected and drove Aeros's face

into the granite plateau.

"You haven't slowed down a bit in your old age."

Aeros laughed as he pulled a knee up beneath him. "An artful distraction."

The Old Man nodded and leaned back against the nearest boulder. "You could have killed me with any one of those strikes."

"I know you better than that, Old Man. We all do."

"I must say," the Old Man said, "you don't give away your target like you used to. Back in the Civil War, I could dance around every attack you threw."

Aeros paused and studied the small man before him. Small to Aeros, at least. "Some of us were not born to fight."

"When the options are fight or die, everyone was born to fight."

My eyes trailed between Aeros and the Old Man. I had broken memories from when I'd touched the Old Man's power with my own. Fragments of the time he'd spent as a Centurion were in my head. I had broken visions of Aeros, and cannons, and blood, from the Civil War.

"When will the wars stop?" Aeros said. "It is no better than the gods of old. Petty, greedy, and destructive."

"There are some things that are better in this world," I said quietly. "People who stand up for victims and try their best to help others, to protect others …"

"To avenge others," the Old Man said.

When my gaze travelled from Aeros to the Old Man, I was surprised to find a smile on his face.

"Try to smash him," the Old Man said. "We'll find out if he was paying attention."

"You mean paying attention to how you blocked everything at an angle?" I asked.

"You make it sound so easy," the Old Man said, and I was damn sure that was sarcasm in his voice.

"Begin," Aeros said.

Aeros was not fond of warnings.

He took one step forward and threw a hook. It was one thing to watch the Old Man and analyze his defense. It was quite another to have a fist larger than your head, made of granite, hurtling at your face.

"Impadda!"

The angle wasn't good. Aeros's fist still glanced off the shield, but I caught enough of the blow that it slammed me into the boulder at my back. I cursed and ran into the open area of the granite plain.

Another hook.

Another shield.

Electric blue energy exploded across my vision as the shield turned his attack away. He stopped mid-punch and threw a left immediately after the right. I was wholly unprepared. My shield flashed up, but the punch landed squarely. I watched in amazement and horror as my shield failed.

I dove backwards and Aeros's fist narrowly missed my chest. I held my neck forward so I wouldn't give myself a concussion when I landed. The hit was hard. I rolled to the side and rose to my feet, gasping for air.

The Old Man was laughing. I found myself irritated beyond reason at that.

"Come on!" I said to the pile of rocks.

Aeros looked to the Old Man. I saw him nod out of the

corner of my eye. Now Aeros was taking cues from the Old Man? Oh, hell no.

The Old God swung at me with a hook again. I crouched and summoned a shield. His eyes widened as his blow was deflected upward, leaving the right side of his body exposed.

"Pulsatto!" My voice was almost a snarl as the wave of force exploded from my hand. I didn't hesitate as it hit Aeros in the head. It wasn't enough to damage him. I swung around behind him, drew the focus, and summoned a soulsword.

"Yield," I said. The golden blade licked the air beside my head.

"Well done," Aeros said, turning to face me. "Very well done. You are outside of my reach. Of course, should I choose to travel through the rocks, you are never out of my reach, but well done."

"You learn fast, but not fast enough," the Old Man said.

Out of sheer frustration I snapped out, "Oh, I need to learn faster?" I let the blade vanish and turned to face him. "What do you suppose I need to learn? Something like you did at Roanoke?"

He stiffened, his shoulders tightened ever so slightly. I wouldn't have seen it if I hadn't been looking for it. Some small part of me gained a glimmer of satisfaction before the sane part of my brain told me not to poke the bear with its paw on the big red nuclear button.

He didn't even move. An enormous boulder stood beside him, and then it was simply gone. Shattered. The burst of ley line energy was practically an afterthought. The damage was already done, and the calamity of falling stone was a deafening accompaniment. Stones the size of people and small cars collapsed to the plateau and slid off the edge. Smoking holes riddled several of them in regular patterns.

The Old Man let out a breath, somewhere between a sigh and a fit of rage. He turned slowly and met my eyes. An ancient memory, his memory, boiled and churned in my mind, showing me the promise of violence behind his gaze. I reached for my focus, because I knew the depth of his fury.

"The old wolf's been talking about things best forgotten," the Old Man said, his voice flat.

Aeros banged his hands together. It shook the entire granite plateau. I could have sworn the huge boulders, balanced beside each other, started to shake. The greenish yellow filaments that formed his eyes blazed into brilliant light. He gave us both the most irritated look I'd ever seen grace his rocky face.

"I will tolerate many things, but you must not put my domain at risk. I respect you both, but the power that lies within the Old Man is beyond anything you can imagine. Do not tempt him into using it."

The Old Man's shoulders sagged slightly. "My apologies. I should not have reacted like that."

My eyes trailed across the names carved deeply into the surface of the granite boulders. Men who didn't know better and thought to summon an Old God. I saw Aeros as a friend, but he was still a being I may never fully understand. It wouldn't do anyone any good for us to get pancaked today. I nodded to them both.

"Now then," Aeros said, "you have enough energy to enrage the Old Man, let us see how you use it against me."

That mountain of granite could move. He came at me with his arms raised, fingers laced together. My first instinct was to throw up a shield. My next thought was that he'd expect it. My mind flashed back to some unfortunate necromancers who'd tried using a shield, and then I remembered the Old Man. I dove to the side instead.

"Impadda!" The shield came up beneath my hand, and softened the blow as I hit the granite plateau hard.

Aeros changed the angle of his attack, using his momentum to pivot his entire body further than any human could possibly move.

I cursed and raised another shield. He caught the edge of it as I tried to jump away, propelling me even further. I sailed several feet through the air before meeting up with the earth again. My feet slid through one of the standing pools of water as I lowered my hands to catch my balance. The rock was smooth, but still cut into my palms as it passed beneath them.

I heard the Old Man laughing. He stood on top of one of the larger boulders, his feet an arm's length above my head.

"How do I fight him now?" I asked.

"I have no clue," he said.

The earth shook as Aeros ran at me. The thunder of his granite feet pounding across the plateau caused my heart rate to spike. The friendly smile I'd come to know was entirely absent on the face of the Old God. If I did something stupid, he was going to add my name to his fucking wall.

I braced myself to move, so the rock pile punched the ground. The Old Man was laughing again as I lost my footing and hit the ground hard. The grinding wail of an avalanche filled the air.

It took me a moment to realize it was Aeros screaming as he ran at me again. He didn't have a weakness I could see. The only times I'd ever even seen him stunned he'd either been struck by another god or hit by one of Philip's soularts.

Soularts.

The focus was in my hand a split second later. Timing would be everything. Maybe two more steps and he'd be on me. The soulsword ignited in my hand and I struck the plateau in front of Aeros's next step. There the plateau was a shallow angle where the rock sloped toward the tree line. I leapt to the side. I saw his glowing eyes brighten as he put his foot down and a three-foot section of the plateau slid away.

The Old Man slapped his leg and started laughing.

The Old God actually cursed as his leg went out from under him. He fell onto his back and sheer inertia carried him off into the trees in a stream of shattered rock, cursing, and the deafening crack of broken trees.

I let the soulsword fade and looped the focus back into my belt.

"You alright?" I said into the hollow of smashed trees that led down the hill.

I heard an exaggerated sigh as Aeros started picking himself up. "Yes. And a fine strategy, Damian. There was little chance I could stop my movement."

"You were going to flatten me."

"That would be unwise. I do not believe I would like to deal with your master if I flattened you."

"Well done," the Old Man said. "Gather some wood. We need a fire. Help convince some of these damn mosquitos to go somewhere else."

"Are we staying here?" I asked.

"For a while," the Old Man said.

"We're meeting an old friend," Aeros said, lowering himself to sit on the ground.

"Pretty damn young friend compared to us," the Old Man said.

CHAPTER TWELVE

T HE FIREWOOD REQUEST didn't annoy me nearly as much as I would have thought. I'm guessing it was the small compliment the Old Man paid me. Even something as simple as "Well done" almost seemed like a glowing compliment. Damned manipulative bastard.

I let Aeros and the Old Man exchange quips about just how old they were as I started down the hill of shattered trees to gather some wood. I was hauling the third load of broken branches when I realized we weren't alone.

Something rapped three times on the asphalt path near the bottom of the hill, near the destroyed boulder. I seriously considered asking if there was raven in the park, but managed to keep my mouth shut.

"Ah've never seen this place such a mess.

My face split into a wide grin. "You're just in time. The Old Man and Aeros are talking about how old they are. They're waiting for their 'pretty damn young friend' to show up. Any idea who that could be?"

A gray-cloaked figure climbed nimbly through the rubble until it was standing beside me.

Zola pulled back her hood and smiled. "Ah might have an inkling." Just listening to her old-world New Orleans accent was like coming home. All the insanity of the coming war faded, if only for a moment.

I laughed, dropped my bundle of branches, and hugged my master.

"Hugs?" she asked. "How bad has he been, boy?"

"Oh, he's not so bad." I paused for a moment. "Although Dell might disagree with that."

"Ah suspect he would," she said before she smiled. I couldn't see her eyes very well in the dark, hidden within her sunken face as they were. Only a glimmer caught the moonlight, a flash that made her dark, wrinkled skin seem more like the drawn cloak of a deadly predator.

"Come, let us visit," she said.

I quickly gathered up the branches I'd dropped a minute earlier. Zola's knobby old cane cracked loudly on the granite surface as she climbed the last few feet to the plateau.

"No fire?" Zola asked as Aeros came into view. "No food? No greeting?"

Aeros's rocky face fractured into a smile. "Adannaya, our young friend."

"Ah'm afraid the only reason you'd call me young is to soften me up for some bad news. Or a favor." She stopped a few feet away from the Old Man and rested her hands one atop the other on her cane. "Which will it be today?"

"We seek only answers," Aeros said.

"From times forgotten," the Old Man said.

"So the light does not wither." Zola frowned at the pair. "That is a very old code. Older than me."

"Older than me," the Old Man echoed Zola's words.

"What news?" Aeros asked.

"Do you know of Hern's rivalry with Glenn?" Zola asked as

she sat down on a stone closer to the Old Man.

"Yes," Aeros said.

"No," the Old Man said.

"Vaguely. Sort of," I said. "Cara's mentioned it once or twice."

Zola gestured at the pile of branches I was setting up in one of the dry pools. "You going to light that or keep rearranging it like a damned flower pot."

I let out a short laugh. *"Minas Ignatto."* The thin rod of flame ignited the wood in a heartbeat.

"Ah knew you weren't useless." She gave me a sideways glance.

"Hern is not the most stable of gods." Aeros crossed his arms and the sound of grinding rocks filled the quiet night. "It was not always so."

"What happened to him?" I asked.

Aeros's glowing, yellow-green eyes rolled to meet my own. "A great many things, Damian."

"It was probably Glenn that sent him over the deep end," the Old Man said. "Glenn won the rights to the Wild Hunt and banished Hern."

"Why would a king care about the Wild Hunt?" I asked.

"Foster would stab you in the eye for asking a question that stupid, boy," Zola said. "It's one of Cara's favorite stories. Glenn led the Wild Hunt to destroy the Nameless King."

I frowned, and then I realized what she was talking about. "Hern's story is woven into Glenn's ascension? The Wandering War?"

"Yes," Aeros said. "Hern fought on the side of the Nameless King, even after Glenn conquered him and displaced him as the leader of the Wild Hunt."

"Most of Hern's power was tied to the Hunt at the time, wasn't it?" the Old Man asked.

Aeros nodded. "Yes, he was weakened to near-mortal levels."

"What reason could he possibly have to stand against Glenn like that?"

"Zealots rarely use reason," Aeros said. His voice had become more quiet than I'd ever heard it before. "Hern was one of Faerie's mightiest lords. Glenn destroyed him. His mercy was no mercy at all in Hern's eyes."

"But he serves Glenn," I said. "One of his generals or some such thing, right?"

"It's easier to stick a knife between a man's ribs if he trusts you."

"Glenn is soft," Aeros said. "He may go to war with Ezekiel, but I do not believe all of Faerie will follow."

I glanced at Zola. Her face was stone. "You agree with Aeros, don't you?"

She nodded. "Ah've seen it. Hern still has followers loyal to him. You will need to step softly in Faerie. The Queen of the water witches would support Hern."

"She is long a fool," Aeros said. "She will lead her people into oblivion."

"Not if Nixie has anything to say about it." The heat in my own voice caught me off guard.

"Do you understand, young one?" Aeros asked as he stared at me. "A civil war among the Fae could destroy this world faster than Ezekiel can dream it. If the Seals fall, the Old Gods walk the earth once again." Aeros's whisper broke into a gravelly explosion of sound as he gestured with his hands. "The dark-touched devour humanity. In the end, the Eldritch rise. When the shadows we abandoned to the darkest reaches of existence find us. This. World. Will. End."

I shivered. The passion in Aeros's speech terrified me. Completely and utterly terrified me.

The Old Man flipped a smoking twig into the fire as he took a drag off his freshly lit pipe. He smacked his lips and spoke from the side of his mouth. "This is going to be interesting." He blew out a breath and turned to Zola. "Anything else to share with a couple old men?"

Aeros laughed softly, and I had a feeling it was because the Old Man referred to *him* as a man.

"Falias," Zola said. Her tone was reserved, sober. "Ward saved many lives there, but the city was lost. Cara spoke to me of Falias, but only briefly. Glenn will use it to gain sympathy."

The Old Man nodded and blew out a streamer of smoke. "It would be a practical rally cry. Everyone in Faerie, and even some of us not in Faerie, want Ezekiel's head for the loss of that city. Among other things.

"Would I only have the chance to carve his name into my walls ..."

"You can be somewhat scary, you know that?" I said to the mountain of rock beside me.

"Keeps the neighbors away," Aeros said.

I blinked, and then I was laughing so hard no sound was coming out. The Old Man juggled his pipe when it fell out of his mouth, casting lit tobacco across the stones in his surprise. Zola chuckled and shook her head.

"Ah must say, Ah needed that." Her mouth curled up into a

broad smile. "Just remember, boy, step carefully in Faerie. The Fae are not always the most reasonable creatures."

"You probably could have asked Nixie to tell me that."

"Perhaps, but Ah needed to get away for a time."

"I'm sure Nixie is busy with the war effort," the Old Man said.

I nodded and looked around the circle. Orange and red light flickered around us, casting everyone in and out of shadows. These three people were my inner circle, outside of the wolves and the fairies. They needed to know.

"Do you all know what Nixie is doing?" I asked.

Zola nodded, and a small knot untied in my gut. I despised keeping things from her.

"If I had to guess," the Old Man said, "she is working to dethrone the Queen of the water witches."

"As well she should," Aeros said.

I narrowed my eyes at the Old Man. "You're not guessing at all, are you?"

He laughed and lit his pipe again, using a burning twig from the fire. "No, son. No I'm not."

"We should still keep quiet about the revolution," Aeros said, his voice nearly as quiet as the buzz of a cicada in the distance.

I shook my head. "You're all in on it already."

"I have known much of what happens in the courts of the water witches since I … helped them."

"Helped them," Zola said before she snorted. "You destroyed a continent."

"It was a small continent," the Old Man said.

"Hmm …" Aeros's voice vibrated the stone I was sitting on.

"Atlantis."

"The most advanced civilization in the world," Zola said. "No match for your temper though, were they?"

The Old Man man's expression didn't change. He pinched his pipe between his teeth. "Queen wanted to drown the world. Ezekiel thought to help her. I took care of it."

"Atlantis?" I asked. "As in *the* Atlantis?"

"You destroyed man's greatest wealth of knowledge," Aeros said.

The Old Man's eyes moved to meet the Old God's. "I saved as much as I could. Once I realized that damned contraption was all that was keeping the island afloat, I saved what I could."

"Only to have it burned," Aeros said.

The Old Man pointed at Aeros with the stem of his pipe. "How was I to know Caesar's war-mongering would burn that library down?"

"Alexandria?" I asked. It was the only famous library I could think of from the Old Man's time.

"Yes," he said, drawing out the word. "Alexandria."

"You were in the library at Alexandria?" Zola asked. "You did not tell me this."

"I was in many places," the Old Man said. "Most of them have been destroyed, or lost, or forgotten."

Zola was quiet, and focused her gaze on the Old Man. For some reason, perhaps the same as me, she didn't prod the Old Man any further. His face looked drawn, and I was fairly certain he had a good idea of what had been lost.

"We saw Aideen," I said, trying to draw the conversation in a different direction.

Zola nodded.

"How's Foster doing?"

"Foster's fine," Zola said, "as are Cara and Aideen. They are worried, of course, but why don't you ask what you really want to ask?" She turned her head toward me, a knowing smile on her face.

"Whatever do you mean?" I asked, gesturing with my palm up and eyes wide.

She snorted. "Nixie is well. Fact of the matter is, she won't stop asking me how *you* are. It is quite … annoying. Ah imagine it will be better for everyone once you two are together again. Some of the stories Foster told me …" She rolled her eyes.

"He shouldn't have listened in to our private conversations," I said.

"He may be scarred for life."

"I seriously doubt that."

"Ah don't know. He asked Nixie about your phone sex habits many times."

The Old Man and Aeros looked at each other before the Old Man coughed over a laugh.

"What?!" I said. "He what?"

"In the river?" Zola said. "Foster says you two had some long distance—"

"Oh, stop," I said as I groaned. "That was just an experiment. I didn't know there was anyone else around."

The Old Man burst into laughter at that point. "Serves him right for dropping eaves."

I growled and flicked a twig into the fire. It hissed for a moment and then popped. "Have you met her Queen?" I asked, turning back to Zola.

Zola was biting her lips and smiling as she nodded. "One crazy bitch."

The Old Man blew a stream of smoke through his nose. "You aren't wrong about that."

I stood up and walked away from the fire. Something skittered away from me on the rocks. I could see the shadows of some of the stones the Old Man had shattered. A furry form scratched at one of the fragments and then vanished. The Old Man had put on a frightening display by destroying that stone. I could scarcely imagine what kind of damage he could do when he lost control. I walked slowly back into the circle of light.

Zola was shaking her head. "Ah saw the stone. You lost your patience."

"There was no risk," he said. "I have it in check."

"What was it like when you didn't have it in check?" I asked. "What did you do?"

The Old Man stared at me for moment before he sighed and turned his gaze to the fire. "There was a long, long time I didn't know what I was. I travelled from war to war, hunting for any trace of Ezekiel. When I found war … I became war."

"How did you recover?" I asked. "The first time you lost control to the gravemaker … I saw it, when I fought Prosperine."

"I'm sorry you had to see that, son." He looked away. "It was an Old God that imprisoned me. Stayed with me for almost a month, as I recall—or that is what he told me—until the rage eventually subsided. I still wonder if it would have been easier for him to kill me."

"Who?" I asked.

"Camazotz," Zola said.

"Rest assured he had his reasons," Aeros said from beside me.

"Oh, I've no doubt he had his reasons," the Old Man said. "I just doubt whether or not I'll like those reasons when I discover what they were."

"Have you heard from Mike?" Zola asked.

The Old Man shook his head.

"I have not," Aeros said.

Zola looked to me. I gave a small shake of my head to let her know I hadn't heard anything either.

Zola rubbed gripped the top of her knobby cane and rapped in on the granite at her feet. "He has been gone a long time."

"The demon will not betray us," Aeros said. "Give him time."

Zola nodded slowly. "Perhaps you are right."

"Okay, I think we've had enough doom and gloom," I said unzipping my backpack. I chucked a crinkled package of graham crackers to Zola, an enormous chocolate bar to the Old Man, and a bag of marshmallows to Aeros.

Aeros held up the bag, pinched between his rocky thumb and index finger. "What … is this?"

"S'mores!" I said.

"Why in the world was all this in your backpack already?" the Old Man said.

"Uh, s'mores, obviously," I said, snatching the bag of marshmallows back from Aeros.

Zola just sighed and shook her head, but that didn't stop her from opening the graham crackers.

CHAPTER THIRTEEN

Z OLA DIDN'T STICK around long after the s'mores were gone. The Old Man and I made it back to the cabin around two in the morning. He actually went into the cabin to sleep before I did. I was used to him staying up well past the time I was out cold. Maybe Aeros had actually taken a little something out of him.

The pond connected to a thin underground river. Depending on the height of the water table, I could reach Nixie. I made my way toward the pond, leaving the nicely trimmed yard and wading through the taller reeds that surrounded the water. I took off my boots, rolled up my jeans, and stepped into the chilly pond.

The symphony of frogs immediately shut down when my foot broke the water's surface. The crickets and cicadas still sang from the trees. I slid the blue obsidian disk out of my back pocket and laid it on the bottom of the pond, keeping my fingertips on the disk's surface.

All I had to do was think about Nixie, and the surrounding ley lines flooded the pond with electric blue light. The disk grew warm beneath my fingers as the water above the disk began to bubble. I would have said it was boiling, but the water was nowhere near that warm. A curious frog flexed his legs and swam around the bubbles. It tried to swim faster when the bubbles rose into a dome above the water, but the frog was pulled up into the swell.

Slowly, a face formed in the rising water. I waited as Nixie's sharp features materialized in the swell. Her eyes were unfocused at first, and then they rolled up to meet my own. The water sending didn't do her bright green eyes justice, but a flood of warmth rolled over me being able to look at her again.

"Damian." Her lips curled into a smile. Nixie's voice was musical, even in the sending. Her image grew undefined, flowing back into a dome of water before sharpening again a moment later.

"Reception kind of sucks down here."

"You're in the middle of nowhere, you brainless lunk."

I pulled my lips back in an exaggerated grin. "It's good to see you too."

"I'm afraid my head is the best you're getting tonight," she said.

I waggled my eyebrows.

"Pig."

"Pig?" I said. "Pig? Where did you learn that? You've been talking to Sam again, haven't you?"

"That's between me, Sam, and Jasper."

"What?" I said in such a loud voice that the insects around us fell silent.

Nixie giggled and blinked several times. It took me a second to realize she was batting her eyelashes.

"Where did you find Jasper?" I asked.

"He is here," Nixie said before she frowned slightly. "I was hoping you would have called earlier."

"Did something happen?" I asked. "You could have sent out

the emergency bat signal. Also known as the freeze my ass off with your disk signal."

"If you weren't near a water source, you would have worried."

"What is it?"

"Sam is here," Nixie said, "and Jasper. Though I don't believe she knows Jasper is guarding her from the shadows."

I stared at Nixie, my mind an absolute blank.

"Damian?"

"How?" I said. "Why didn't she tell me? What happened?"

"Glenn invited some of the Pit to the Concilium Belli. They came early."

"Who else is with Sam?"

"Vik is here, and I am checking on her when I can."

"Thank God for small favors," I said. I trusted Vik more than any of the other vampires. He'd shown his loyalty to Sam and Zola both on more than one occasion.

The scars on my left arm began to tingle. Lately I'd come to realize it meant something significant was happening with the pack. I ran the fingers of my right hand over the scars and met Nixie's gaze. "The River Pack?"

She nodded, her image collapsing and reforming in the motion. "Yes."

I needed to be at the Concilium Belli. Somewhere in the back of my mind I knew this gathering was growing more and more significant, but Zola's words stuck in my head. "I have to finish my training."

"Yes. I know. The day grows near when I can hold you in my arms again."

"That's awfully touchy feely." I said, cocking an eyebrow.

"You have no idea."

Both my eyebrows shot up and she giggled again.

"How is Levi?" she asked.

"Whoa whoa whoa, let's get back to Jasper."

"Jasper," Nixie said. Her eyes closed slightly and her head hung forward, as though someone had placed a great burden on her shoulders. "Jasper was with Ward at the fall."

"Falias," I said under my breath.

"He has lived in Faerie since you and Sam no longer needed him. He is one of the few survivors of Ezekiel's rampage."

My fingernails bit into my hand and I ground my teeth together. So many lives lost. So many Fae I didn't know. So many Fae I'd never have the chance to meet. Rage warred with the desire to keep my family safe. Keep my friends safe. I could almost understand why the Old Man had lost himself. If everything you live for is taken away …

"Damian."

I looked up and the expression on Nixie's face almost tore my heart out.

"Do not lose yourself."

I took a deep breath and nodded.

"It's gotten worse, hasn't it?" she asked. "The temptation?"

"We have to kill Ezekiel," I said. "Look at what he's done. We have to stop him."

"The Old Man is the most powerful necromancer ever to walk upon the earth. Even he was barely a match for Anubis." Her voice began to get shaky. "If you lose yourself, Ezekiel wins."

"I won't leave you," I said.

The water along her cheeks shimmered and flowed downward. I wasn't sure if it was just a stutter in the sending, or she was crying.

"How's the Queen?"

Nixie's face shut down. That was really all the answer I needed. "We'll talk about it when you get here. Focus on your training. When you use the hand of glory, do not let go of it for any reason.

"How is Levi?" she asked.

I laughed a little and rubbed my eyes before looking at Nixie's translucent image again. "I got a bit nasty with the Old Man today. It's like Russian roulette with sarcasm."

"Levi is not someone to fuck with," Nixie said.

"You're picking up some of the worst parts of our language quite well. Mom will be so proud."

"Which mom?" She asked. I could barely make out the rise in her eyebrows.

"*And* sarcasm?" I wiped my brow with an exaggerated motion. "That's sexy."

She grinned at me. "I miss you, Damian."

"I miss you too, Nix."

"How much longer will you be training with Levi?"

"I'm not sure. Until he says so, I suppose."

Her image shimmered, faded, and then resolved itself in a fountain of water. "I haven't felt your warmth in almost a year."

"You have a frog in your head."

She narrowed her eyes. "Are you changing the subject?"

I laughed and held my hand beside her image. The frog swam out of her cheek and onto my hand before it croaked and I set it down. "Really, you had a frog in your head."

She blinked and said, "Oh."

"I wish the world would calm the hell down so we could take a vacation together or something."

"We'll have some time here. You can see one of my homes!" She smiled, and it was warm, even in her watery state. "I love you."

A small smile crossed my lips. "I love you too."

She faded into the water and the light left the blue obsidian disc. I picked it up, shook most of the water off, and slid it into my jeans. In some small way, it felt like Nixie was still close.

I WALKED BACK to the cabin after strapping my shoes on. It wasn't a great idea to walk around southern Missouri without shoes. Copperhead snakes have a nasty bite. At least the ticks weren't out in force. I hate those bloodsuckers.

I ducked through the front of the cabin and eased the door shut. The s'mores hadn't cut it and I decided to indulge in one of Dell's most amazing of gifts.

I was on the couch about ninety seconds later, freshly microwaved chimichanga in hand. It was fantastic slathered in sour cream, but my mind was focused on far more troubling subjects.

Sam was in Faerie.

Glenn had brought the pack and the Pit.

Jasper was with Sam.

Mike was nowhere to be found.

Neither was Ezekiel.

I blew out a breath, turned awkwardly on the couch, and set my dishes on the counter. I smiled at a brief memory of Zola scolding me as a child for leaving my dishes in that exact same spot instead of the sink two feet away.

I stared at the backpack beside me and my smile faded. I unzipped it and pulled out the thin, black leather journal. My index finger slid to a random page and prodded the book open. Philip's looping scrawl was almost familiar now. I hoped to find some new insight into Ezekiel buried in those pages, but we'd long since studied everything useful.

I flipped further back into the journal. My eyes skimmed the text until I realized what I was reading. It was a page I'd read more than once. I started at the top again. There was a faint coppery stain at the top edge of the page. At some level, I knew it was blood.

January 1st, 1862

I have never seen death on such a scale. The Chicago boys are calling it the Slaughter Pen. We were some of the first to retreat. Without Aeros's quick thinking and Sheridan's response to the Confederates' flank, I don't know if anyone would have survived. They closed on us from the north. We expected them from the east.

Sheridan inspires a loyalty in his troops I can scarcely comprehend. They hold their ground, charge, and die, at his whim. His strategies are sound, methodical, but how can someone send so many children to their deaths?

Zola spun the most fantastic tale around the fire. A man who could step from nothing and vanish into the same. I had my doubts, but Aeros claims he saw the same. I do not know who the stranger was, but I fear my love would have been run down in the retreat if not for his intervention.

I was not fast enough to help them. Not strong enough to protect the woman I love. It won't happen again. It can't happen again. I will never let Zola suffer again.

A man who chased power to protect the people he loved. How did he fall so far? My eyes drifted closed. The night was haunted with dreams of what Philip Pinkerton had been, and what he had become.

CHAPTER FOURTEEN

"I WILL STAB you in the face," I said as someone shook my shoulder, waking me from the first decent dream I'd had all night.

"You can try," a gruff voice said.

My eyes shot open and found the Old Man about a foot away. I groaned and winced as I straightened my neck. Sleeping on a too-short couch is generally not recommended.

"Let me see that journal." He pulled out a thin pair of reading glasses.

"The what?" I said before I realized Philip's journal was lying beside me on the couch.

I tried really hard not to smile as the Old Man tilted his head down and looked at me over the rim of his glasses. I failed.

"I'll start the bacon," I said, handing him the book. I flicked my wrist as I passed the old wood stove and said *"Minas Ignatto."* A thin spiral of flame leapt from my hand and began to consume the wood. The burst of fire rattled the top of the stove.

"A little less energy next time," the Old Man said. "Modifiers help you control the power of the incantation, but your control of the energy will refine it. Or burn the cabin down. And I do not want to have that conversation with Zola."

I laughed as I pulled the bacon and eggs out of the fridge. "You and me both, Old Man. You and me both."

He focused on the journal as the bacon sizzled in the black, cast iron skillet.

"Coffee?" I asked as I pulled a Frappuccino out of the fridge.

"That's not coffee," he said without looking up. "That's milk and sugar with a hint of coffee flavor."

"Uh huh, what's the problem?"

"I'll take it black."

"You know Zola's coffee maker practically churns out asphalt, right?"

"Perfect." He turned a page.

I grimaced as I flipped the bacon and began prepping the old coffee maker. It smelled good, but I knew better than to attempt drinking it.

I flipped a TV tray out and set it next to the Old Man as breakfast finished cooking. He nodded as I slid a plate chock-full of bacon and eggs onto it.

"One mug o' sludge," I said, setting the bowl-like coffee mug beside his plate.

"Thank you." He closed the journal and set it down on an end table.

After a few bites, my eyes trailed from the journal to the Old Man's scarred and bearded face. "You knew Zola? In the war, I mean?"

The Old Man's gaze lifted slowly from his plate to my eyes. He had the same gray eyes as me. "Finish your breakfast, and we will talk."

It sounded so much like something Zola would say, I

couldn't help but chuckle.

We finished in silence. I gathered up the dishes and set them in the sink as the Old Man walked outside. I found him on the front porch, sitting on one of the steel chairs I hadn't flattened in training with Zola.

"You knew her back then," I said.

He nodded once as embers flared in his pipe and smoke curled slowly around his beard.

"Then you knew Philip too."

"Yes," he said. "I knew Philip and Zola. Not too well at the time, but I came to know Zola very well after the war. She helped me regain some of who I was after Sherman's march."

I nodded. One day I hoped the Old Man would tell me his stories, the stories I'd heard only through Zola of a time he'd almost lost himself. He'd been Sherman's secret weapon, and had carved a bloody path to the sea as he burned the south to the ground.

My thoughts trailed back to Zola. "Philip wasn't always …"

"Evil? No one sets out on a path to become evil. No sane person, at the least. Philip was not always the faceless monster you think of now."

I frowned and looked out into the field in front of the house. A quiet wind rustled the branches of the old oak. A doe and her fawn wove their way through the edge of the woods, not giving us so much as a glance.

"Philip's destiny is not yours."

I turned my eyes back to the Old Man. "There's a lot in that journal I can relate to."

"There is much in that journal anyone can relate to. It does not bind you to his mistakes."

"I know."

"And then there was Hinrik."

I nodded.

"Hinrik was an anomaly, or so most of us thought. A dark necromancer who would lay down his own life to protect people he barely knew." The Old Man took another breath from his pipe and exhaled slowly. "I thought I was damned to walk the earth as a dark necromancer. I'd spent five hundred years convincing myself I was one of the worst beings living in this wretched place. There was always one worse. Ezekiel. He was my enemy, and my salvation, in one tidy package.

"Hinrik changed that, Damian." The Old Man looked down at the embers in his pipe. "Hinrik changed a great many things."

"Why? What made him change?"

The Old Man emptied his pipe. "Koda, perhaps." He looked up at me. "What's important is that he did change."

"Could Philip have changed?"

"You've read the journal," he said. "No. He knew exactly what he was doing with every atrocity he committed. There is no hope for someone who loses themselves to righteousness."

✦   ✦   ✦

DAYS PASSED. THEN a week vanished, and then more. More things than bruises became routine as the time passed. I would wake up before the Old Man, usually right at sunrise, and cook up some bacon and eggs in the old cast iron skillet.

This morning I rubbed my shoulder and winced while I cooked breakfast one handed. I was a convert to asphalt coffee, and I sucked it down gratefully. "Wasn't one of the fairies supposed to come heal us by now?"

"You said Nixie told you they'd be late."

I frowned as I remembered. She'd just told me a few days before. "Dammit, how hard did you hit me on the head?"

He changed the channel on the small TV and asked, "Which time?"

I laughed and started slopping breakfast onto some chipped plates, eggs covering the sunflower pattern along the edge.

"Her again?" I asked, setting the plate of fatty breakfast goodness on the Old Man's TV tray and looking at the small, pixelated reporter. "What was her name?" It hadn't been long since she'd been standing in my shop harassing Frank. "What's she doing in southern Illinois?"

"Showing us our enemy," the Old Man said. The arm of the couch creaked as he clenched his hand around it.

"We're covering the murders on the bridge between Brookport, Illinois and Paducah, Kentucky. As you can see behind me, the police have the area surrounded and the suspect has made no move to run. We have evidence of the murders, and it is not for children. Roll it."

Shaky video played on the TV. The Old Man leaned forward and I stared in horror. Ezekiel stood in the center of a narrow blue bridge. Ten Watchers hung from the top of the steel structure. At least half of them were already dead, either from hanging or from the large, bloody gashes etched across their chests. Some, still alive, hung suspended in crude rope harnesses.

Ezekiel raised his arm toward one of the dead women. I couldn't see the flow of power, or the change in the auras, but I had a good idea of what was coming. Her pale face twitched and the swollen tongue vanished into the corpse's mouth before her arms flexed, and the bonds broke.

It was faint, being so far from the microphone, but I could hear the man next to her scream "No!"

The dead Watcher reached up and grabbed the noose around her neck. She pulled herself up the same old rope Ezekiel had used to hang her. I watched in awful fascination as she chewed through the rope. She shimmied along the ledge to the next rope, and slid down to the screaming man. He thrashed and screamed as she started to chew his face off.

The video feed swung back to the reporter, who stared at the monitor in the van beside her. I knew she was watching the rest of the event unfold. "Oh my God," she said. "Oh my God." She turned away from the screen and vomited. She glanced back toward the bridge. Ezekiel still stood there, motionless.

The reporter wiped her mouth. "What's that sound? It's a … we're hearing a rumble and—"

The camera shook violently.

"Earthquake?" asked a voice from off screen.

"They failed," the Old Man said. He sighed, and that mild expression of emotion sent a chill into my bones. "She should be running. That's a summoning ritual."

The camera panned away from the sick reporter and then zoomed and blurred momentarily until Ezekiel's form filled most of the screen. His lips moved in his pale, sandy face. His eyes were entirely black on the pixelated screen, and I didn't think it was a trick of the light.

The river boiled.

"So rises a Leviathan." The Old Man stood up and walked away.

I stared. My jaw grew slack as the first tentacle wrapped itself around the bridge behind Ezekiel. The supports began to bend and screech. There was a roar … but it was more than a roar. It was a thousand lions, distorted and tortured and crying for blood. My skin crawled as the light reflected off a dark, dripping form.

Screaming joined the raucous screech of tortured metal and the Leviathan's roar. The reporter and the cameramen came to their senses. The cameras panned back to the bridge, where dead Watchers devoured living ones. Ezekiel casually swept his fingers in the direction of the Leviathan. The camera locked onto another of the dead Watchers when she moved. The bullet holes in her chest and a blown out cheek—a good sign the police hadn't been sitting idly by—didn't seem to be slowing her down as she shambled toward the edge of the bridge.

The reanimated Watchers abandoned their gory feast and dropped to the pavement below. A trio of hideous beaks revealed themselves in the black mass of the river monster. The undead Watchers stepped over the railings one at a time and reached out to the beast. Tentacles snapped out, crushing them and dragging the remnants to each of the beaks in turn. The Leviathan roared again, and the beast's flesh seemed to grow, expanding to dwarf the bridge, then shrinking. I closed my eyes and looked again.

The Old Man walked back into the room. "You cannot see the entire creature on film. Only its non-magical shell. It is hunger and destruction incarnate."

"What the fuck is that?" I asked as I started to gnaw on a piece of bacon, looked back at the TV, and set the whole plate down in disgust.

"Where Philip was cautious and secretive, Ezekiel will be merciless and bold."

"He's Anubis," I said. "He's a necromancer, not Aquaman for fuck's sake!"

The Old Man actually laughed and settled on the couch again. "The reason I am so hard on you in training. The reason Zola was so diligent. However unlikely, we knew this could happen in your lifetime. When a Seal falls, through the death of Ezekiel, or Edgar, or any of the Guardians, the Old Gods of the Abyss will begin to break through into this world. You will yearn for the days when Philip Pinkerton was all that haunted your dreams."

An ear-piercing scream drew our focus back to the television. The camera was sideways on the ground, and a rubbery tentacle was dragging a man in headphones toward the river.

The reporter wasn't forming words anymore. She screamed and vanished into the van before it barreled out of the frame. As the camera refocused, another tentacle, a dozen feet thick, wrapped around a small car, dragging it into the river. The bridge began to give way. Metal screamed and the earth shook. Another tentacle shot out of the abyss and swung toward the camera. The picture dimmed into shadow and was lost in an explosion of static.

I clenched my jaw and turned to the Old Man. "We should be out there helping. It could be my family out there dying."

"Croatoan." The Old Man almost growled after he said it.

"What?" I glanced at the static on the TV. "That was Croatoan?"

"No," He rested his chin on his fist and leaned forward. "I killed Croatoan. This one is of his ilk."

I wanted to ask him what it was like to battle Croatoan, to fight a Leviathan. How did he do it? How in the hell did one man kill an Old God? "What happened in Roanoke?" I asked, even though I half expected the Old Man to stop talking again.

"I lost my temper."

I slowly raised an eyebrow.

"I'm not trying to be humorous. It is something you'll have to be careful of too. You've read Koda's manuscript, yes?"

"I … yes. How did you know?"

"Last year, in Boonville, you seemed very concerned with becoming a dark necromancer. I haven't heard you mention it once since."

I nodded. "I spoke to Koda about soularts at great length. I see those arts differently than I did before."

"You spoke to him?"

"His ghost, yes. He's still around."

The Old Man looked down at his hands. "I did not realize he was still with us. Koda was one of the first to realize a dark necromancer may not always be a hellish blight upon humanity." He met my gaze. "Koda's manuscript gave Hinrik hope when he had none. Such a sacrifice. All to banish a demon. He saved many lives."

"So did Maggie and Carter," I said. "And they were good people."

CHAPTER FIFTEEN

W E'D JUST SQUARED off to begin training when I felt a small surge in the ley lines behind the cabin. The Old Man and I exchanged nods and headed around back, past the old stone well.

"My shoulders are so happy," I said. "It's got to be one of the fairies."

A small white and gold figure fluttered out of the woods and exploded into a seven-foot colossus, trailing a cloud of fairy dust. Foster threw his arms out to his sides, golden chainmail tinkling as he moved. "Damian!" He crushed me in a hug, at which point I realized my ribs hurt like a bitch.

"Ow," I said, but I hugged him back anyway.

"Sorry, sorry," he said, slapping my shoulder.

I winced again.

"Damn," he said. "You've been getting a good workout."

"Even trained with Aeros," the Old Man said.

Foster extended his hand and traded grips with the Old Man. "I bet that kept him on his toes."

"Kept him diving around like a drunk duck."

Foster laughed and turned back to me. "It will be good to have you in Faerie."

"It's damn good to see you," I said.

"Is Glenn aware of the Leviathan?" the Old Man asked.

Foster nodded and his face shut down. "We saw."

The Old Man nodded, and they both fell silent.

"How're Aideen and Sam and, well, everyone?"

"You mean Nixie?" Foster asked. He raised an eyebrow, seeming glad to change the topic. "Nixie's great. Although she doesn't shut up about you coming to Faerie, I'm going to have to put her out of my misery."

That made me smile. "Sam?"

"Sam is safe as safe can be. You never told me what Jasper was." He leveled his gaze at me, eyebrows drawing down over his slightly slanted eyes.

"What he was?" I asked.

"God of dust and bones. He's a reaper."

I blinked.

The Old Man whistled.

"What? But he … no, he's an overgrown dust bunny who likes to make Sam's stuffed animals dance for her."

"He was probably drawn to you both," Foster said. He slid the helmet off his head and ran his hand through his platinum blond hair. "Reapers have a knack for finding people with a whole lot of shit headed straight for them."

Foster set his helmet on one of the stones Aeros had raised.

"Yeah," I said. "That pretty much describes our lives." I shook my head. "I thought all the reapers were killed in the Wandering War."

"So did I," the Old Man said.

Foster turned to look at each of us in turn. "Reapers aren't really Fae, you know? We're not sure where they came from. They can use ley lines, they can feed from them, but they don't have to be near them to survive."

The Old Man scratched at the scars on his arm and said, "Their bones are supposed have useful properties."

Foster looked at the Old Man. He started to open his mouth, and then he looked away.

"What?" I asked.

He looked up at me. "Nothing, it's nothing." His eyes flicked to the Old Man, who concentrated on his pipe.

I nodded. Apparently Foster had something to add, but he wasn't talking in front of the Old Man.

"Let's see how much damage you've managed to take on," Foster said. He started prodding at my shoulder.

I winced away at the sudden, sharp pain.

"You've either got some screwed up muscles or a torn rotator cuff." His hand moved from my shoulder and poked my lower rib cage.

I gasped. It felt like I'd just taken an uppercut in my abdomen.

"Buck up," he said.

"Buck up?" I said between gritted teeth. "Did you seriously just tell me to 'buck up'?"

"Yes," he said, jabbing another rib.

I cursed and glared at him. "Why are you hanging out in super-size mode?"

Foster stepped around me before stretching his back. "I've been small since we went to Faerie. You can't just walk around in your Proelium state. That's considered a challenge, at best, and an act of war at worst.

"Alright, you're not looking so bad. Two cracked ribs are the only real damage. That shoulder won't do you any favors if we let it go.

Foster stood up. "You better take off the kid gloves, Old Man."

"Kid gloves?" I said. "Bloody hell, you just said I have two cracked ribs."

Foster flashed me a grin. "The Concilium Belli is going to convene in two days. That means you're coming over to Faerie tomorrow."

"It was only a matter of time," the Old Man said.

Foster nodded and cracked his knuckles. "Let's patch you up. Ribs are going to hurt."

I took a deep breath and braced myself.

"*Socius Sanation!*" Foster said, extending his right palm. Warm white light bathed me for a split second. My breath hissed out between my teeth when it felt like Aeros had just jabbed me in the ribs.

I gasped for air, grabbed my chest, and groaned.

Foster shifted his focus to my shoulder. My arm spasmed and there was a tremendous pop before the light of his incantation began to fade.

"Do you have the hand of glory?" Foster asked. He was nonchalant, as though he hadn't just healed my cracked bones in a span of seconds.

I nodded. My teeth were still clenched.

"Good. I know Nixie told you not to let go. Seriously, do not let go. No one will come to fish you out of the Abyss." He turned and scooped up his golden helmet before seating it on his head once more. "You need to watch your tongue when you're in Faerie."

I stuck out my tongue and tried to look at it. "Difficult."

Foster groaned. "Don't make me call your mom."

I smiled as Foster crossed his arms. "As long as you don't call *your* mom, I'm good."

Foster laughed quietly.

I think the Old Man was getting bored. As he walked away, he turned and said, "Meet me in the front field once Foster leaves."

I watched him walk around the side of the cabin where the sheds used to be. Smoke trailed after him, and it reminded me of the smoldering crater from our fight with Azzazoth.

Foster snapped back into his smaller form. "Levi still kind of creeps me out sometimes."

"What didn't you want to say?" I spoke into the wind, making it unlikely any sound would carry around the cabin.

Foster fluttered to my shoulder and his voice was not far above a whisper. "The bones of the reapers are tied to a very old legend."

My mind flipped through a dozen of the oldest Fae legends I knew. None of them matched up with the description of a reaper.

"They're Magrasnetto," Foster said.

"What?"

"Their bones. When they die in a certain form, they leave bones behind. The bones bond to iron and form Magrasnetto.

I narrowed my eyes. "The Magrasnetto in the shop that was shaped like an irregular cone?"

Foster nodded. "It was probably a piece of a tail."

"That's interesting, but why didn't you want the Old Man to hear?"

"I just …" He looked away. "Damian, you've never seen him lose it. I don't like the idea of him knowing even more things he could use to gain power."

"He seems pretty stable these days," I said.

Foster glided out in front of me and hovered with a slow flap of his wings. He shook his head and pointed at me. "Do you remember how close he came to losing it at Rivercene?"

The Old Man's encounter with Ezekiel at Rivercene. The thunderbird had prevented any real fighting from happening, but the Old Man had practically been frothing at the mouth.

I nodded.

"When we fight Ezekiel, and you know damn well it's coming, will he be able to hold back? Would you?" Foster crossed his arms. "After two thousand years of hatred …" Foster frowned and his brows drew down beneath his helmet, hiding his eyes in shadows. "I wouldn't hold back. I would break the world."

I thought about Azzazoth and Devon. How, for all intents and purposes, they'd enslaved Sam and turned her against me. I'd gone head to head with Azzazoth. I'd brutally dismembered his lackeys and used their auras against him, along with a metric fuck ton of dynamite. If it hadn't worked … If it hadn't been enough … If I'd lost Sam …

I shivered and closed my eyes.

"No, I don't think I could."

Foster nodded and glided to the nearest protruding stone. "How are you dealing with the dead?" he asked.

I shrugged. "They're a bit more active than usual, but it really hasn't bothered me. They've kept their distance. Maybe it's the Old Man?"

"Maybe," Foster turned his armored head toward the pond. "Aideen said Dell was in pretty bad shape. Why didn't the dead leave him alone?"

I frowned. "I don't know."

"You should ask the Old Man. He may have some idea. Don't know if he'll actually tell you if it was his doing in the first place. He can be a pretty secretive son of a bitch."

"Says the fairy who wouldn't talk about Magrasnetto in front of him."

Foster cast me a lopsided grin. "I didn't say it didn't have its uses."

"How long can you stay?"

"I can't," he said. He glanced down and frowned slightly. "The courts are divided, Damian. Some of them think Ezekiel's actions will benefit Faerie."

"What?" I said, unable to keep the utter disbelief from my voice. "How could any Fae support Ezekiel? After what happened in Falias?"

"There is a lot about Faerie you do not understand. If Ezekiel destroys humanity, or enslaves it, the Fae will be free to walk the earth with abandon."

"What does that have to do with Ezekiel?" I asked. "They could do that regardless."

"If Ezekiel succeeds, he will be the only god left outside of the Old Gods."

"He is not a god," I said.

"He is as much a god as any man can become. Take that for what it's worth, but he is a god." Foster sighed and lifted his helmet slightly to scratch his head. "I have to go, Damian. Take care of yourself. I'll see you in Faerie."

✦　✦　✦

FOSTER LEFT WITHOUT circumstance. He glided into the woods, there was a brief spike in ley line energy as he entered the Ways, and he was gone.

My eyes looked after the path he'd taken, up through the rut Zola's fiery execution of Philip had created. I sighed and started around the cabin. The longer grass whispered along my jeans. A small brown lizard scampered up the cabin's shingles. It blinked once, and then vanished behind some firewood.

The Old Man stood with his hands behind his back. The lower branches of the oak tree framed him in the afternoon sun, a mottled image of sunlight and darkness.

"Why was Dell so heavily affected by the dead here?" I asked.

"There are reasons," the Old Man said before he turned to me.

"No shit," I said.

His thick beard curled up and I knew his scarred face was smiling. "What you may not know, and your master may not have realized until recently, is that you are no mere necromancer. We seven sons of Anubis are all something more. The Fae teach you arts no born necromancer should be able to access. Using those arts breaks the very concept of necromancy. Why do they teach you these things? To what end? It's best not to trust any Fae that can still draw breath. Even dead Fae can be … problematic."

"I trust my friends," I said, thinking of Foster, Aideen, Cara, and Cassie. My friends who fought with me, laughed with me, died beside me. "You're wrong."

He crossed his arms and walked up onto the porch and into the cabin. "Come, let us talk indoors."

I followed him inside and sat down on the green couch as he leaned back into the old orange chair.

"Let us hope you are right about your friends. Regardless of what you believe, you are changing."

"What do you mean?" I leaned forward, elbows on my thighs and hands hanging in the empty space between.

"Tell me," he asked as he leaned forward, "when was the last time you studied an aura? The last time you needed the Sight to tell you exactly what you needed to do?"

His words hit me like a slap in the face. "I …" When I'd trained with Zola, I always had to focus on the aura to perform any remotely complicated incantation. It had been so damn hard to use the vampiric zombie auras to injure Azzazoth, but I was pretty sure I could do it blindfolded now.

"When was the last time you really had to think about manipulating an aura?"

When did that change? "When?" I said aloud. *When?* I thought to myself.

"When?"

My eyes widened as my mind pinpointed the exact time. "When I killed Prosperine."

The Old Man leaned back in his chair and smiled. That smile made my skin crawl. "Welcome to godhood, brother."

CHAPTER SIXTEEN

I SNORTED AT the Old Man's claim.

"It is time to leave your playthings behind," the Old Man said as he walked to the front door. "Come."

"What did you mean by 'godhood'?" I grimaced and lifted my bruised yet recently healed ass off the couch. The glorious, glorious couch that I missed immediately. I don't think godhood meant the same thing to me as it did to the Old Man.

"Bring your staff."

I grabbed the staff as I passed by it on my way out the door. The screen door slammed shut behind me and startled an unsuspecting bat. It climbed deeper into the darkness in the corner of the porch, squeaking in what I can only imagine was annoyance.

"That it? Are we done talking about this?"

"Bring up a circle shield," he said.

"Why?" I asked.

"Because I would prefer this not kill you."

I groaned and began dragging my staff through the dirt to form a circle. I touched one of the Magrasnetto ferules to the indention and said *"Orbis Tego."* A flowing dome snapped into existence, distorting my vision of the Old Man ever so slightly.

"This is called the Hand of Anubis." He closed his eyes and reached out with his right hand.

The earth rumbled. For a brief moment it felt as though Aeros was speaking. Then the earth around my feet exploded. Five gravemakers rose up around me, slamming into the shield, and I screamed as lightning bolts of electric blue energy shot off into the air. The shield began to bend, and then I rose into the air. My heart thudded in my chest as the flashes of power illuminated the gravemakers.

But they weren't gravemakers.

Oh, it was the stuff of gravemakers, looking like worn and rotten bark off a dead tree. But each of the five was connected below me. One was shorter than the others. I realized I was standing on a hand made up of gravemakers' chaff.

"Fuck. Me."

I heard the Old Man's quiet chuckle, but I couldn't see him through the arcing power and the darkness around me. I felt myself being lowered before the fingers began to disintegrate. Slowly they degraded into piles amid the grass before seeping back into the earth.

I slammed the end of my staff into the ground to break the circle. It fell, and I stared at the Old Man. "What. The hell. Was that?"

"There are only eight beings that have walked this earth that can control a gravemaker. Anubis and his seven sons."

"Bullshit," I said. "If necromancers are destined to become gravemakers, some of them had to be able to control the damn things before Anubis."

"None that I am aware of," the Old Man said. "And I *have* looked. A butterfly does not control the caterpillar that bore him."

I stared at the Old Man. "That sounds like something Hugh

would say."

The Old Man nodded. "It is something Hugh said to me a very long time ago."

"What will you do when we find Ezekiel?" I asked.

"I will fight him. I may defeat him, or he may defeat me. It is a long road we have walked. It is time for that road to end." He turned and walked toward the pond. "Come, show me the Fist of Anubis."

"You haven't explained it yet," I said.

"You have seen it. I doubt you need more than that. It is one of the few gifts you will enjoy from our father."

It was night by the time we finished training. I was pretty sure the Old Man had been right. Between shield training and close quarters combat, he had me focus on the Hand of Anubis as he summoned it and showed me its variant, the Fist of Anubis. I was sure I could do the same, and that frightened me, and exhilarated me, which frightened me even more.

The Old Man settled onto the couch. "The world will try to beat you down. It will steal your will. The best thing you can do is kick it in the balls."

I raised my eyebrows.

"You saw the Leviathan." He stayed silent until I nodded. "You need to understand something. You are not strong enough to face a creature like that. You need more power."

"How?" I asked. "Where do I even begin?"

"Soularts will be your best weapon. Study Koda's manuscripts. See if the old ghost will train you. I'm afraid, at some point, you will become an immortal, or you will let this world die."

I sighed and stared at the old wood stove. "Super."

✦   ✦   ✦

IT WAS LATE when I felt the enormous ley lines around us shift as *something* arrived within the perimeter Zola had setup so many years ago. The Old Man's eyes met mine and he simply nodded. I pointed to the back door as I moved to the front.

He moved silently. The door that normally squealed opened quietly, as if he had willed it to be silent. I took a different tact and let the front door slam behind me with a thunderclap of wood slamming together and the metallic echo of rusty springs.

A bulky shadow stood at the edge of the forest, beyond the old oak. Something pulsed out from the figure as it pulled a thin blade from the darkness to its side and held it to the sky. I didn't even have to concentrate to see the nova of power emanating from the blade. The shadow stepped forward into the moonlight as it sheathed the object once more.

Mike's features took shape and I started to smile. In the moonlight, I could see the dark streaks on his arms disappearing beneath the leather blacksmith's vest he wore. He drew the hammer from the belt loop as his side. The Smith's Hammer ignited, expanding into an enormous war hammer as smoke began to climb from the demon's eyes. I took a step backward as I realized his eyes were flame.

"Mike?"

"Prove your worth to me Anubis-son. God-child. Only a worthy god can wield the Splendorum Mortem."

That's what the blade had been. Gods, that thing was power incarnate.

Thought left me as the flaming hammer of death streaked

across the field. Mike released an inhuman growl. For the first time since I'd come to know the demon, fear lived in my gut instead of our usual camaraderie. My shield was up in a split second. My training with Aeros kicked in. I adjusted the angle and Mike's first strike glanced off it. Fire and lightning erupted from the shield's surface.

The demon knew what he was doing with the heavy weapon. His momentum carried through to a spinning strike and caught my shield squarely. Flames exploded across my vision as he growled, shifted, and connected with an overhead strike.

A shield can take a lot of abuse. It can't take direct hits from the Smith's Hammer. My safety net vanished in an explosion of electric blue lightning. The explosion lit up the field and something flickered across Mike's face, something like regret, as he pulled back for a killing blow.

I caught a glimpse of the Old Man. The bastard was leaning against the corner of the cabin with his arms crossed. The Old Man. Fuck. Yes. I'd only seen it a few times, but I was sure, for this magic, it'd be all I needed.

My growl turned into a scream as I sent my aura blasting out to every dead thing I could find within a half mile. It came to me by the time I punched my fist into the air. The ground exploded in front of Mike. His eyes widened before the grisly fist the size of his entire body made contact with his chin. The hammer fell from his hand, the flames vanishing in the blink of an eye, dropping the entire field into darkness.

A current of power lit my senses on fire. In that moment, I knew nothing could stop me. Nothing could touch me. I laughed, and it was a horrible, wretched sound. I stalked toward the demon and barked at him. "Is that all you have? Is it? I could kill you so easily …"

I stared at Mike, unconscious and bleeding on the ground. That wasn't right. Something felt wrong … and then my senses began to return. I raised the palm of my right hand to my forehead and swayed.

"What the fuck?" I fell onto my knees by Mike's head. He was face down in the field of grass. I reached out and touched his neck. He still had a heartbeat. His back rose slightly. He was still breathing. I wasn't sure if any of that mattered with a demon.

"Mike? Dammit, Mike, are you alright?" I rolled the demon over and winced at the blood running down his face as his eyes slowly focused on me.

"What … what happened?"

"I think I knocked you out."

"It didn't take you." His eyes trailed from me over to the Old Man. "You were right, Leviticus." Mike's bloody face curled up into a smile. "You were right."

Things started clicking in my head. "This was a test?" I looked at the Old Man.

"Yes. I lost myself to the Fist of Anubis once, during Sherman's March to the Sea. We had to be sure you were stronger than me."

"What?" I asked.

"You summoned the power of a gravemaker, and it did not take you. You didn't lose yourself in it."

"Bloody hell, is that what I felt? The raw power? The absolute need to kill something?"

"You didn't," Mike said. "I wouldn't have believed it if I hadn't seen it." He sat up and rubbed his face. He blinked and looked at the blood that came away on his hand. "Damn. That was a hell of a punch."

"You did great, kid," the Old Man said. "There was a time I failed to resist." He started to light the pipe in his hand, paused, and set it on the porch railing instead. "You have seen my past, son. You know what happened to my family. You probably know more than you even realize. The memories and life you absorbed when your power siphoned away my own."

I nodded, remembering the battle with Prosperine. Remembering the terrifying power that allowed me to reach out to the Old Man while he was some five hundred miles away.

"Unless I miss my guess, you already know what happened in Roanoke."

"The Leviathan?" Mike sniffed and climbed back to his feet.

"Croatoan," the Old Man said. "I will always have regrets for what happened there."

"I've heard the story," Mike said. "If you hadn't stopped that thing when you did, it could have ended this entire country. The Watchers weren't in the States yet. Outside of the Native Americans, this country was lost when it came to magic."

"Croatoan was not magic," the Old Man said as he picked his pipe up and finished packing it. "Croatoan was an Old God."

"Some believe he was Eldritch." Mike rubbed his jaw and winced.

"You alright?" I asked.

He nodded his head and gave me a thumbs up.

"Old Gods and Eldritch Gods," the Old Man said. "There is little difference."

"Are you nuts?" I asked. "If one of the Eldritch Gods ever came here, we'd be lost."

"No," he said. "If they come here, we will kill them. Koda believes the line of Anubis was born to defend this realm from the Old Gods. I cannot help but believe he was right."

"You'll be attending the Concilium Belli soon, yes?" Mike asked, turning to me.

I nodded.

"Do not reveal the Splendorum Mortem to them. There are several beings who would take the blade and use it to their own ends to do great harm. With the oath I swore on my hammer, never to kill an innocent, it could very well be the end of me."

Mike pulled a simple leather sheath off his belt. He took a deep breath, and then held it out to me. "Regardless of what you fight, this blade can kill it."

I held out my hand and Mike gently placed the sheath in my palm. I smelled oil and leather. Stitching edged the sheath and ended in two copper rivets. I snapped the strap off the dagger's hilt and stared at the braided metal beneath.

Two fairy Blessings had been married. The hilt's wide, flat base reminded me of the dull end of an old railroad spike. The metals wove together, one slightly lighter than the other, even in the moonlight. The hilt curved and ended in a wicked-looking blade. It was rough, with forge and hammer marks along either side, but the edge glinted, ready for blood.

I slid the Splendorum Mortem back into the sheath.

"The blade alone can kill an immortal," Mike said. "It can channel a soulsword, just like your focus does, but I would urge you to avoid that. You may not be able to control the amplification of power."

"I'll avoid it as best I can," I said. "Unless I need to roast some marshmallows really, really fast."

Mike nodded and wore a serious expression. "It would work pretty well for that."

"Idiots," the Old Man said. I could have sworn the ghost of a smile crept onto his face.

"Rest well tonight, Damian. I understand Gwynn Ap Nudd declared you must travel by way of the hand."

I nodded.

"Don't—"

"Let go," I said. "Yeah, I've heard that once or twice.

Mike laughed quietly, his massive chest moving with the sound. "Rest well. It will not be long before war is upon us."

"Will you be at the council in Faerie?" I asked.

"Glenn invited me, but I do not know if it would be wise. The courts of the undines are in turmoil. A fire demon may draw too much attention."

"Plus I'll cut his balls off if he goes," a voice said from the vicinity of the old oak tree.

We all turned.

Mike's little necromancer stood there with her arms folded across her chest.

I grinned and turned back to Mike. "I think I see the reason pretty clearly now."

The Old Man coughed in what I'm fairly certain was a failed attempt to hide a laugh. "She's had a leash on you for almost two hundred years. Hephaestus indeed!" He laughed in earnest and the little necromancer giggled.

Mike sighed and gave me a very put upon look. "I can't win."

"Seems unlikely. At least you still have your dignity." I paused and pursed my lips to the side. "Mostly."

CHAPTER SEVENTEEN

THE OLD MAN was gone when I woke in the morning, but the routine didn't change much. I still cooked a few eggs and enjoyed the last few slices of bacon. Three of Dell's chimichangas were still in the freezer, but I didn't think they'd travel well. Not to mention I had no clue if Faerie put much stock in microwaves.

Philip's hand of glory was still stuffed in my backpack and sitting on the rounded corner of the counter. My staff was leaning against the backpack. My hand wandered to the pepperbox holstered at my side, slid over the bump of the concealed sheath that held the Splendorum Mortem, and eventually came to rest on the focus. I was both intrigued and filled with dread when it came to the hand. I was *pretty* sure Glenn wouldn't ask me to do something that would result in my immediate death. But dammit, he was Fae, and sometimes they surprised the hell out of you. Sure, some days they were surprisingly benevolent and generous, but on a bad day? Immediate death.

I finished washing the dishes from last night's dinner and the morning's breakfast. Once the last plate was in the drying rack, I wiped my hands on my jeans and started shutting down the cabin. I made sure the lights were out in the bedroom and I unplugged all of the appliances except for the fridge. Hell if I knew when we'd be back.

All the while, I'd catch glimpses of the backpack from the corner of my eye. On my second trip through the cabin to check the plugs, I realized I was just delaying the inevitable.

"Let's get this over with already." I couldn't avoid touching that awful hand any longer. I grabbed the staff and the backpack. I stepped toward the back door and left the cabin, letting the screen door slam behind me. I paused and tried the door to make sure I'd actually locked it.

The thick soles of my shoes caused my footsteps to echo as I crossed the wooden deck. The woods were quiet. It was odd to hear so little in the country after living in the city for so long, but this was even quieter. A calm wind rustled a few leaves and bent the longer blades of grass around me, but the animals didn't make a sound. It felt like the forest was just as apprehensive as I was about what was to come.

I dropped the pack onto one of the stones Aeros had raised. The hand of glory felt cold when I pulled it out of the backpack. It wasn't room temperature, it was more like an ice pack. I took a deep breath and looked down the scorched, u-shaped depression Zola's incantation had left behind. Time was wasting.

I grimaced as I laced my fingers into the dead hand. The cold flesh warmed and I felt the flow of power a moment before the dead fingers flexed and grabbed onto my hand.

I swore I heard the Old Man say "I hate those damn things," and then the world vanished into darkness.

I had a brief moment of panic before warmth flooded my entire being. It flowed through me like the rhythm of a heartbeat. A faint golden glow took shape to my left.

Motes of light drifted down onto the severed hand as it began to bleed. The light coalesced and brightened, calling more sprites that gathered like snowflakes drawn to a tiny world. In moments, there was a woman, born of the purest light, holding my hand.

"Ah, I have a new master." Shoulder-length hair flared out slightly when she turned to look at me. "Where do you wish to go, child of Anubis?" Her eyes were golden light.

My grip loosened on the bloody hand, and then her fingers locked into my own.

"Do not release me here, for there is nothing but death in the Abyss between."

Nixie's warning came screaming back into my mind. *Do not let go.*

"What?" I asked, my hand tightening on the woman's. "Who are you?"

"You may call me Gaia."

"The spirit of the Earth?"

"In a way," she said with a tiny nod of her head. "Where do you wish to go? I would imagine you wish to join the King at the Concilium Belli."

I nodded and looked at our intertwined hands. Ever so faintly, I could see the dead hand within the warm light. "Are you bound to this hand?"

"It is my hand," she said. I waited for a smirk or some kind of indication she was joking with me. Nothing came.

"Why are you helping me?" I asked.

"It is my purpose."

Purpose. I wasn't sure if she was being vague, or blunt. "Are we within the Warded Ways?"

"Yes."

"I've never experienced them like this before."

"If you have travelled the Ways, you have experienced this. It simply happened so quickly in your perception that you cannot recall it."

The thought of those twisted moments of violent movement and light being the same as this was hard to imagine. Travel in the Warded Ways normally made me sick as hell.

"Your purpose is to help whoever brings the hand of glory?" I asked, as much to myself as to her. I moved my thumb and felt the smooth skin of a young woman beneath it, not the dead hand I'd started with. "If you're bound to the hand, then you're compelled to help the bearer?"

"It is a compulsion, yes. I am not meant to help a false bearer."

I glanced at her as we walked forward through the darkness. Did she mean she'd kill a false bearer?

"Not necessarily," she said.

I blinked. "Did I ask that out loud?"

"You did not need to. You are in my realm."

I couldn't stifle a shiver. "Whose compulsion drives you? Am I asking that right?"

She nodded. "He was known as the Mad King."

"The Nameless King?" I said. "The forger of the Warded Ways?"

"Yes. The Mad King was not so terrible. His compulsion rewards me with joy when I help you through the Abyss."

"You have no free will," I said.

"And do you, child of Anubis?" She smiled and turned her gaze back to our invisible path as we took one slow step after another. "Or do you walk the path of your destiny?"

"Bloody hell, lady. I'm kind of in shock here. I don't think I can ponder the great and wonderful meaning of life right now."

She gave me a small smile.

"The Abyss you mentioned?"

"Yes?"

"Is it the Burning Lands?" I asked.

"No, it is this place," she said as she swept her golden arm before us. A gown of light draped from her wrist. "Endless darkness filled with the tiniest hope."

"I don't see much hope in this place." My eyes wandered over the endless night. Tiny pinpricks of light shone like scattered stars in a moonless sky. Nothing so great as to warrant the name hope.

"You are that hope."

I turned my head to stare at Gaia. "What do you mean?"

"Were you to stand in this spot for several days, the Old God beside you would devour your existence. Look carefully. Do not be afraid. It cannot harm you now." She held out her left hand and the glow around her brightened.

A dark, slimy tentacle caught my peripheral vision. I turned slowly, my heart racing despite Gaia's promises that I was safe. I shivered and winced away from the monstrosity beside us.

The tentacle was one of many. All joined to a grayish body made golden by Gaia's light. A great eye sat above an enormous beak. Within the beak I could see three smaller beaks. Smaller is an odd word, considering each beak was ten feet long. The eye followed us, raised as it was along a circle of gray flesh, pocked with scars and bumps. The oblong pupil slowly widened in a blood red iris.

"It is known as Croatoan," Gaia said. "I believe you already of this beast."

My jaw slowly fell open as I realized Croatoan's tentacles vanished into the black space a hundred feet above us. I could scarcely comprehend its size, and I was standing beside it.

"Why is it here?" I asked.

"Banished here by your brother when he could not kill it."

"The Old Man killed Croatoan."

"Leviticus may have believed Croatoan could not survive the Abyss, but he was mistaken. There are a thousand foul creatures that dwell here. Many are more powerful than the savage devils of the Burning Lands."

A Leviathan a fraction the size of the thing beside us had torn down a steel bridge in moments. Ezekiel truly did mean to destroy the world as we knew it. I shivered and looked away from the mass of tentacles and the beaks that looked as though they could swallow Aeros whole.

"Your father is a madman, Damian."

"Ezekiel is not my father," I said.

"Perhaps he is not, in your heart, but you are the seventh son of Anubis."

I wanted to drop her hand and scream in protest and disgust. She squeezed my hand more tightly. She already knew what I was thinking.

"You cannot imagine the things that will be hunting you before the war is over."

"You sure know how to make a guy feel special."

She gave me a sideways glance and a small smile. "Once Ezekiel has fallen, one of the Seals will fall with him. Did you know one of the minor Seals has already fallen?"

"What?" I looked into Gaia's eyes.

"Philip was part of the Seal of Anubis."

I slowed my steps. "Because Anubis was his father?"

"Ah, you do learn quickly. You and Leviticus are also minor Seals. While the death of Anubis could be enough to unleash the Old Gods upon the earth, the Seal will still hold much back, so long as the sons survive."

"But I won't live that long," I said. "What happens when age catches up with me?"

"Dark times, Damian. The darkest of times." She gave me a small smile. "There was a golden age of Faerie. After the Nameless King was struck down by Gwynn Ap Nudd, and the Seals were laid upon all the lands, peace reigned for thousands of years.

"It was not until Anubis betrayed Ra and damaged one of the Seals that the others began to decay."

"How did he betray Ra?"

"One of Anubis's sons was under Ra's protection. Once Anubis realized he could become stronger by eliminating his first born, it became his mission. After many years of combat, he succeeded in killing the man. The man had been one of Ra's closest friends for millennia, and had trained Leviticus in the darkest of arts."

I began to have an even clearer understanding of Edgar's hatred for Ezekiel. I glanced to my right, expecting to see the Leviathan looming over us, but it was gone. I looked behind us and could see nothing.

"It is left behind, on the other side of the world. Pray you never need face that creature. I have enjoyed our journey, Damian. Fare thee well."

Gaia released my hand.

CHAPTER EIGHTEEN

A S FAST AS the world had vanished into darkness when we began the trip, torchlight exploded into my vision. My staff hit the floor and clattered to a rest. I heard the hand of glory land with a dull, fleshy thud. The light was nearly blinding, although I was quite certain the hall I was kneeling in was actually quite dim. I took a deep breath. My palms were flat against the cold stone tiles. I could see another hall branching off to the sides of the room I was in, and another trailed off into the distance. Two pillars stood to either side of me.

The hand of glory was between my own hands. It was a dead, gray thing once more. I swung the backpack off my arm and unzipped it. I picked up Gaia's severed forearm, cringed at the chill in the dead flesh, and tucked it into the backpack. I checked to make sure I still had the Splendorum Mortem and the rest of my portable armory.

I heard footsteps echoing through the hall. The echo made it hard to pinpoint, but I thought it was coming from my right. I pushed off the marble-like floor. There was no sense in being sprawled out on the floor when those footsteps arrived.

"Shit," I said, realizing the marble column beside me was the lower calf of an enormous sculpture. My eyes trailed up to the stone kilt and outstretched sword. Some thirty feet above me, the sculpture was locked in battle with another monolith.

One wore a horned helmet. The other's head was faceless. A smooth, swirled stone surface.

"Welcome, Damian Vesik." The voice was musical, enticing, and some part of my brain screamed that it shouldn't be.

I turned my gaze to the entryway. A creature stood there, more beautiful than I can describe. She was tall, like Nixie, and her skin was almost as pale as the marble floor. The color of her eyes seemed to shift between an array of prismatic colors. She held her hand out and I almost reached for it.

"Glamour." I frowned and raised my staff instead.

"I'm sorry?" she asked. She tilted her head to one side.

I bared my teeth, grabbed the rune at the three quarters mark on my staff, and smacked the ferrule into the stone.

The creature screamed as its glamour was stripped away. Reptilian skin reflected the dim torchlight when the glamour fell from the woman's body. Only her white dress remained as the woman raised her arms to cover her face. "I do not wish to frighten you, Damian Vesik. Do not look at me."

"You obviously haven't met my friends," I said as I extended my hand. I hadn't meant to frighten her, either. Well, at least not once I realized she actually *was* there just to greet me.

She peered out from between her scaly fingers and blinked her yellow eyes. The blink was slow and methodical. She looked down at my outstretched palm and then up to my eyes.

"But you are a necromancer," she said, her voice barely above a whisper.

I smiled. "I get that a lot. I'm sorry if I frightened you."

She reached out and took my hand, her movements slow. I really had scared her.

"You don't know what I am."

"I assume you are Fae."

Her lipless mouth curled up into a smile. "I am Utukku."

"Utukku?" I asked as I let her lead me from the chamber I arrived in. "I know that name from somewhere." And I did, but damned if I could remember where.

"My kind are not many," she said before she paused briefly. "Anymore."

"What happened?" I asked. I stopped dead in my tracks when we turned a corner.

She laughed quietly. "It is impressive, no?"

Enormous sculptures filled the entire hall. Every column stretching to the ceiling was an elaborately carved figure. I started walking again, counting the steps between one monolith's base and the next when Utukku spoke again.

"Your people killed most of us in the war with the werewolves."

"Those were not my people."

"I am sorry, Damian Vesik, but I have no reason to believe you. I have seen the most noble of you become death incarnate on this earth. There were more of us, once. In Atlantis."

"Fuck, I'm sorry." I already knew where the story was going.

"The darkness that took Atlantis into the sea took the lives of my people."

The Old Man.

"We harbor no ill will for what he did so long ago, Damian Vesik. The water witches would have killed us all eventually. Gwynn Ap Nudd gave us sanctuary in Faerie after the fall of Atlantis. It is why we survive to this day." She released my hand. "And this is a beautiful place to live."

"It is at that," I said. My eyes followed her gesture to another hall. This one was shorter and ended in two massive doors. A sun was carved into the left door, surrounded by jewels and what looked like gold. As we got closer, I could see there were thousands of runes carved into the door as well.

"One of the court has requested an audience with you," she said. "You may wait in your chambers so you have a modicum of privacy."

"That?" I said, hooking my thumb at the door.

"Yes," she said. "You seem sincere, Damian Vesik. I feel as though you meant your apologies for the actions of another man. Perhaps the Queen of the water witches is indeed wrong about you."

"What do you mean by that?" I asked as I reached the doorway.

She pushed a translucent veil to the side and I easily walked past her in the huge doorway. "It is nothing to be concerned with now. Please, make yourself comfortable." The Uttuku's voice echoed in the room. "It was … nice to meet you." She nodded once and her footsteps clicked on the marble floors as she disappeared through the veil in the doorway.

I stared after her for a moment, wondering what she'd left me to. I turned my attention back to the room itself. The light from the sconces barely reached the ceiling of the room. If I had to guess, I would say the stonework was at least twenty-five feet above my head.

The bed was just as massive as the room itself, looking like at least two king size mattresses pushed together. Four stone posts stood at each corner of the bed, each intricately carved with vines and flowers. I didn't realize how high the bed was until I got closer. The top of the mattress was at my waist.

I set the backpack on the long marble dresser beside the bed. I blinked and looked again before I realized it was the end table.

"Damn." I laid my staff behind the bag to keep it from rolling off.

"You do leave an impression."

I jumped at the woman's voice behind me. When I spun around, I found Cara hovering just inside the doorway. She swooped down on her black and white atlas moth wings and landed nimbly on the end table.

"Mom!" I said.

She laughed. "You will only confuse the Fae, calling me that here."

"Is that a bad thing?" I asked.

She frowned slightly. "I suppose not, now that you mention it." Cara adjusted the two swords sheathed on her back. "You met an Utukku."

"Yes, I think I scared the crap out of her."

Cara nodded and a broad smile lit the sharp features of her face. "I think that encounter was a test from our illustrious king."

"Did he think I was going to turn into a slavering monster and eat her because necromancers used to be at war with her people?"

"It sounds silly when you put it like that, but yes, I imagine that was exactly the point."

I hopped backwards to land my ass on the bed. "Why would he do that?"

She walked closer to the edge of the end table and sat down

on the ferrule of my staff. "It is so odd to see you in Faerie." She paused and ran her hands over the golden greaves covering her legs. "You need to understand something, Damian. You are the first necromancer to be invited to Faerie since Glenn became king."

"I thought the Old Man had been here."

"I said invited, not 'kicked in the front door.' There is a subtle difference."

I scratched the back of my neck and laughed. "Not so subtle, methinks."

"Your encounter with the Utukku went well. Admittedly, I would not have removed the glamour from the first Fae I encountered in the Royal House, but I am not you."

"When you put it like that …" I said under my breath.

Cara just smiled. "It worked out surprisingly well. The Utukku is already speaking of how different you are. Something else you might like to know—Edgar has taken a stand squarely against the other Watchers."

I raised my eyebrows in question.

"In support of you, Damian. Glenn invited you here, and half the water witches would support you just to stay on Nixie's good side. The word of the *Sanatio* isn't half bad either, so I hear."

I smiled at Cara as she mentioned her own title in the courts.

"Calling the Demon Sword a friend may have even more pull in the coming days."

"I got the impression Foster is getting a little stir crazy."

"Oh," she said with a slight stutter as she laughed. "That may be considered an understatement."

"He's doing alright, though?"

"Yes, yes," Cara said, waving her hands. "Leave your weapons here. The Concilium Belli convenes in minutes."

"I thought it didn't start until tomorrow," I said.

"It *is* tomorrow. Time does not move evenly in the Warded Ways. You're also in Europe now."

"Oh, right." I unfastened the holster for my pepperbox. I didn't like leaving the gun behind, but I did. I laid the focus beside it. I left the Splendorum Mortem concealed in its slim sheath.

"Good." She ushered me to the door before looking back at me and frowning. "What are you wearing?"

I glanced down at my shirt and smiled. "It's the shirt Vicky got me for Christmas. Nice touch, right?"

"It's a vampire skull."

"I thought it might make a statement."

I half expected her to tell me to change it, but her expression turned thoughtful. "It is a good day for statements."

"Vicky will love this story," I said as I followed Cara into the hall.

CHAPTER NINETEEN

"**H**AVE YOU SEEN Nixie?" I asked Cara while I walked briskly behind her.

"Yes, she's already in the hall. Please, for the love of Nudd, don't blow her kisses or anything childish like that? We don't need an incident."

"Me?" I asked. "Cause an incident? I'm not the one who set a reaper to guarding my sister, now, am I?"

"Shush," Cara whispered and the look on her face was fierce. "That is exactly the kind of thing I was talking about. Glenn knows. If his opposition knew that was here, it would be an *incident.*"

"So Sam really doesn't know?"

Cara shook her head. "I doubt Jasper will reveal himself here unless your sister is in grave danger."

"Grave," I said with a laugh. "You're funny."

Cara blew out a breath and glared at me. "Sometimes I wonder why Glenn invited you to this."

"Damian!" a voice screeched from down the hall. "Oh my God Damian it's you I can't believe it's you they said—"

Sam continued to babble for several seconds, but I tuned her out and smiled.

"Shut up," I said.

She blinked and I grinned at her before I hugged her like I

thought I'd never see her again.

"Damian, thank God you're alright. Did you hear about Ezekiel?"

"The bridge?" I asked.

She nodded and squeezed me until I thought my ribs would crack. And then she squeezed a little harder.

"Ribs!" I squeaked.

"Sorry, sorry," she said with a laugh.

"Did you know Jasper is here?" I asked.

"Dammit, Damian," Cara said.

I pouted at her and she couldn't stop a small chuckle.

"What?" Sam asked. "No, where?" She looked around the hall, eyeing the figures far above our heads and the stone rafters above those. "I want to see him."

I lowered my voice. "Cara doesn't think he'll reveal himself while we're here. He's too busy guarding your ass. Ninja-like."

Sam's smile fell a little. "I'd really like to see him again."

"Maybe later," I said, putting my arm around her.

"Did you know he's not the only one watching over me?" she asked, her voice darkening as we turned the corner. "*Vik* is here. Like I need his protection? Please. Oh, you know who else?"

"No, who else is—" The wind rushed out of my lungs as a bristly green missile knocked me to the floor. The panting bark felt like it shook the stone floor beneath me a moment before my world vanished behind an enormous pink tongue.

"Bub– Ack! Bubbles!" I finally managed to spit out.

"Oh dear," Cara said. "Did I forget to mention Bubbles?"

Cara and Sam both burst into laughter.

The cu-sith pulled her head back and cocked it to one side,

ears flopping over on top of her head. Her tongue rolled out and hit the ground with a wet smack.

I looked up at Sam.

"See?" she said.

"Barely," I said without emotion. "Bubbles was so subtle I almost didn't realize she was here."

Sam smiled and offered me a hand up. She easily pulled me to my feet.

"Come, children," Cara said, her voice growing serious. "We're only two halls from the Royal Court."

"Yes Mom," Sam and I echoed together.

WE TURNED DOWN a plain hall. It was entirely void of the stone monoliths that stretched to the ceiling in all the other halls. Through the open door I could see a massive, curved table on the far side of the room. Elevated seats stood to our left and right, each a comfortable distance from its neighbor.

The voices echoing around the chamber were incredibly loud. I paused in the doorway and took it all in. The explosion of sound was deafening. There were arguments and laughter and death threats spewing from a thousand different faces. Some of the Fae wore glamour, and they were almost too beautiful to look at. Others sat in bulky, roughly hewn armor. A row of women were clad in intricate gowns that captured any light that dared come too close, only to release it again in orbiting spheres of color.

The central throne—a mighty throne I would have sworn was iron—stood empty. A helmet rested on the curved bench before it. Enormous horns rose from the sides of the helmet, gray, and silver, and menacing.

"Come, Damian. You and Sam will be sitting by the King's Guard."

I followed Cara through my peripheral vision alone. I couldn't stop staring at the ranks of creatures and mortals and gods. Sam's hand was cool when it grabbed mine and squeezed. I squeezed back and gave her a small smile.

We cleared the entryway and stepped onto the main floor. It was a wide-open space between the seats beside us up to the throne. I turned my head to catch a glimpse of what was behind us.

My heart rate increased when I found Nixie staring down at me, her hair pulled back into an intricate design that looked something like a fleur-de-lis. She was surrounded by her sisters. Some of them I recognized—our allies at Stones River, and Euphemia from Boonville—but others were strange to my eyes.

Behind Nixie, an older undine sat upon a larger seat, a throne in its own right. It had to have been Nixie's queen, and I could barely keep a snarl from my lips. The woman was glaring at me. She gave me a smile fit for a gravemaker.

I blocked it out and turned my gaze back to Nixie. A sincere smile lit her pale features. She gave me only a tiny nod. I grinned like an idiot and then tripped over my own feet.

The resulting stomping stumble brought the entire room into silence.

Cara just sighed.

Sam giggled.

The whispers started up anew. Only this time they were filled with venom.

Necromancer.

Destroyer.

Murderer.

"Silence!" A voice boomed from nowhere and everywhere. "Do not demean my guests."

Gwynn Ap Nudd. He wasn't in the room, and yet he was. As we made it to the other side of the auditorium, I realized there were dozens, if not hundreds, of small seats lining the wall behind Glenn's throne. Foster sat in the small central seat, and more fairies filled the rest. Another small seat sat on the bench beside Glenn's helmet.

My eyes followed the bench around to the other end. Twenty Watchers were there. Edgar was looking right at me. He nodded once and then returned to his conversation with the bulky-looking man beside him.

"Take your seats," Cara said as she gestured to the empty chairs just below the far left side of the bench.

I looked at who we'd be sitting next to and smiled. Zola was on one side and Dominic started the ranks of vampires on the other. I wondered if Zola had received the same warm welcome I had. I reached out, traded grips with Dominic, and nodded to Vassili, the lord of Sam's Pit.

The old, white-haired vampire returned the gesture. Vik was sitting on the opposite side of him, looking reserved until his eyes trailed down to my shirt. He sucked in his lips and it looked like he was fighting not to laugh.

I politely took my seat. Zola patted my knee as Sam sat down beside me.

"Ah think this should prove interesting," she said.

"As long as it's the kind of interesting we can live through," I said.

"Mmm," was her only reply.

I watched Cara glide to the elaborately carved bench. She took a few steps and sat down in the small throne beside Glenn's. Somehow, I wasn't surprised.

Movement above her caught my eye. It was an elderly Fae standing up behind an ancient podium. His voice was smooth and loud, though it did not contain the authority of a king.

"We now call to order the Concilium Belli."

The room fell silent.

I blinked my eyes a few times, thinking I had a floater in my vision, before the spot expanded into a black, swirling maelstrom. There was a sound like a crack of thunder and Glenn was suddenly standing before his throne.

He wore a black robe, but it was more than black. It didn't reflect any light. It was more like he wore a void that curled around him in rising and falling wisps of power. An enormous golden mantle hung from his shoulders, made from a hundred Celtic knots, all intersecting at the edges, that came down to meet in the center of his chest. I knew what was mounted on his chest, I just didn't understand why it was there. A soulstone the size of a baseball gleamed from its setting.

I stared across the chamber at Nixie. She was focused on Glenn, but I eventually caught her eye. She smiled slightly. I didn't miss the glare from the Queen behind her. I could tell she was going to be one of my biggest fans.

CHAPTER TWENTY

"T HE WATCHERS WILL speak first," Glenn said, drawing my attention back to the bench. His voice was just as unnerving as I remembered. It was closer to Aeros's basso rumble than any human's. "They are the latest to suffer a loss in this conflict."

The older man to Edgar's right stood up and removed his bowler. He had a thin, white beard that trailed along his chin. His gaze was piercing, even from across the chamber. It took me a moment to realize he was glaring at *me.*

"You invite *him?*" The Watcher's hand shook as he pointed at me, and then it began to glow.

I started to move, but Zola's hand snapped out and stopped me.

Glenn moved faster than I could see. One moment he was seated on his throne. The next, he was on top of the Watcher. The punch would have removed the head of a mortal. The Watcher stared up at Glenn. I couldn't see the King's face, but judging by the absolute terror on the Watcher's face, I didn't need to.

Edgar wore a smug half-smile beside the two. I wondered why.

"He is here at my request, Geb. If you take issue with that, I will remove you."

Somehow I didn't think he just meant remove him from the council.

Glenn leaned in closer to the Watcher, but his voice was still clear. "I invited Leviticus to this council, Geb." Whispers and protests rose throughout the hall. "He thought it unwise to attend, due to the inclusion of certain council members. He is a wise man." Glenn let go of Geb's suit and Geb flopped into his seat. "War is upon us, Watcher. You should rejoice in the knowledge we avoided it so long."

Glenn walked slowly back to his seat. His eyes scanned the chamber as he spoke. "We've witnessed the madness of Anubis unleashed on this world before. And now? Now he raises a Leviathan in the middle of a Nexus. Do not lose sight of your true enemies. Vesik is an ally, and a weapon."

"Have we forgotten The Wandering War and all its darkness?" Glenn asked as he spread his arms. "How many lives did that conflict cost?" He let his arms relax, curling his hands into fists. "How many centuries did it take to clean up the aftermath? Yes, Falias is lost, but we will rebuild it. For now, we must prevent a disaster like Falias from engulfing all of Faerie. We will need many allies."

The chamber grew restless as a hundred voices muttered support and objection to the King's words.

"So many dissenters," Glenn said as his eyes swept the room. "Have you forgotten what will happen when Ezekiel falls?"

"No," a bulky Fae said from the edge of the bench. "That is why we stand against you."

Glenn nodded, acknowledging him. "I understand your concern, Hern, and you are right to be afraid."

"I am not afraid of a deathspeaker."

Glenn's calm façade cracked slightly as he glared at Hern. The brief exchange lingered, and then Glenn's focus returned. "The Seals have been fragile for almost a millennium. Ezekiel was able to summon a Leviathan barely three hundred miles from the Storm Seal."

My ears perked up. I'd never heard of a Storm Seal.

"Lies," Hern said. "Nothing can be summoned so close to the Seal."

"And yet it is done," Glenn said.

"Lies upon lies, my *King.*" Hern leaned forward in his seat. "You weave insane tales of this *unavoidable* conflict. The return of the Piasa Bird. The Old God, Aeros, working with a pathetic, powerless, necromancer. You're a fool, Nudd." He raised his arm and pointed directly at me. "And you will damn us all with that deathspeaker."

"Still your tongue," a man said, rising from a seat far to Hern's right. Despite his shaved head and creased forehead, he didn't look much older than I was. Celtic knots, tattooed into his flesh, vanished into the sleeves of his cloak and reappeared on his neck. Each pattern bore a cache of runes. His nose was steep above full lips and a prominent jaw.

He slammed his fist into his palm and a small explosion of electric blue lightning flashed into the air. "You did not stand to help Falias, Hern. You let them die. You, who has wielded enough power to lead the Wild Hunt. Instead of proving your worth, you let innocents die by the thousands. Still. Your. Tongue." The man's rage was palpable.

"Thank you, Ward," Glenn said as the other man slowly took his seat. An edge of violent promise snaked into Glenn's words as he focused on Hern and said, "Do not force my hand in this place."

Hern relaxed into his seat and folded his arms.

So that was Ward. I kind of thought he'd be taller. I cursed silently to myself as I thought about the exchange. Hern was intimidated by Ward. Possibly frightened of him. What the hell did that say about Ward?

Glenn turned to face the rest of the chamber. "Allow me to put this in the simplest terms, should you share the misguided opinions of our noble Hern." Glenn's form darkened and the light fled the room. The King seemed to grow taller as he spoke. What miniscule light there was illuminated him and him alone. His voice deepened into an abyss of sound that rattled the stones beneath us.

"I give my vow in support of Damian Valdis Vesik. He wears the blessing of the *Sanatio* and her Demon Sword. Those who betray him betray Faerie, and invite their doom." His gaze locked on a fixed point when someone hissed one simple phrase.

"You know what he is."

I followed his gaze and found it led directly to the Queen of the water witches. I could barely make her out in the shadows, but her lips were flattened into a thin line.

The room brightened as Glenn seated himself on the throne. His back lay straight against it as he said, "You would do well to remember that."

Ah, here's to hoping I don't outgrow my usefulness.

Whispers circled the chamber once more. Hern's frown was even deeper, matching Geb the Watcher's beside him. Hern laid his leather-clad arms on the bench and leaned forward. I caught a glimpse of light reflecting off something above his head. As I looked closer, I could see a translucent pair of antlers rising from his skull.

On the opposite side of the chamber, Nixie's Queen stood and drew the focus of the room. "We have all seen the failings of the *Lord of the Dead.*" She sneered as she spoke Glenn's title. "It is time to throw down this madman as we did the Nameless King."

Glenn's voice was an icy calm. "Most who have the same level of respect for the Concilium Belli as you are already dead."

Nixie's Queen looked as if she was ready to bolt. She may have a big mouth, but not many beings could stand up to Glenn. She gathered herself. "Come, sisters. Let this *King* lead his people into death." She began to storm down the aisle when Nixie stood up behind her.

"No." She paused and after a beat added, "My Queen."

The Queen stopped and glanced at Nixie over her shoulder.

"You are wrong," Nixie said.

The Queen turned to face Nixie. "Dear child, let us discuss this at a more—"

"Your reign is done."

The Queen shifted and took a more aggressive stance. Her right hand vanished into the layers of fabric at her waist. My heart rate spiked as I realized she must be going for a weapon.

From the corner of my eye, I saw Ward stand.

The room was thick with ley line energy. Behind it, I could feel the pulsing auras of the dead. I could reach out with my necromancy and summon any dead thing I could dream of into this place. My fingers curled up slowly and caught on the resistance of the gravemakers just outside the walls of the Royal

Court. It would be so easy to summon the Hand of Anubis and turn the Queen into a smear.

Sam's hand pulled on the side of my face. She wrenched my head until I met her eyes. "Stop. I can feel it. Stop. You must not hurt her here."

I blinked and stared at my sister. Her fangs were out. She was ready to attack something. The Hand of Anubis … bloody hell, I didn't even know if that would work on a water witch. I shook my head and took a deep breath as Sam released me.

I caught Edgar looking at me. He gave a brief shake of his head. I got the sense he didn't mean it as an admonishment, but more of a 'not now' gesture. He turned and said something to Ward in the noise that followed.

Ward frowned slightly, nodded, and took his seat once more.

My eyes trailed back to Nixie.

"Leave us, traitor," Nixie said to the Queen. "You no longer lead us into the future. You leave us to drown in the past while the world moves forward without us."

"You will die," the Queen said, and her voice held nothing but ice and promise.

Euphemia stood up behind Nixie, on the same tier as the Queen. She'd been at Stones River when we'd fought Prosperine. Her hair had grown some since I'd seen her at Boonville, which made her look even more like Nixie.

"Nixie does not stand alone," Euphemia said.

Another witch stood up just behind the Queen, blocking her exit. I recognized Alexandra's black hair before I heard her speak. She was just as bedazzled as the rest of the witches. "Leave this place before you taint the realm of the undines. We are done with you."

The Queen looked over her shoulder before her eyes trailed back to Glenn. She walked quickly out of the aisle, shoving Alexandra out of the way. At first, I had a warm rush of satisfaction. As half the undine contingency stood and left with the Queen, that warm rush turned to ice. At least half the court of the undines was against Nixie.

"When the Concilium Belli has concluded," Glenn said, "I will close the Warded Ways to all beings save the Lords of Faerie."

Whispers and nods of agreement rose with shouted objections around the chamber. Glenn held up his hand and the room fell silent. The drama unfolding around Nixie's Queen was immediately lost with Glenn's announcement.

"You are a fool, Nudd," an old woman said.

I could almost feel the gaze of every creature in that room shift to the diminutive Fae sitting behind Hern.

"Speak, Morrigan," Glenn said. "You have no enemies here."

She laughed, and it was a terrible sound. "Perhaps not, but you certainly do." She added, "My King," after a pause. It didn't feel like a slight, the way Nixie had put her Queen down. It sounded more like an afterthought, as though she knew Glenn on less formal level. "Now you intend to close the Ways. To cut off all travel for your allies just as effectively as your enemies. It's as though you do not trust your own kind."

"The Ways will close," Glenn said, leaving the accusation unaddressed.

Glenn turned his gaze upon me. "You will be forced to travel over land, Damian Vesik. Be sure your wolves are organized and the vampires truly stand by your side." His face pulled down into a small frown and his eyes swept around the room.

I was sure he wanted to say more. It just wasn't the time to say it.

"You have erred on the side of the commoners," Hern said, cutting off any further exchange. "I will not stand for it. Even Anubis has more sense than to do what you propose."

Glenn stared at Hern. "Then join him. I will cut you down when we meet in battle."

Hern stood. "You are a foolish King." His antlers materialized, the blackened points gleaming in the light as they extended from the brown base at his skull. The crowd gasped as Hern crossed his arms and cracked his neck.

"The world will know us, as the dying know death," Hern said an instant before he vanished into a black vortex and crack of thunder.

Glenn laid a hand on his helmet. His mouth compressed into a flat line as he looked out across the chamber. "Prepare yourselves. Meet with your local clans. The Seals will fall, and we must be ready. So ends our Concilium Belli."

CHAPTER TWENTY-ONE

THE BUZZ OF chatter filled the chamber once more. I looked toward the Watchers. Edgar nodded and I returned the gesture. The others were already filing through the walkway beside their seats.

A small swarm of fairies swirled around us. They were all talking at once and I just raised my eyebrows.

"Silence," Cara said. "You can meet him later. There is work to be done."

Petulant chatter filled the air as fairies slowly flew away.

"Foster has been talking about you," Cara said. "They're simply excited to meet a demon slayer." She leaned forward and whispered into my ear. "Glenn will be coming to talk to you later. For now, return to your chambers."

Someone grabbed my arm from behind and I turned to find Vik. I smiled at the old vampire and traded grips. Hugh had gotten us all in the habit of shaking hands by gripping forearms instead of hands. I had to admit, it felt like there was more of a bond with the gesture. Dominic did the same.

Vassili offered only a nod and then hurried through the closest exit.

Vik followed close behind me with Sam and Dominic.

"What's up with him?" I asked when Vassili disappeared.

Vik smiled. "Old habits die hard. The last time Vassili attended a Concilium Belli, one of the questions was whether or not he should keep his head."

"What?" I asked, my eyes scanning the balconies for Nixie. I hid the disappointment when I couldn't find her. "Why would they kill Vassili?"

"Rumors, mostly," Dominic said from the other side of Vik. "He was suspected of allying himself with the dark-touched."

"No one found proof," Vik said. "I admit, I have always kept an eye him, though he is our Lord."

"Me too, old man," Dominic said with a laugh. "You're not the only one who's paranoid."

Sam briefly scratched my back and I gave her a smile.

I heard a fairy yelling in the hall before I saw movement. "Bubbles! No!" It was Aideen. "Peanut! Dammit!"

I could hear the claws before I saw the pups come streaking around the corner. Sam blurred into motion to greet them as they hopped and jumped and showered her in so many doggy kisses she was going to need an actual shower.

I was surprised when Dominic went down on one knee and Peanut hopped off Sam to playfully attack the vampire. Dominic grunted as the pony-sized cu sith hit him in the chest and took him to the floor. "Holy shit," he said between laughs as Peanut growled and nipped and smacked him with his tongue.

Aideen glided in behind them. "They weren't supposed to be seen in the chamber," she said, looking around the room behind us. "It's somewhat difficult to control them when I have to stay small."

It took me a moment to realize the chamber had fallen silent. The few Fae left in their seats were staring at the cu siths.

Some of them wore a wide-eyed, awestruck look of astonishment. Others looked terrified.

"Dominic," Aideen said. "Sam, please help me get them into the hall."

"Sure thing," Dominic said as he picked Peanut up effortlessly. Peanut's floppy ears stood straight up and he sucked his tongue in, scoping the room from his new elevation. Curiosity sated, he began licking Dominic again.

Sam just patted her thigh and Bubbles began following her out of the room.

"I was going to have them escort you to your room, Damian." Aideen sighed and watched the vampires leading the cu siths away. "I think they were excited by all the noise."

"Why can't they be in the chamber?" I asked.

"Oh, they can, it's just that some Fae are terrified of cu siths."

"Let me guess," I said. "Some old war where some old Fae got licked by a cu sith and some bad thing happened."

"Pretty much," Foster said, gliding past my shoulder to join us.

"Your highness," Sam said, grabbing Bubbles's ruff. Probably not a bad idea considering the cu sith's occasional tendency to snap Foster up with her tongue.

"You're hilarious," Foster said, circling her head.

Bubbles began crouching on her hind legs.

"She's going to eat you again," I said.

The tongue lashed out and Sam caught it in her left hand. "No." She looked Bubbles in the eye. I swear the cu sith was glowering at her.

"Are you okay to get back to your room?" Aideen asked.

"I'd rather get Bubbles and Peanut locked up for a while. I don't like the looks they were getting."

"Sure thing," I said.

"I'll make sure Damian doesn't get lost," Foster said.

We said some brief goodbyes and I watched as the vampires trailed after Aideen with the cu siths. Sam smiled as Bubbles leapt around her in circles and Peanut tried to nip at her from Dominic's arms. Seeing her happy made me smile.

A dark form moved through the rafters. It was nebulous, and only a tiny gleam of silver caught the light. I knew those teeth.

My smile broke into a grin as I watched Jasper flowing across the ceiling, ever hidden, ever watchful.

✦   ✦   ✦

IT WASN'T LONG before Foster and I were back in the ancient monolith-lined halls. It was quiet there, and my footsteps echoed across the marble. My eyes trailed up to the top of one of the bulkier statues. Horns adorned its head and its face was contorted into a permanent scream. Its stone sword pierced the monolith facing it.

I frowned slightly and glanced at Foster. "What's the story with Hern's horns? They were invisible until he made a show of it."

"A show of it?" Foster said. "That's an understatement. Hern's antlers were hidden because they are considered a weapon. He has a … reputation for goring people."

"Ugh," I said. "What's with him, anyway?"

"Hern?" Foster asked as he raised his eyebrows.

I nodded. "Seems like a pretty grumpy guy. And that is

seriously saying something after training with the Old Man."

"You don't understand," Foster said. He shook his head and his wings moved in shorter strokes. "Hern wants the world to be what it was."

"What it was?"

"Yes, in ancient times. Ruled by Fae. Ruled by magic."

"I'm guessing he's pretty devoted to the idea? Considering how much trouble he was giving Glenn."

"He is insane for challenging the King like that," Foster said. "It proves only one thing, in my mind. Hern will stop at nothing."

"Another single-minded nut job. That is *exactly* what I was hoping to find here."

Foster laughed at my grumbling.

"That seemed like an awfully short council," I said. "They didn't even discuss attack plans or defenses or anything."

Foster glided to my shoulder and leaned into my ear. "That was not the council, Damian. That was Glenn showing off his allies to the dissenters in the Court. Claiming Levi as an ally was a bold move. Everyone in that room is aware of the mass destruction he has caused throughout history. The real council, the Concilium Belli you won't see, will include only Glenn's oldest allies. They, in turn, will pass the orders down the line."

My eyes widened. "Fucking hell he's tricky."

"You have no idea."

We turned another corner. The next hall was a dead end with an open doorway and a thin veil hanging across it.

"Ah, my quarters," I said, unable to keep a regal inflection from my voice.

Foster laughed. "It's good to have you here, Damian. I hope

you don't lose your humor in this place." He hovered in front of the door as he spoke. "It can be a dark place without friends."

"You coming in?" I asked as I pulled the veil aside.

He shook his head. "I have to attend to the … follow-up meeting."

I nodded. "Well said."

"I'll tell you everything I learn. For now, keep your head down."

Foster glided down the hall, disappearing around the corner we'd just come from.

I pushed the veil to the side and then let it fall as I entered the room. My footsteps didn't echo as much inside. It was a bit more homey, I suppose. Certainly it was more homey than the halls had been. I walked to the dresser and ran my fingers over the Magrasnetto inlays on my staff.

What was Glenn going to do? It seemed he had a lot of support, but there were some outspoken dissenters in the Concilium Belli as well. I had a feeling they were like cockroaches. For every one that made itself known, there was an ocean of them hiding in the walls.

Footsteps sounded as someone walked through the veil behind me. I left my staff where it was and turned to find Nixie. As soon as she cleared the veil, the fabric became an endless waterfall. It pooled on the floor, then flowed back up the door frame only to fall back to the stone once more.

Nixie's face was angled downward slightly and she wore a grin like nothing I'd ever seen. Absolutely wicked.

"It's been almost a year," she said as she came closer, pulling the elaborate pattern of braids out of her hair. She turned around and lifted her hair. "Unzip me, would you?"

"It's a real dress?" I asked, surprised she hadn't conjured one instead of wearing actual fabric. The salty smell of the ocean hit me as she got closer.

"Yes, we always wear them for these damned councils."

The zipper ran all the way down to the small of her back. She turned around and stared at me. "Off." She pulled on my shirt.

I grinned and pulled the vampire skull off, leaving a white t-shirt beneath it.

Her hands oozed under my shirt, becoming translucent before she moved her arms out, shredded the shirt, and tossed me onto the bed. She shuffled her shoulders out of the dress and all of our talking stopped. She held her hand out to one side and the lights in the room dimmed.

I kicked my shoes off and fumbled with my belt, finally shaking my jeans off my ankles as she finished strutting up to the bed. Her nipples were pale and tight. Her hair was still pulled up slightly, leaving her smooth, pale waist exposed.

"Oh, yes," she said, leaning down and wrapping her mouth around my erection. Her lips made a popping sound as she raised her head and repeated the motion. She went back to moving her head up and down with a firm grip on my shaft, and I flopped onto my back.

I groaned, and then stared as her weight began to shift. Nixie's body grew translucent. She flowed up onto the bed and covered my mouth before becoming solid again, her mouth never losing its rhythm. She tasted salty and sweet and I leaned into her as her groans joined my own.

She stopped and slid forward, casting a glance over her

shoulder. "I'm on top. You can be on top next time."

"Okay." I was quite agreeable.

She spun around and locked her mouth on mine. Her tongue was soft and warm, and everything I'd been missing for almost a year. She hovered above my erection, taunting me by brushing her warmth against my own.

Nixie leaned down to kiss me again. Her soft tongue became more and more demanding as she lowered herself onto me. I started to wrap my arms around her, but she pinned them to the bed. Her body appeared eerily still as she pressed her lips against mine, but the parts she wanted to move continued to shift and undulate.

Her hands finally slid off my arms and, no longer restrained, my hands found their way to her ass. I pulled her in as close as I could. Her tempo increased as she raised her butt slightly, slamming herself against me with more and more urgency. She purred, and it was a sound I'd missed so much.

Her thrusts grew more frantic and I matched her pace until I felt her begin to tighten.

"Not our bed to cleanup," I said between breaths as her movements shook the mattress beneath us.

She grinned and instantly her body became moist and supple, as slick as her sex. Her lips were soaking wet, salty, and her liquid warmth surrounded me, enfolding us both. Her breath hitched as her body spasmed, and I joined her in ecstasy.

"Oh, gods, you need to move here," Nixie said into my chest. She started to roll off me, but I wrapped my arms around her and held her tight. She buried her face in my neck and sighed.

"You know anyone who's renting?"

She laughed and slapped my shoulder. "Smart ass."

CHAPTER TWENTY-TWO

"DID YOU KNOW there was a hot tub in the room?" Nixie asked.

"I saw the bath in the corner." I toweled my hair off. "I try not to take too much at face value here."

"Smart." She closed her eyes and her flesh was suddenly covered in skintight blue jeans and a black t-shirt to match my own.

I frowned. "You are *much* less naked."

"Glad you noticed." She began rooting through the dress she'd left on the floor. She made a happy sound and then hopped onto the bed. "I have something for you."

"Really?" I asked as I placed the towel on its rack. I crawled up onto the drier side of the bed beside her and crossed my legs.

"It's just an old book," she said with a serious expression. "You may not be interested."

" 'Old book' may be the only phrase that can distract me from my other favorite phrase."

"The chimichanga is done?" she said with a sideways smirk.

I smacked my lips. "Uh huh, and who's the smart ass now? Though I occasionally indulge in the changas, they don't have much to do with a naked Nixie."

She laughed, the dim light catching her crystalline eyes as

she smacked my arm.

"Now you're just trying to kiss my ass."

I waggled my eyebrows.

She narrowed her eyes and handed me a thin, green book. I thought it was leather, but the texture felt odd as I took it from her hands.

"What?" I asked as I stared at the volume and then read the name aloud. *"The Deathspeaker, Leviticus Aureas, and the Fall of Atlantis.* What is this?"

She cocked her head to the side and gave me a blank, wide-eyed stare. "Why, it's the story of the deathspeaker, Leviticus Aureas and the fall of Atlantis." She then proceeded to blink several times.

I laughed and turned the book over in my hands.

"It is one witch's account of what happened. There are only three copies in existence that I am aware of."

"Deathspeaker," I said as I ran my hand over the name on the cover. "Why deathspeaker? Why don't they call us necro-mancers?"

"You're not just a necromancer, Damian."

The Old Man's words played back in my mind, 'Welcome to godhood, brother.' I stared at the book and frowned.

"There are a few races that still refer to all necromancers as deathspeakers," Nixie said. "In the time of Atlantis, death-speaker was the name we gave to the sons of Anubis."

"Azzazoth called me a deathspeaker. How could he have known what I was?"

"Your bloodlines, if I had to guess."

I laughed. "A demon with a knack for genealogy? That seems … unlikely."

Nixie shook her head. "Ask Zola about Ronwe. Demons are obsessed with genealogy. It's how they predict when the arch demons will be born and reborn."

"Damn." I fanned the pages of the book. It had that old, gloriously musty smell.

I smiled at Nixie, her crystalline eyes catching the dancing candlelight. "Thank you for this." I held the book up.

She leaned forward on her elbows and kissed me. "I'm glad you like it."

My eyes trailed back to the book. "It's amazing, Nixie. Really. Did you ever see Atlantis?"

"Oh yes, I lived there for a time."

"You *lived* there?" I said.

She nodded and rolled onto her stomach, propping a pillow beneath her chin. "It was a beautiful place. Tragic that it was destroyed in the war."

"The Old Man was really there."

She nodded. "Levi fought against Ezekiel at Atlantis. Might have killed him too if Levi hadn't been so busy trying to save the humans and their knowledge."

"What?" I said. "He could have killed Ezekiel?"

"Yes, it was possible, though if he had seen the fight through to the end, most of the humans would have died on Atlantis. All of their knowledge would have been lost. You may learn some things about Levi he'd never tell you himself," she said, gesturing at the book.

"He lost his chance at revenge to save people?"

"Yes. He may be a ruthless man to those who don't know him, but there is more to Levi than you'd think."

My mind churned through what I knew about the Old

Man. I knew he could be benevolent, but he was one of the most ruthless warriors ever to walk the earth. I'd seen why when I'd touched his essence during the battle with Prosperine at Stones River. Now I realized that essence must have been the gravemaker elements within him. What Ezekiel had done to the Old Man's family … The visions came back to me, vivid, violent, and terrible. The screams of his children would never leave me.

"What's wrong?" Nixie asked.

I closed my eyes and shook my head. "You know what made the Old Man into what he is?"

She nodded, and her voice was sad as she said, "Yes."

"I saw it, Nixie." I met her eyes. "In the battle with Prosperine. I lived his memories like they were my own." I could feel my eyes starting to burn as I remembered his daughter's blood running down his back. The soldiers laughing as they violated her and finally discarded her like a ragdoll. "I felt him go insane, Nixie. I felt him lose everything he'd ever loved. I watched the darkness take him."

She had her hand over her mouth, but I could still tell her lips were trembling. "He doesn't tell anyone that story." Her voice was quiet. "There were only four water witches with us when he told me. Just before the end of the war, when he killed our Queen. Damian," she said as tears began to flow. "How much he loved his family …" she sniffed and rubbed at her eyes. "He wanted us to understand what we were doing, what happened to the families when we took away their fathers and mothers and children. It was then that I realized we murder people with so much to live for. His story changed me."

I wrapped my arms around her as she cried.

"We killed so many …" she whispered as she squeezed my chest.

"Think of how many you've saved," I said. "Think of Hugh. If Haka had died. If you hadn't saved him, I don't think Hugh would have continued on. Haka is Hugh's world."

"Honiahaka," Nixie said, drawing out the name.

"Look at how many water witches stand behind you now. If it wasn't for you, all of them would still be drowning commoners for fun."

"The Queen will never let us live in peace. She wants us to return to the Dark Ages just as much as Hern."

I frowned and looked into the mirror across the room. We looked small sitting on the huge bed, the four stone columns dwarfing us as I stared.

"Carter may be right," I said. "Everything is changing."

Nixie took a deep breath. "Did you ever hear from Mike?"

I leaned back and held a finger over my lips, just in case someone was listening. I reached into the concealed sheath until I found the hilt of the Splendorum Mortem.

I held it out in my hand as it siphoned and bent the ley lines around us and Nixie's jaw dropped open. I slid it back into the sheath and the lines returned to normal.

"Yes, I heard from Mike."

"We have a chance," she said. "We have a chance."

The room dimmed in my peripheral vision, and the darkness began to spin. At first I thought it was in the mirror, but it grew beyond the borders of that ancient glass. As I turned to look at it, I could see it was just a few feet past the edge of the bed.

A hulk of a man stepped through. His eyes glowed red and

massive bronze antlers stretched toward the dim light of the ceiling.

I didn't have the focus in my hand, but that didn't stop me from summoning an aural blade. If our visitor didn't know what it was, it might be of some leverage.

"Peace," Glenn's voice said as he lowered his arms. He twisted his wrist to one side and the vortex vanished without a sound.

"Glenn?" I asked.

The half of his face I could see wore a thin smile. He removed the helmet of antlers, and when he released it above his head, it dispersed into a black mist.

"Most would call me King here, but Glenn will do fine." His voice didn't have the earsplitting volume I was used to.

"The portal didn't make a sound," I said. "Usually it's all thunder and calamity."

Glenn crossed his arms and offered a sincere, if small, smile. "Are you asking a question? I believe you already have the answer."

"It's for show," I said. "Out there in our world."

He nodded. "A Fae who fears you is more likely to be loyal than a Fae who believes himself more powerful."

Patterns within patterns within schemes. Trying to follow the ways of Faerie did nothing but give me a headache. I let the aural blade vanish in much the same way Glenn's helmet had.

"My King," Nixie said, bowing her head.

"Formalities have no place here," Glenn said. "I must be brief and return to the council."

"Why come here on your own?" I asked, emboldened by his statement of this being a casual meeting.

"Can you think of no better question for the Lord of the Dead?" Glenn asked.

"So, are we underground here?" I asked.

He nodded. "We are not so much beneath the ground as we are within it."

"Huh?"

Glenn actually smiled a little as Nixie tried not to laugh at me. "It may be simpler to think of it as another dimension. A sideways step into a realm beyond your own."

"Your definition of simpler, and my definition of simpler, are vastly different."

Glenn nodded. "Nonetheless, we are there, within the earth." He paused for a moment and looked at the bronzed vambrace on his wrist. "There are many realms beside your own. The Frozen Waste, The Burning Lands, and what we call Faerie are but the tip of what we know.

"I am of the opinion there are many more. The void you walked with Gaia?"

I nodded.

"I believe that is a realm all its own, and perhaps a junction from which you can access an infinite number of realms."

"Like an alternate, *alternate* dimension?"

"Just one alternate," Nixie said. She curled her fingers around my upper arm. "An infinite number of realms, only one dimension away from our own."

"Exactly," Glenn said. "I believe it is where the Old Gods and the Eldritch things have been sealed away for so many millennia. We don't truly know where they were sent when we banished them from the known realms. Other than the few seen within the void, we do not know where they've gone. The dark-touched have not been seen since Camazotz drove them from your realm.

"Regardless," Glenn said, "Ezekiel is the immediate threat. You have the Splendorum Mortem." It wasn't a question.

"Yes," I said.

He nodded. He didn't ask to see it. Didn't insist I hand it over. Just nodded. "Leviticus will not stand idly by when the time to face Ezekiel is upon you. If it comes to it, you must be ready to strike him down."

"No," Nixie said. "That's terrible."

"I am aware of that," Glenn said. "You know what he's capable of. We must be ready."

The thought had crossed my mind before. What if he truly lost control? There was scarcely a being that could stand up to him, much less defeat him.

"I hope it doesn't come to that," I said.

"As do I," Glenn said. "You will not travel to Gettysburg alone. I have arranged for some of Samantha's Pit to travel with you. Hugh insists that Alan guard you. I am sure the Ghost Pack will be close to you." He looked away as he said, "There are others that will be guarding you, but you will not see them."

I had a feeling he meant Jasper, but perhaps there were more?

"I have discussed the rift between the packs with Hugh," Glenn said. "They are making good progress gathering allies, and the help of the Irish Brigade has been invaluable."

"They'll never have enough wolves to face Ezekiel," I said.

Glenn shook his head slowly. "You are right. It is why I am sending Ward to walk among them."

"Ward agreed?" Nixie asked as she leaned forward. Her

eyes were wide.

"Yes," Glenn said before he turned his gaze to the stone floor. "Ward witnessed a terrible event with the fall of Falias. I know we've had our issues in the past, but we are both wise enough to know when to set those differences aside."

He looked back up with his pitch black eyes and met my own before he said, "Aeros will join you in Kentucky. I have other business for him to address in the meantime. There are a few things in which I believe Hern is in the right. It is time we reclaim our place as Guardians of this realm." He raised his hands as if something was between them. Black mists drifted from his shoulders, spinning in the void between his fingers, and finally obscuring his face as they formed the semblance of ghostly horns. Slowly the mist solidified. Glenn opened his hands over his head, leaving his face in shadows behind a dark bronzed helm. A curved faceplate showed a violent streak of white that faded and wound into the textured antlers rising from his head. Two red orbs began to glow within the darkness. "It is time."

I stared at the Lord of the Dead, and he stared back. I wasn't afraid of him in that moment, but I respected the ever loving hell out of his power.

"Nixie, Damian, be wary. I am sorry to have interrupted."

I blinked, and my vision returned just in time to see the black whorl vanishing behind Glenn. He was gone, as silent as he'd arrived.

"You ever feel like he is scary beyond all reason?" I asked as I looked at the empty air where Glenn had vanished.

"I thought you weren't afraid of him anymore," Nixie said. She hopped off the bed.

"I didn't say that out loud, did I?"

She grinned and shook her head. "Just a feeling I had."

"I kind of didn't think I was afraid of him, but my common sense is coming on strong."

"We should find Zola," Nixie said. "I'd like to hear what she has to say about all of this too."

"It's late," I said. "Let's get her in the morning. She gets grumpy without her beauty rest." I grabbed Nixie around the waist and tossed her onto the bed.

She crossed her arms and frowned at me. "And just what do you think you're doing?"

I grinned as I hopped up on the bed and kissed her.

Her frown cracked into a smile as she said, "Morning would probably be fine."

CHAPTER TWENTY-THREE

W ITH NIXIE BESIDE me, I slept better than I had in a year. Once we got to the sleeping part, anyway.

Nixie was still asleep when I crawled out of bed, donned my jeans and t-shirt, and slid *The Deathspeaker, Leviticus Aureas, and the Fall of Atlantis* off the end table. I was anxious to read it, and was pretty sure I'd be combing through snippets of the book as I could over the next few days.

I sat back down on the bed and leaned back into the oh so perfect pillows. The cover crackled slightly as I gently pried it open.

IF THERE WAS one thing I never expected to say about the fall of our beautiful city, it would be a word in the defense of Leviticus Aureas. Yet the fall may have been triggered by his mighty battle with Anubis, but at what fault of his? Had he not been there, what chance would the people of Atlantis have had?

With our sisters spread across half the world, engaged in a war with no apparent end, Ezekiel would have taken Atlantis and buried it in the sea regardless. Our Queen was a fool to cross swords with Gwynn Ap Nudd. He is the rightful King of Faerie, slayer of the Nameless King.

Here, I will record the story as I remember it. The story of a lost soldier, a new King, and the final days of our terrible

Queen.

NIXIE SLAPPED ME on my stomach and I almost dropped the book in my surprise. She grinned at me and said, "Good morning."

I leaned over and kissed her. "Good morning to you." I eyed the explosion of hair running off in every imaginable direction.

She narrowed her eyes at me. "What?"

"Nothing." I opened my eyes wider, trying to achieve an image of absolute innocence.

She tugged on the explosion of hair. It came away easily from the tangle of sheets. She shook it out once or twice, and it looked like she'd been styling it for hours.

"Sam would be so jealous of that," I said with a laugh. I turned back to the book and closed it. "Does Zola know about this?"

Nixie had crawled out of bed and was pulling her dress on from the day before. "Zip me up, would you?"

I stood up to help her. "Does she?" I asked again as I zipped Nixie's dress up the rest of the way.

"She knows of them, yes, but she does not know I've given you one." She paused. "I don't see any harm in showing her. She already knows Levi, and probably knows almost everything in that book already."

"Yeah, Zola's like that." I slid the book into my backpack. "You ready? Let's track her down."

"She was staying close to the vampires," Nixie said. "It's a bit of a walk."

I nodded. "Nothing like a romantic subterranean walk to

start the morning."

Nixie narrowed her eyes at me. "Are you possessed?"

"What?" I said with a half laugh.

"You've had no coffee, or caffeine of any kind, and you're almost … chipper."

"Don't tell anyone," I said in a serious tone.

She took my arm when I offered it. I escorted her immaculately dressed self down the hall in my slightly wrinkly vampire skull t-shirt and jeans. We turned the corner, walking beneath the embattled monoliths towering above us.

I'm not sure if they built the place so large to intimidate the guests, or simply to accommodate the largest of the Fae and their guests. I imagined Aeros would be quite at home with the oversized dimensions.

"Wait," Nixie said. She pulled on my arm. I glanced at her, and she was staring down the hallway to our left. "That's where we need to go."

A man stood at the end of the hall. He wore a dark cloak with a hood pulled low over his eyes. His entire face was lost in the shadows. My hand brushed the Splendorum Mortem concealed at my waist. The rest of my weapons were in the room, in accordance with the laws of the Concilium Belli.

"Though I am sure whatever you have concealed at your waist could kill me, there is no need to draw it." I recognized the voice as the figure began walking toward us.

"Ward?" I asked.

He reached up and flipped the hood of his cloak back as he nodded.

"Ward," Nixie said. "You scared us."

"I apologize for that," he said.

I heard the cackle of an old Cajun before I saw Zola step out from behind the pedestal of an elaborately carved knight's boot. The click of her knobby cane on the marble grew louder as she approached. "Ah think that may have been the most insincere apology Ah've ever heard."

Ward's mouth curled up into a small smile. "It was her idea."

I crossed my arms and cocked an eyebrow at Zola as she settled in beside Ward. The dark gray fabric of her cloak looked new in the light from the sconces around us.

"Somehow I'm not surprised," I said.

"Why are you still here?" Nixie asked as she looked at Ward. "The King said you'd be travelling to meet … allies."

Ward nodded. "I will be.

"He came to warn you," Zola said. "Ah believe you've been marked for execution, Nixie."

"What?" I said.

"I am not surprised," Nixie said. "I declared my opposition to my Queen today."

"Zola is right," Ward said. "One of the King's … men, heard the order issued."

Nixie almost snarled, her lips curling back. "She means to go to war with the King. She issued those orders here, knowing they would be overhead."

"She wants you to see her coming," I said. My hand trailed over the Splendorum Mortem. I had a sudden urge to test it out.

"No," Zola said. Her eyes trailed from my hand back up to my face. She frowned slightly as her gaze passed between me and Nixie. "Do you have one of the blades?"

Nixie shook her head.

"Ah'm afraid you'll need it." Zola gestured toward Ward.

Ward pushed his cloak aside. I caught a glimpse of a leather jerkin adorned with bronze rivets. Every rivet had runes carved into it. As I focused my Sight more intensely, I could see the ley lines around us being bent towards each ward, ever so slightly. It was subtle enough as to not be noticed by a casual observer, and those wards were channeling enough power into the man to burn most practitioners to a crisp.

He unbuckled a sheath at his side and pulled a gray blade from it. It was wide like a small spade at one end and it tapered down into a bronze hilt. Twisted knots and runes formed wards all over the knife. Ward looked around before he handed it to Nixie.

She nodded, not verbalizing her thanks as she slid it into the folds of her gown.

"It is not one of the originals," Ward said. "Most of those have been lost. It is a copy I made to the best of my ability. It should work just as well as the ancient tools."

"What is that?" I asked.

"We do not speak of it," Zola said. "Not in this place. Gather your things and meet us in the Royal Court. Glenn will open the Ways for us. Sam already left with her Pit" She motioned down the hall with her head. The Magrasnetto charms in her hair clinked together as her braids moved.

Ward extended his hand to shake mine. The sleeve of his cloak slid back, revealing flesh so densely covered with tattoos and wards. It was jaw dropping. I eventually raised my eyes to meet his.

"That must have stung a bit," I said.

Ward blew a short breath out through his nose. "You are not mistaken." He smiled as he shook my hand in three short, controlled cycles.

I watched Ward and Zola turn left down the hall toward the Royal Court. He was taller than the old Cajun, but not by a large degree.

I didn't offer my arm, and Nixie didn't take it. We didn't have to speak to each other to know it would be idiotic to be tangled up out in the open.

"Damn, I've never been to Europe before," I said, glancing up at the ceiling far above. "Now all I've seen are these damned hallways."

"You've see the Royal Court of Faerie, Damian." She glanced at me, and then turned her attention back to our surroundings. "Think of how many commoners wish they could say the same."

"You're right," I said. "I know I should appreciate what I've seen, but …"

"We'll come back," Nixie said. "I'll take you sightseeing." She smiled at me and I couldn't help but smile back.

I heard footsteps echoing, out of rhythm with our own. My pace slowed, and Nixie's slowed beside me. The footsteps died away.

"How much of a threat?" I asked.

"Serious," Nixie said. "I betrayed our own royalty. They will strike soon."

"But here?" I said. "Under Glenn's nose?"

"Yes. By his own laws, he cannot retaliate." Her eyes scanned the intersecting hall as we passed it. It wasn't long before we reached our room.

I walked through the doorway first, my right hand never leaving the hilt of the Splendorum Mortem.

"Do not draw that in this place, Damian. We don't have the time to deal with the repercussions. If you must act, use one of those." She nodded to my pile of weapons on the end table.

"Faerie's laws are a bit odd, aren't they?"

"Pfff, like you have room to talk. Commoners have insane laws just as much as we do. The stories Frank has told me ..." She held her hand to her forehead and moved her head slowly from side to side.

"Oh yeah, he's got some stories all right." I strapped my holster and belt on. I pulled a loose black button-down shirt out of my backpack and slid it over my shoulders. It covered the focus and the pepperbox quite well. Satisfied, I slung the backpack over one shoulder. It would be easier to drop in a hurry that way.

I picked up the staff and tapped it on the marble floor.

"I don't think you're hiding that one," Nixie said.

"Nope," I said with a smile. "That's just fine by me."

She nodded. "Let's go. We should be able to get back to the Royal Court in ten minutes if we hurry."

Nixie took off walking so fast I almost had to jog to keep up.

"What is it?" I said.

"We are being followed."

"By who?" I asked.

A throaty, feminine laugh was my answer.

An undine stepped out of the shadows before us. Her body was translucent. "Dearest Nixie, I'm afraid your death has been ordered by our great Queen."

"Like hell," I said as I slid the pepperbox from my holster and poised my palm above the shield rune on my staff.

"Leave us," Nixie said. "I will not warn you twice."

"The Queen wishes you to suffer, child. We will start with the demon beside you."

I didn't hear the undine behind us. I just saw a sad smile lift Nixie's lips, and then she moved like a viper. She was facing one way, and then her body simply *changed*. The knife whipped forward in her left hand with terrifying speed.

The first indication I had that something was behind me was a brutal kachunk as the blade impacted … *something*.

I turned my head and cursed. The blade was half buried in another undine's chest. She was mostly translucent, except where the blade bit into her flesh. Nixie's face no longer wore a smile. Her face was utter rage.

"*You dare!* You who betrayed Atlantis to its end!" She snarled as she stepped closer to the witch's face. "You are lost to the waters, *sister.*" She shoved the blade deeper into the undine's chest.

The water witch cried out as her body became solid. Her cry was lost after Nixie plunged a second dagger into the witch's throat. Nixie released her grip and the witch hardened into something resembling gray stone. Nixie pushed the body over and it shattered on the floor before it slowly flattened into a thick, gelatinous ooze. It thinned and spread until there was nothing left but a wet stain on the marble floors.

In the time it took me to turn around, Nixie had grabbed the closest dagger and whirled back to the first undine.

The other witch was shaking, an expression of sheer terror etched across her face.

"Come, assassin. Prove your worth upon my blade."

She ran. By the gods did she run.

"Don't follow her." Nixie bent to reclaim the other dagger.

"You had two," I said.

She nodded. "Ward gave me two."

"What are they?" I asked. "It made her solid."

"Damian, I love you, and I trust you with my life, but it is a sworn oath that we do not speak of these." I caught another flash of the gray metal as she tucked the blades away in her dress. "I have already broken one oath today. I do not wish to break another."

I nodded. "Let's move. We're almost there."

Nixie glanced back at the wet stain on the stone floor behind us as we resumed our trip.

CHAPTER TWENTY-FOUR

G LENN WAS WAITING for us when we jogged into the Royal Court. He wore deep black metallic armor, etched with elaborate scenes of war and magic. Small spikes accented his forearms, seamlessly worked into the designs so they seemed to be raised by the images etched around them. He glanced between us and his black eyebrows drew together slightly. "Is the assassin dead?"

"Yes," Nixie said.

Glenn nodded. "You both have a choice to make. Nixie, your entire race is about to fall into conflict. They see you as a leader."

She sighed and closed her eyes. "Don't say it," she said.

"Without you, the entire revolution may die away before it begins. I will not order you to do this, but for the good of your kind, you should stay in Faerie."

My heart sank. The thought of being separated from Nixie again so quickly was awful.

Glenn turned to me. "Damian, we need you in the fight against Ezekiel. You think on your feet, and you're more powerful than you believe."

"How long do you need me to stay?" Nixie asked.

Glenn looked away, his eyes focused on the distant side of the Court. He inhaled through his nose before turning his gaze back onto us. "You don't intend to stay, do you?"

Nixie crossed her arms and leaned against the stone bench beside her. "If you give me access to the Ways, I can travel between all the realms. There are enough waterways near Gettysburg that I can access any number of portals in minutes."

Glenn nodded slowly. "I know. If your Queen wins the will of the people, this war will become all too bloody. After the loss of Falias, we can ill afford a conflict on two fronts."

"You already have a conflict on two fronts," I said. "I don't see any way around that. Even if you don't go to war with the undines, you've called for Ezekiel's head. You're going to bring down one of the strongest Seals between us and the Abyss."

Glenn laughed, a quiet, menacing sound. "Gaia has spoken to you of the Abyss."

"While showing me the sights, yes."

He nodded and met my eyes. "We will need the undines to fight the Leviathans. On land, yes, we may be able to slay them with the help of demons and Fae alike. In the seas and rivers ..." He shook his head. "I do not know if I would be capable of defeating a Leviathan in the seas."

"Happy will be with us. And Vicky," I said as I stared at the Lord of the Dead.

"And Vicky," he said.

"Did you know what was happening to her?" I asked.

Glenn eyed me for a moment before he said, "No. Not at first."

"What happened to Vicky?" Nixie asked.

"Nothing has happened to her," Glenn said. "Not yet."

"When an arch demon falls, another must rise to take its place."

"Okay?" Nixie said. "What does that have to do with …" She grabbed my arm. I turned to look at her, and her eyes looked almost panicked. "It cannot be Vicky. She is no demon."

"She is darkness," Glenn said before he let out a sigh. "She is a powerful ally, but I fear she may be lost to you once she fully embraces her role as the Destroyer."

"There has to be a way to stop that from happening," I said through gritted teeth. "She's been through enough."

Glenn frowned. His eyes glanced at Nixie, and then fell to the floor.

"What?" I asked as I stepped closer to the King. "You know something. If it can help that girl, you tell me now."

"I would like to convey the fact I have more patience for you than I have had for others," Glenn said in an even voice.

I caught the unspoken threat behind those words and nodded. "Please tell me about Vicky."

Glenn paused. "Very well. So long as the seven devils rule the Burning Lands, arch demons will continue their endless, immortal march. It cannot be stopped."

"Everything can be stopped," I said.

"What would you have me do?" Glenn said as he leaned against one of the stone benches and spread his palms across it. "Attack the Burning Lands? As we join together to hunt Ezekiel? Invite yet another enemy into the conflict?"

I clenched my fists. I knew he was right, bloody hell, I knew he was right.

Glenn nodded. "After this fight is done, perhaps we can discuss the child once more."

"If the devils were to die?" I asked.

Glenn looked at me with a stern expression etched across

his face. "It is unlikely the laws would continue if the creatures who enacted the rituals were dead. If you wish to commit suicide in the Burning Lands, I would request you do it some other time."

Nixie's hands slid from her gown and her posture visibly relaxed.

"I have no quarrel with either of you," Glenn said. "I would prefer it remain that way. Nixie, please, stay for now. Rally your people. Join Damian at Gettysburg, but let him make the trip alone. Those loyal to you are gathered at the river Styx.

Nixie gently placed a hand on either of my cheeks. "I love you, Damian." She kissed me lightly, but the rush of emotion I felt was anything but light. "You have the Wasser-Münzen?"

I slid the blue obsidian disk out of my back pocket. "Always."

She curled her hand around my own. "Be safe."

"I love you."

Nixie didn't look back as she vanished down the hall slightly to Glenn's right. It felt like she'd walked away with a piece of my soul.

"What now?" I asked of Glenn.

"You do not seem to be afraid of me, Damian Vesik."

"That's misleading," I said. "I just assume Cara will cut your balls off if you do anything to me."

Glenn's mouth twitched a moment before he burst into laughter. It was a full, deep, laugh. A small smile lifted the edges of Glenn's lips. "I suspect you are correct."

I nodded. "You want to send me on my merry way?"

"In a moment." Glenn turned and glanced down the hallway Nixie had disappeared through. I had a feeling it was just for show. I doubted Glenn needed his eyes for much of anything in the Royal Court.

"What?" I asked.

He turned his gaze back to mine. The infinite pits of black were not as unnerving to me as they'd once been. "Ezekiel was spotted in Cumberland, Maryland by the local pack."

"Doing what?" I asked.

"The Cumberland Pack has long been an ally of my reign. After Ezekiel's latest attack, most of them are dead. I can only guess that Ezekiel made such a spectacle out of it to dissuade any other werewolves from joining the fight."

"A spectacle?" I asked.

Glenn nodded. "You will see the broadcasts when you return to your realm."

I ran my fingers through my hair and gritted my teeth. "And you didn't say this while Nixie was here, because you didn't want her to follow me."

"We need the undines on our side. If their Queen destroys the rebellion before it begins, we will be left alone to battle the Leviathans and their brethren."

I frowned slightly and stared at the stone bench behind Glenn. "She's probably safer in the middle of a goddamned revolution anyway."

"You are a mystery to me, Damian." Glenn narrowed his eyes and leaned forward slightly. His black armor was as silent as cotton against the stone. "You can be brash, and ruthless, but you maintain a head for strategy. You proved it in the defeat of Azzazoth, and you proved your ability to improvise with Prosperine."

"And?" I said.

"Most of the brash warriors I have known did not survive more than one or two battles.

I looked away and laughed, but it was flat. "I would have been dead without Foster and Aideen." My eyes trailed back to Glenn. "I would have been dead without you, as I recall."

Glenn nodded. "I know."

"I know" was all he said. Not, "you owe me your first born," or "don't worry about it, we're pals." I'm not sure which one would have scared me more.

"Take the road through Lexington," Glenn said. "Break your travel into two days. I do not want this battle to end before it begins by having an uncoordinated arrival in Gettysburg."

"No plan survives contact with the enemy," I said.

"Moltke?" Glenn asked as he raised an eyebrow. "And here I thought you were an uneducated heathen." The Lord of the Dead stepped forward and clasped my shoulder. "Damian, we are on the cusp of a great darkness. I hope you will fight for us until the end."

"I will fight with you," I said. "*Who* I fight for, that's an entirely different story."

"That will do." Glenn lowered his hand. "Come, let us get you back to your realm."

We walked to the center of the Royal Court. I stared at the intricate Celtic knot in the center of the room. Glenn took up a position on the other side.

"You should know your shirt made an impression."

I raised my eyes to meet Glenn's as my lips slowly curled up into a smile.

He laughed once more. "I rather thought that was the

point." He waved his arm and reality broke into a sickly vortex between us. "Travel well."

"And you," I said as I adjusted my backpack and stepped into the Warded Ways.

CHAPTER TWENTY-FIVE

"OH, YOU SON of a—" I squawked as the river came rushing up to meet me from twenty feet below. I performed a graceless, flailing belly-flop while I kept an iron grip on my staff, remembering the Leviathan I'd seen not so long ago. Water is not overwhelmingly soft at that height. I grunted as the cold river cut off my cursing. Its dark, wet chill closed over my head. It only took two quick strokes to surface.

My backpack was water resistant, but I still pulled it off and held it above my head as I reached the shallower part of the river. The roar I'd heard while beneath the surface was once again the peaceful, relaxing flow of the Missouri River.

All of my clothes dripped onto the muddy shore and I began slogging my way back to my staff. The river had carried me a fair way from my drop point. I heard someone laughing, and I looked up to see two kids pointing at me. Their dad was shushing them both. I gave him a small wave and he nodded. I ran my fingers through my drenched hair and pushed forward, jerking my feet out of the mud as I went. Some small part of my mind was impressed with how not sick I was after travelling the Warded Ways. Maybe Glenn was just being nice. By dunking me in the river?

I blew out a noisy breath while I wiped the mud off my staff and shoes as best I could on the nearby grass. In the future I'd have to remember not to piss off the fairy king who's in charge of my travel arrangements.

I looked up toward the old brick buildings at the top of the embankment. "Damn, Glenn. Practically door-to-door service except for the whole river thing." I walked up to the cobblestone street and smiled as Death's Door came into view. I crossed the parking lot and waited for a minivan to pass on Main Street before I walked over to the front door. I glanced to my right, looking at the newer stretch of cobblestones that formed the street. Ashley had done a number on them during the battle with the blood mage, but the city had been quick to repair the road.

The shop's sign was flipped to open. I pulled on the door and the familiar chime of bells welcomed me home.

"Take them off," a stern voice said from above me.

I looked up to find Cara hovering with her arms crossed. "What, these old things?" I asked as I shook my muddy foot at her.

"Yes," she said with a small laugh.

"I was totally going to do that anyway." I grimaced as I undid the muddy laces. "What a mess."

"We don't normally take that path," Cara said.

"I can see why."

"Damian!" I heard Frank say. "Have you been in the river? Sam's not going to let you into the SUV looking like that."

I leaned my staff on the doorway. "The SUV?"

"Yes," Cara said. "Sam is bringing one of the Pit's SUVs to drive you to Gettysburg."

I nodded. "I just need to towel off and change. I'm good. Glenn said we should go through Cumberland on the way. Are you coming with us, Mom?"

Cara shook her head. "Aideen and I are travelling to Gettysburg with Vik and some of Sam's Pit. Zola, Sam, and Foster are coming with you."

"I'm staying here with Ashley and her coven," Frank said. "Cara's leaving some furry muscle behind for us."

"The cu siths?" I asked.

"Yes," Cara said. "I don't want them in the battle. They made an appearance in the courts. I don't want them targeted on the battlefield. Their job is done for now."

"Have you heard from Happy and Vicky?"

Foster swooped into the room and glided to a running stop by the register as I walked by. His golden armor gleamed as the chain mail slithered around his waist. "They're travelling with the Ghost Pack."

I nodded. "Makes sense. Keep the Harrowers together." I turned back to Cara and asked, "How soon are you leaving?"

"Now," Cara said. "They're waiting on me."

"Are you going to fly to the Pit?" I asked, only half joking.

"I'll take the Ways."

"The Ways are shut."

"Not to everyone," she said. "Be safe, all of you." She looked at Foster and Frank as she said the last.

"You too," Frank and Foster said at the same time.

Cara glided to the back and I didn't see her again that day.

"Perks of knowing the King?" I asked.

Foster hesitated, and then said, "No doubt," as he glanced toward the back room.

"What? What aren't you saying?"

"It's not always perks you get from knowing the King.

Sometimes you just get dead."

I didn't think Foster was trying to be dramatic at all, which just made that statement all the more scary. I rubbed my face. "How soon are *we* leaving?"

"Sam should be here in less than five," Frank said.

"So, after a thirty minute goodbye between my sister the vampire and her tasty mortal snack, we should be out of here in an hour."

"Ha!" Foster said. "It's funny because it's true."

Frank laughed and I caught a smile as I passed through the saloon-style doors. I slid the duffel bag off the second shelf and dropped it on the Formica table. The grandfather clock's rhythmic clicks made the shop feel even more like home. I really just wanted to go upstairs and curl up in one of the overstuffed leather chairs with a good book, but that wasn't going to happen for a while. I took a deep breath and pulled out some fresh, dark jeans.

I removed my belt and holster before stripping out of my muddy pants and dropping them into a plastic grocery bag. I slid the duffel bag back onto the shelf. A moment later, I decided I'd take the spare clothes with me. I piled some snacks and bottled water into the empty space in the duffel bag, rearmed myself, and headed back out front.

I pushed through the doors. "If things go south, stay with Ashley. Protect what you can."

Frank nodded. "I've been talking to some of the Watchers."

"Really?" I asked as I set the duffel bag on the counter.

"Edgar's right hand man, er, woman," Foster said.

"Who?" I asked, having no clue what he was talking about.

"I'm glad Mom left," Foster said, as he slapped his hand on

his thigh. "She'd beat your head in if she knew you hadn't been paying attention. I told her not to say anything when you were focused on talking to Nixie. But what do I know? Nothing. That's what! I don't know a damn thing."

"Foster!" I laughed and asked, "Who?"

He blinked at me. "I don't remember her name."

Frank and I exploded into laughter.

"Oh, shit," I said as I rubbed the bridge of my nose. "That was priceless."

"She's a blood mage," Foster said. "I just don't remember her name."

I nodded. I remembered Edgar telling us they had at least one blood mage in their ranks. A horn beeped in three quick beats from the front door. "That must be—"

Sam crushed Frank in a hug before I could finish my sentence.

"Yep," Foster said. "Sam."

Sam leaned into Frank like she was going to swallow his face. I grimaced, and smiled, and then grimaced again.

"I know how you feel," Foster said.

"Shut up, bug," Sam said. "Are you lazy bastards ready?"

"Aye-aye, captain."

She glanced at my feet. "You don't even have shoes on."

"Ezekiel doesn't stand a chance against my toenails of doom."

Sam rolled her eyes and turned back to Frank.

"I'll miss you," Frank said.

"I love you, Frank." My sister wrapped her arms around Frank and I wondered just how much his ribs could take.

"Eww," Foster said. "Here we go. I'll be in the car. Watch

your ass, Frank."

"You too," Frank mumbled around Sam's hair.

Frank extended his hand and I gave it the forty-five degree thumb wrestling shake. "Watch over your sister for me."

"I will, you silver-haired bat."

Sam started giggling.

"Who told you about *that?*" Frank said, horror obvious in his voice.

"About your vampire nickname?" I asked with as much innocence in my voice as I could. "Vik." I laughed a slightly evil laugh.

"Bastard."

"At least they didn't call you the silver caterpillar."

Sam laughed and brushed one of Frank's eyebrows.

"I'll meet you in the van, Sam."

She nodded, and I carried my backpack and assorted weaponry out the front door. I blinked as I looked at my shoes and staff. They were perfectly clean, and my socks were dry. Clean, dry socks are like magic after have frigid river water socks.

"Thanks, Mom."

CHAPTER TWENTY-SIX

I OPENED THE back door to the SUV and found Zola staring at me from behind the driver's seat. Her eyes were almost glowing in the darkness until the overhead light brightened.

"You don't want shotgun?" I asked as I stuck my head in.

"Is your sister driving?"

I looked up and to the side as I thought about it. "Probably."

"Then Ah'd prefer not see my imminent death on the roadway."

I laughed and tossed the duffel bag onto the floor and backpack onto the back seat. I slid my staff into the far back. It fit fairly well at an angle.

"She's not the best driver," Foster said from the dashboard.

"She has vampire reflexes," I said. "We'll be fine."

Zola blew out a breath, and something told me she wasn't so sure about that. "The Old Man tells me your training went well."

I nodded as I closed the back door and then let myself into the front seat. The SUV smelled like new leather. I shifted so I could look back at Zola. "Well, at least I survived it."

"The Hand of Anubis is no small thing, Damian. Ah know of no one outside of the bloodline able to do that."

I nodded. "How long have you known what I was?"

Zola met my eyes as the overhead light began to fade, leaving her in shadows once more. "Ah suspected early in your training. Hinrik alone raised my suspicion. Ah did not truly know until Edgar told me."

"When?" I asked.

"Long ago, Damian. Ah hoped to keep it from you. Hoped it would never come into your life, but Ah trained you as if it one day would."

One part of me was hurt that she'd kept a secret from me for so long. The other part was grateful she'd let me live as normal a childhood as possible, without worrying about the real monsters that would be crossing my path.

"I understand," I said. "Thank you."

She leaned forward and patted my shoulder. "You've done good, Damian. Lots of good."

I began to notice the voice on the radio and turned up the volume. "… not a hoax and have declared martial law across both sides of the river. The bridge over the Ohio River was indeed destroyed and the casualties have not yet been identified. We've been unable to get an answer as to what, exactly, the creature was. We understand the local authorities are speaking to the world's most accredited marine biologists, but no more information is available.

"Two dozen men and women have been confirmed dead in Cumberland, Maryland. The attack there, some say by the same creature, destroyed a small section of downtown. To make matters more confusing, several eyewitnesses are claiming to have seen several bigfoot-like creatures. Others are calling them werewolves. Terrorists, radicals, or rabid bears? More after the break."

I turned the radio off and stared at Foster.

He flexed his wings and shook his head. "This can't be covered up anymore. Ezekiel is bringing us into the open."

"We'll worry about that once the war is over," Zola said. "Humanity has witnessed worse men than Ezekiel. The Fae have defeated stronger enemies than him."

"Some of those Fae are on Ezekiel's side now," Foster said.

The driver's door opened and Sam slid in. She smacked her lips and grinned at me.

"Did you leave him some blood?" I asked, thankful for the change in topic.

"Breakfast of champions." She started the SUV.

"Let me get my blindfold on," Zola said.

Foster and I chuckled. Sam looked at me, and then into the rearview, before she said, "My driving is not *that* bad."

"Mmm," was Zola's only response.

Sam started to pull out of the parking spot when we noticed the traffic backed up on Main Street. "Hell no." She made an overly quick U-turn that sent us all hurtling into the right side of the car. She turned right onto Adams Street.

"That's a one way street!" Foster shouted as Sam zipped down the short road and cut right onto Riverside Drive.

"It's short," Sam said. "No one's ever on it."

I glanced at Sam from the corner of my eye. "Maybe, uh … Maybe I should drive."

"No way, Demon. I love driving."

"We're going to die," Zola said. Her right hand dug into the edges of Sam's seat and her left strangled the oh-shit handle. "Ezekiel won't even get the chance to kill us himself."

"Oh, stop it," Sam said.

Foster clung to the rearview mirror. "Is it safe to come down now?"

"You might want to wait until we hit the highway." I watched the back lots of the Main Street buildings zip by. Foster grunted his agreement. Several of the old brick structures had wooden decks and staircases leading up to the second floors. Ancient faded signs painted onto the bricks graced a few walls.

The river was on our left. Tourists wandered along the paths and the riverside. A few relaxed on benches and gathered in gazebos and pavilions along the Katy Trail, talking animatedly about god knows what. Most were probably talking about the Leviathan. With the radio and television coverage, people weren't going to think it was a hoax.

The SUV bounced down the cobblestones briefly, as Riverside Drive became Boone's Lick Road. I rolled the window down and leaned close to it, taking in the smell of the river and the nearby brewery. Tourists milled around the shops, but the crowds were light at this end of Main Street.

"Which way are we going?" Sam asked as she pulled onto Fifth Street.

"Take Seventy to Sixty-Four East," I said. "We'll take Sixty-Four all the way to Lexington."

"Why Lexington?" Zola asked. "It would be a shorter route to stay north."

"Just outside Lexington, actually. Glenn told us to take the scenic route through Frankfort."

"Oh, Ah'm sure Ah know right where Glenn wants us to go. That's fine. Ah could use some bark juice."

"Some what?" Sam asked.

"Whiskey," Foster said, rubbing his hands together from his perch on the mirror.

"That doesn't sound half bad," Sam said.

"You are so not driving if you whiskey up," I said.

"Hey, my whole vampire thing lets me drink you under the table, Demon."

"Yeah? Well my whole necromancer thing makes you slap yourself in the face."

"Don't even think about it."

Zola chuckled from the back seat. "Children, children. Let's just drive to Frankfort and see what Glenn wants us to see. Though Ah suspect Ah know *who* he wants us to see. It's an old rendezvous point for an old friend."

I eyed Sam as she glanced at me and grinned.

"So," I said. "If Cara and some of the other Fae can still use the Ways, why are we driving all the way to Gettysburg?"

"Probably timing," Foster said. He glided from the mirror to Sam's shoulder. "If we show up at different times, and there's a large enough force waiting, we could be in deep shit."

"Ah agree," Zola said. "Not to mention whatever is waiting in Lexington. Glenn would not send us there without reason."

✦   ✦   ✦

WE WERE HALFWAY to Lexington by three in the afternoon when we zipped by a sign pointing to Jasper, Indiana. Sam and I looked at each other and laughed. Foster sat with his legs crossed, watching the world pass by through the windshield.

I thought back to what Foster had said about Jasper. A reaper. A goddamned reaper. I shook my head. I wished I could ask Koda about reapers. That old ghost would answer anything you asked him, no matter how mind-scarring the answer may be. And then there was the book Nixie had given me. What else did Koda know about the Old Man?

I glanced into the back seat at Zola. Her chin rested on her fist as she stared out the window.

"Do you know where Koda is?" I asked. "I haven't seen him since he gave me the manuscript."

Zola turned her head and held my gaze. The metal in her braids tinkled as she cocked her head to one side.

"And why would you be asking of Koda now?" She narrowed her eyes slightly. "Some new question?"

I nodded and gestured at the backpack beside her. She handed it up between the seats. I unzipped it and slid the book Nixie had given me out of one of the inner pouches.

"Oh, Damian," Zola said as she carefully lifted the book from my hands. "Did Nixie get this for you?"

"Yes."

"Do you know how few of these exist?" she asked.

I nodded. "Nixie said they didn't make many to begin with, and they only know of three still in existence."

Zola's voice was almost reverent as she read the title aloud, "The Deathspeaker, Leviticus Aureas, and the Fall of Atlantis."

Foster hopped up from the dashboard. "Holy shit. I didn't think *any* of those were left."

"Atlantis?" Sam asked.

"Yeah," I said. "The Old Man sank it back in the day."

She cursed and muttered something I couldn't make out before she finally said, "I'm glad he's on our side."

"No shit," Foster and I said together.

"That's why I was asking about Koda. I thought he might

have some more insight into the Old Man."

"You have touched the darkest part of the Old Man with your necromancy. You have more insight into him than most would ever want to have."

"Hadn't really thought about it like that," I said, turning my attention back to the flat landscape.

Zola started reading the old book, and the car fell silent again. I couldn't keep thoughts of the coming war out of my mind. What if we failed? What if Ezekiel unleashed the old and eldritch things onto our world? What if we won? Ezekiel himself was a Seal. What would *we* be unleashing?

I took a deep breath and tried not to think too much as Sam started humming along with some horrendously catchy pop song on the radio. I smiled at my sister and let my eyes fall closed.

CHAPTER TWENTY-SEVEN

"**D**EMON! WAKE UP!"

Something hit my arm like a sledgehammer. I pried one eye open and found Sam grinning at me.

"We're in Lexington."

"What?" I said.

She nodded enthusiastically. "Well, just outside of Lexington in Frankfort. We made awesome time."

"And we're still alive," Zola said. She opened the back door.

"Only three or four near-death moments," Foster said. "Usually have more than that just driving through Saint Charles with Sam."

Sam narrowed her eyes and Foster flashed her a grin.

A sign in the gas station window said "Hot Pretzels."

"Pretzels," I said from my half-awake state. I stumbled out the door and squinted in the still-bright sun.

"Ah swear you could wake him from a coma with food alone."

I hopped onto the curb and said, "I heard that." I held the glass door for Sam and Zola. Foster glided through with me.

We all headed straight for the restrooms. That done, I scoped out the next priority. "Ah, yes." I opened one of the cooler doors and lifted out two four-packs of Frappuccino.

I set the blessed Frappuccino on the counter while I

grabbed some napkins and a few hot pretzels.

"Grab some water, boy," Zola said as I checked out.

"Good idea." I handed her the Frappuccino. The clerk rang up four bottled waters along with the rest of our stuff and we hauled our loot to the door.

"I'll wait for Sam," Foster said.

I only nodded, since the cashier was still staring at us. I pushed the door open with my back and held it for Zola.

Once we were back in the car, I offered one of the pretzels to Zola.

She shook her head. "Ah'll stick with Frank's jerky."

"Ooo, you brought some?"

She lifted a gallon bag out of the back of Sam's seat. It was filled with jerky. She opened the bag, and pulled an inner bag out, and then another. When she finally cracked open the bag with the jerky in it, I thought my eyes might melt.

"Just a light snack, I see."

She laughed and started gnawing through a thick chunk of beef.

I could smell the heat from the front, but I still managed to focus on the pretzels. Granted, they were no Auntie Anne's, but they were soft, warm, and salty. Sam was still walking around inside the store. I wasn't sure what she was looking for.

I shifted in my seat so I could get a better view of the back. "Zola," I said, and I waited for her to look up at me.

"What is it?"

"Have you read all of Philip's journal?"

"No," she said.

"I think … I think you should." I attacked the pretzel again. "At some level, I think he knew what Ezekiel was doing was wrong."

Why?" she asked. "What else do Ah need to know?"

I fiddled with the napkin that had been wrapped around the pretzel. "Up until some of the last entries in his journal, it seemed like everything he was doing he thought he was doing for you."

"Ah know, Damian. Ah know."

"If that's true, why would he have let Agnes hurt you? It makes no sense."

"To us?" she said. "No, it does not make sense. To a man entirely focused on one mad quest? The ends always justify the means." There was a sadness to her voice, but there was also an acceptance. I think on some level she knew she had to kill Philip when she did, but she also remembered the man he used to be.

"Why are you looking at me like that?" she asked with a small frown.

I smiled. "I was just thinking about some of the stories you used to tell us."

She nodded. "The past is the past, Damian. Ah'm grateful for the good memories. Philip died the moment he passed judgment on the world. Ah just provided the burial service."

I didn't say anything as Zola handed me a Frappuccino. I turned around and saw Sam walking back from the gas station, Foster fluttering beside her. She had a gummy worm hanging out the side of her mouth.

"*That* is what took so long?" I asked as she sat down and Foster resumed his post on the dashboard.

"I was looking for the good kind." She held up the bag. "They had the good kind."

"Have some pretzel too. Zola's dieting."

Foster snickered and I didn't even see the hand snap forward from the backseat to box my ear.

"Oww."

"You just be glad we need you in working order. Ah would have done more than smack you."

Sam laughed as we pulled out of the parking lot. I glanced at Zola, and she wore a small smile. Things felt right as Foster cut little chunks of pretzel off with his sword. Sam didn't even tell him how gross it was.

✦　　✦　　✦

IT WASN'T LONG before we turned onto a narrow drive called Duncan Road. Ancient trees and wide, green fields flanked us on either side. The leaves were turning, and the autumn reds and yellows seemed more vibrant than what I was used to in Missouri.

"Where are we going?" I asked as Zola told Sam to turn on a road called McCracken Pike.

"It's an old distillery," Zola said.

The road was narrow and winding enough that even Sam almost slowed down enough to match the speed limit.

"There," Zola said as we rounded a corner. "Pull in there."

I could make out some long, ancient buildings at the base of a large hill. Black roofs and barred windows were set into weathered stone, three stories high. There were some newer structures further away, but the old gray shutters flanking each window kept my attention on their elders.

Something moved in my peripheral vision. My head snapped to the right, but whatever had been there in the third story window was gone.

"Did you see that?" I asked.

"Didn't get a good look," Zola said. "Something was up there."

A dark form peeked around the far edge of the stone building and vanished again.

"What the hell?" I said.

"Stop the car," Zola said.

Sam started to slow. We were still up on a slight hill that sloped down and vanished into what looked like a shallow creek. Something moved, deep within the shadows.

"Aeros?" I reached out to open the door. "Who's with him?"

"Looks like Alan," Foster said. "Why is he here and not with the wolves?"

"Let's find out." I hopped out of the SUV as soon as it came to a halt.

"Ah'll check the building," Zola said.

I nodded. "Sam, wait here until we know what the hell is going on."

"Seriously?" Sam said. "Don't go into the unknown. Wait here in the empty car? Oh, and for the record, I'm a *vampire.*"

I blinked.

"I'll go with Zola and Sam," Foster said. He glided out of the SUV behind Zola.

"Damn straight," Sam muttered. She hopped out and slammed her door.

"I'll, uh, meet you down there," I said.

Sam cocked an eyebrow as she walked by.

I waved once to Aeros and he waved back with one rocky

arm. I jogged down the hill. The closer I got, the better everything smelled. I didn't know what, exactly, they were distilling, but damn it smelled good. A rich, yeasty scent followed the light breeze.

I walked along what looked like train tracks, but a glance down the tracks showed barrels sitting on them instead. I guessed it was some rudimentary conveyance system running between the buildings, but I didn't really know.

Up close, the buildings were obviously old. If I had to guess, I would have said right around the time of the Civil War. The stone wasn't uniform, and I was amazed that the builders had managed to assemble a rectangular structure out of the motley assortment of roughly hewn stone.

I turned to my right at the next corner, and could clearly see Aeros down in a shallow creek bed. Alan was talking to him from the edge of the creek, just past what appeared to be a very large, stone-lined well.

"Alan." I smiled at the hulking werewolf.

He extended his hand and our forearms smacked together. "Good to see you, Damian."

"Likewise," I said. My eyes trailed to Aeros. The water was quiet, splashing slightly as it flowed around his massive legs.

The Old God nodded to me and I nodded back. His hands were tucked behind him, which I thought was odd.

"Have either of you noticed some shadows creeping around this place? We saw something in the window when we pulled in." I glanced between the two.

"Yes," Aeros said. "He is nothing to be concerned with." His red granite form was a stark contrast to the pale stone of the short bluff behind him. Aeros's face fractured into a craggy grin as I splashed down into the shallow water. The cold soaked into my shoes. A crawfish scuttled backwards on a flurry of legs and disappeared into a submerged log.

I crossed my arms and cocked an eyebrow. Sam wasn't the only one who knew eyebrow warfare. "And what, exactly, are you not telling us? And why, exactly, didn't Glenn just tell us to meet you here?"

Alan chuckled at our exchange.

"Damian," the old rock pile said. His voice was incredibly deep, and it vibrated the earth and water around me. "Is Samantha with you?"

I raised both my eyebrows. "Yeah, you want me to get her?" I asked, pointing toward the one of the old buildings.

The boulder that made up the god's head ground as he nodded.

"We're safe here?" When he nodded again, I turned around, cupped my hands over my mouth and yelled. "Hey, Sam!"

A faint clack echoed off the buildings as a heavy door fell closed in the distance.

"I could have done that," Aeros said, his hands still behind his back.

Sam skidded to the edge of the creek. "What's up?"

"Greetings, Samantha."

"Greetings, rock," Sam said, leaning forward. "Has my brother irritated you enough yet to be smashed into the ground and have his name carved into your wall?"

Aeros laughed quietly, but the sound still sent vibrations through the cold water. The fish that were slowly regrouping around us scattered. "I wanted to introduce you to a friend. An ally, really."

He shifted his hands out from behind his back. In his right palm sat the largest, furriest, toothiest dark gray dust bunny you could ever imagine.

"His name is—"

"Jasper!" Sam said with a squeal. She jumped down into the creek beside Aeros and held out her hands.

The amorphous pile of fur and lint contracted and then exploded out of Aeros's palm. Sam caught it mid-flight and it swarmed around her. Jasper chittered and clicked as he rubbed against Sam's cheek and ran around her neck.

"He said he knew you," Aeros said. "I did not particularly believe that until now."

"You can understand him?" Sam asked.

Aeros nodded. "It is a dead language." He paused and ground his rocky palms together. "I am understating the truth. Jasper is ancient."

"Ancient compared to us?" I asked.

"Ancient compared to the universe," Aeros said.

A whirring series of buzzes and clicks erupted from the lint ball. Jasper sat in Sam's hands, a perfect gray sphere with two large, unblinking black eyes.

"He says we do not have time for the long stories, and to give you the shorter version."

"Can he understand us?" I asked.

"Of course he can," Sam said as she ran her fingers over the top of the blob. Little bits of gray fluff rose up to meet her fingers as she stroked his back.

"Oh yes," Aeros said.

"Bastard," I said with a smile.

The sphere of furry lint parted and showed me its many rows of teeth. A shiny, metallic gleam reflected the surface of the water below him. For the first time, I realized he probably could have bitten my hand off when we were kids, if he'd wanted to. My fingers flexed at the thought.

"Jasper, and the few like him who remain, are the ancestors of the Old Gods. As you know, some of us became Guardians, some merged into the world to become elementals, and some of us faded into the great sleep." Aeros leaned against the limestone bluff, his shifting feet sending small waves through the shallow creek.

"I didn't know that," I said.

"Oh," Aeros said. "Well, I suppose you do now."

Sam snickered and ran her fingers through Jasper's fur.

"A few were not so benevolent," Aeros said. "Creatures, not of hate, though you may think that is what drove them, but they were creatures of destruction. Everything that exists, exists in opposition to something else. At times, opposition lives within a single being. Imagine Gaia."

"Mother of the Earth," I said.

"Yes, but for Gaia to exist, so must her opposite. Imagine a being with the power of Gaia, whose only nature is destruction. Those are the Eldritch Gods. Those are the devils seeking to devour all existence. I do not say this to frighten you, but Gaia was never a powerful god. Even Ezekiel does not have the power to bind most gods.

"When the Seals fall, some of those gods will find their way here," Aeros said, patting the limestone bluff. "One day, perhaps not in your lifetime, an Eldritch God will fall upon our world."

Another series of clicks and pops rattled out of Jasper.

Aeros turned and looked at the pulsing pile of lint. "Jasper is worried for Samantha. If Ezekiel dies, the dark-touched will return. They will come for those that live in the light."

"My sister won't fight alone," I said, meeting the gaze of Jasper's huge black eyes. "Our allies are growing. Even the wolves of war stand at our side."

Jasper growled and bared his teeth.

I nodded at him. I was fairly certain he was asking if I meant werewolves. "Big werewolves. Like him," I said, jabbing my thumb up at Alan.

"Oh. My. Lord," Zola said when she joined Alan at the edge of the bank.

"What?" Foster asked as he glided down toward Sam. He suddenly jerked back into the air and landed on my shoulder instead. "Nudd be damned. That's a reaper."

"It's Jasper," Sam said, running her fingers through the ball of fur again.

"Ah haven't seen that thing since you stayed with us in Coldwater, Samantha." Zola shook her head and a small smile lifted her lips.

"I'll just stay over here," Foster said.

It sounded like Jasper was purring every time Sam scratched him. "I haven't heard that sound in so long." She looked up at Aeros. "Thank you for bringing him."

"He was quite insistent on seeing you again before he left."

"Where is he going?" Sam asked.

"The wolves and the Fae are not the only creatures in council."

I looked at Jasper and then back to Aeros. "What's going to

happen?"

"I do not know, Damian. I do not believe anyone truly knows. In my many years, I have come to find that great change does not happen gradually. It erupts and burns and the world left behind is forever changed."

Jasper made a chittering noise, and it sounded sad.

"Yes," Aeros said. "Ezekiel has already killed some of the werewolves."

"What?" Zola asked. "More? Where?"

"Ezekiel killed the Voice of the Cumberland Pack," Alan said. "In the open. We don't know how many members are left. Hugh is afraid their Alpha is dead too. He asked me to travel north to the distillery to catch my ride." He laughed quietly. "The way that wolf can coordinate something is damned frightening."

"You know, I never really thought about it, but who's the Voice of the River Pack?"

"Carter didn't need one," Alan said. "He was … is … was?" He looked confused for a second. "Whatever. Carter is damned sociable for a werewolf." Alan pulled a phone from his pocket and glanced at the display. "We'd better go."

Aeros nodded. "Come, Jasper."

Jasper chittered and twirled around Sam's face as she kissed the fur ball before he leapt back to Aeros.

"We will join you in Gettysburg," Aeros said. "Fare thee well."

A pool of green and blue power began to spin and spark beneath the water. Jasper gave us a flash of silver teeth and Aeros gave us a single nod as they vanished into the portal.

Alan stared at the empty space. "That's new."

"Not really," Zola said as she patted Alan on the cheek.

"Did you see those teeth?" Foster asked as he jumped off my shoulder. I'd forgotten he was there, he'd been so quiet.

"Well, if we're driving on to our deaths," Alan said, "we're stopping at Biscuit Emporium."

"Oh, yeah," Foster said.

"Where?" I asked.

"You haven't been there?" Alan asked, his eyebrow rising as he opened the back door. "But you eat everything." He coughed. "Or so I heard."

"Ha!" Sam ribbed me with an elbow. "He knows you, Demon."

I heard Zola chuckle as she crawled into the back beside Alan. They adjusted the bags and shut the doors as I buckled myself into the front seat.

"Picture this," Alan said. "Sausage, egg, cheese, and a hashed brown patty on a flaky, buttery biscuit."

"I love you man," I said.

Foster grinned at me from the dashboard.

"Sam," I said as seriously as I could. "Onward to Biscuit Emporium."

CHAPTER TWENTY-EIGHT

"FOSTER," I SAID. "Have you told Zola about Jasper's bones?"

He glanced at Zola. "She knows. I didn't tell him in front of the Old Man."

I caught her nod from the corner of my eye. "Wise not to tell him. Ah trust the Old Man, Ah do, but when shit goes bad …" She shook her head.

"He's a scary son of a bitch," Alan said.

"That's what I thought too," Foster said.

"What are you talking about?" Sam asked as we started up another mountainside. It hadn't taken long for us to make the Appalachian Mountains.

"The bones of a reaper," Foster said. "They *are* Magrassnetto."

"That thing didn't have any bones that I could see," Alan said.

I glanced at the werewolf, and then back to Foster and said, "Except for his teeth."

"His teeth look like metal," Zola said. "But very shiny."

"They're only shiny when they're alive," Foster said. "But that's just his teeth. That's not the biggest source of their bones."

"Jasper doesn't feel like he has bones," Sam said. "He's all fluff. With teeth." She smiled as she turned the wheel slowly, taking us around a sharp turn in the highway.

"You've never seen him angry," Foster said. "They aren't called reapers because they're cute."

"There!" Alan said.

Sam veered toward the exit.

"Better hurry. They close early. I wish they didn't close early."

"God, you sound like Damian," Sam said.

"Just slam the accelerator to the floor," Alan said through a deep laugh. "I'm sure we can make it."

The SUV surged forward as Sam complied.

"You wolves aren't afraid of a damn thing, are you?" I asked as I wrapped my hand around the oh-shit handle.

"There are some things," Alan said before he fell silent for a moment. "I didn't tell you when we were there, but Stones River scared the hell out of me."

"Really?" I said. "Just because a big nasty demon wanted to devour us all?"

He laughed without humor and was looking down when I glanced back at him. "No, Damian. I had been there before. You must remember, I am not so young as I look."

"Shit," Foster said. "You've aged well."

Alan smiled. "I was a kid back then, you know? I don't remember a lot of it, but I remember losing my family."

"Sorry man," I said.

He shook his head. "They weren't my real family. I lost my real family to the slave trade years before Stones River."

I felt sick to my stomach.

"It was just a nice group of people. They got us into the

Underground Railroad. Took me under their wing. Protected a small group of us. It was actually the first time I ever met Aeros," he said with a laugh as he slapped the back of my seat. "I should ask that old pile of rocks if he remembers me. Hell, I couldn't have been more than seven or eight."

I turned around and Zola was staring at Alan. Her eyes were so wide I could see the whites all around her pupils.

"Alan," Zola said, and her voice was shaky. "What is your last name?"

"Weir. Why?"

"Oh my god." She put her hands over her mouth. "Oh my god. Do you remember two people …" She slowly lowered her hands and placed one on Alan's knee. "Do you remember two people named Sarah and David?" Her voice cracked slightly.

"Sure, but how did you … how did you … no." This time it was Alan's voice that cracked. "Sarah? You're Sarah? You're Sarah!" Alan's eyes glistened and tears started running down his face.

I heard Sam sniff. She was crying, glancing at Zola and Alan in the rearview. Foster hopped to her shoulder and leaned against her neck.

Zola pushed the backpack out the way and slid across the seat to Alan. "We thought you died. We thought you died. We never would have left. I'm so sorry!"

Zola wrapped her arms around Alan. The huge werewolf was crying. I mean, he was bawling, and it brought tears to my own eyes.

"David was," Zola said before she had to stop and swallow. "David was Philip."

"No …" Alan said, his voice trailing off in pain and disbelief. "No … David protected us. He'd never become that thing. There was no trace of humanity left in Philip."

Alan wrapped his arms around Zola. "I can't believe it's you," he said. "How are you still alive?"

Zola pushed away from the werewolf and stared at him. She frowned and glanced at me. I didn't know if she was looking for my thoughts on the subject or not, but I just nodded.

Her eyes trailed back to Alan. "Ah took the souls of eight slavers." Her body was drawn into a tight line. She was bracing for Alan's reaction, and I could see it. "In blood and darkness, Ah took the lives they should have lived."

Alan didn't recoil. He didn't frown. He just rubbed his arm and stared at Zola. "Did they suffer?" There was an anxiousness in his voice, and I saw Zola visibly relax.

"A great deal," Zola said. "A very great deal."

"Good," Alan said. There was a violence in his voice I'd never heard from the wolf, and I'd seen him tear heads off.

I saw Sam shiver out of the corner of my eye.

"That reconfirms my theory," Foster said. "Don't fuck with Zola."

Alan released a slow chuckle and I nodded sagely.

"No shit," Sam said.

I turned around and took a deep breath. "Oh, look. Biscuits."

Sam swerved into the drive thru. "Two minutes to spare. They're going to hate us."

"Ah don't care," Zola said. "Ah need some damn comfort food."

Sam smiled as we pulled up to the window.

A cashier with a forlorn look slid the window open after a

brief hesitation. "Can I help you?"

"Are you still open?" Sam asked.

"Yes," she said with a small frown.

"Oh good, we don't want to make the werewolf angry."

"Hey," Alan said from the back. "I'm not going to rip your arms off if I don't get a biscuit."

The cashier actually belted out a short laugh and smiled. "That's a new one. What can I get you?"

✦　✦　✦

IT WAS DARK by the time we neared our destination. The biscuits were long gone, and Alan had shared some incredible stories of his time with Zola and Philip. Sarah and David. In some ways, I wished I could have known them then. In other ways, I was thankful as all hell that I didn't. Those were some of the darkest of times.

The Old Man's words came back to me. Philip was not always the faceless monster you think of now.

I frowned and stared out the window. Foster was carving something into the top of the dashboard with his sword. I was sure Vik would be thrilled about that. I smiled and watched him work for a while.

"I don't think you should stay in Cumberland," Alan said. "I would normally invite you in as a pack member, but the city is in upheaval. Honestly, I don't even like the fact you'll be driving through it."

"Is it that bad?" I asked as I turned away from the fairy's impromptu art project.

"From what we've heard. It's all secondhand information, but it seems likely."

"Can you recommend a better place?" Zola asked.

"Anywhere," Alan said. "Hagerstown has some decent hotels."

"It would be better to find a questionable motel," Zola said. "Ah don't want to use any of our real names."

"No," Alan said. "There's a safe house in Hagerstown. Neutral territory. Damian, show them your pack mark and they will give you all room and board."

"Can I call it my rabid dog mark?"

"I …" Alan furrowed his eyebrows. "That may not be the best idea." He started to laugh.

"Umm, guys?" Sam said, leaning forward.

Foster turned his gaze away from his carving and dropped his sword. "Nudd be damned."

"Shit," Zola said, and she dragged the word out.

Alan was silent, but I felt him pull on the back of my seat as he leaned forward.

I stared at the horizon. It should have been pitch black other than the light pollution.

The sky burned. Orange and red shadows rose above a half-ruined skyline.

"Do *not* drive into the city," Alan said. "Cross the bridge. Stop on the other side. I'll find my own way."

"Alan," Zola said, "Ah don't think that's the best—"

Alan leaned over and kissed her cheek. "We don't have time for the best anymore. We have to make do with what we have."

Sam slowed as we swerved around a shallow s-curve.

"The fires are on the eastern side of the city," Alan said. "Fucking hell. What a clusterfuck."

Something thundered beneath us and then something else

exploded in the distance as we started over the river. There was a brief flash of light and debris in the distant hills.

"Stop there, Sam."

Sam came to a stop as we reached the opposite side of the river.

"Good luck my friends," Alan said as he traded grips with me. "We will meet again." He locked eyes with Zola for only a moment. "Go. Now."

Sam didn't hesitate. As soon as Alan closed the door, she smashed the accelerator to the floor. The SUV lurched forward. I watched as Alan hurdled the edge of the bridge behind us.

Something was coming down the highway on the other side. It was too big to be a car, and it was driving forward without lights.

"Oh my God," Sam said. "That's a tank."

"That's a fucking tank!" Foster said. He leaned against the windshield. "What the fuck are they thinking?"

I recognized it at the same time Foster and Sam did, and my jaw was on the floor. The tank fired, and the concussion was massive, even shielded in the SUV my ears rattled. The shell exploded in the distant hills, almost exactly where the first had.

"Then, that was another tank earlier?" Sam said.

"Yes," Zola said. "The witch hunt has already begun."

"Those are military," I said.

"No shit," Foster said. "Martial law my fucking ass. They're using tanks!"

Then I saw it surging through the river. Its tentacles swept along the banks, leveling a city block. Its flesh was fiery, lit by the flames and flashes of the falling city around it. Before we cleared the next hill, I could just barely make out the tank held up in the air. The Leviathan hurled the crushed metal into a mass of buildings.

"We can't just leave that thing there," I said. "We have to go back."

"No!" Zola said when Sam's foot eased off the accelerator. "We *must* kill Ezekiel. The thought of leaving Alan to battle that … thing." She squeezed her forehead. "It's … it's almost too much, but we *have* to. We have to, Damian."

"Zola's right," Foster said. "The needs of the many."

"I know, but that doesn't mean I like it, Foster." I glanced at the fading fires and ruins behind us. "I don't think it's the needs of the many. I'm afraid it's the needs of the whole fucking world."

An idea struck me. "I need water."

"For what?" Foster asked.

"For Nixie," I said as I fumbled with my back pocket.

Sam slammed the brakes and we all slid toward the front of the SUV. "Creek," she said.

I was out and running before anyone said another word. I slid down the bank and splashed into the waters, slamming the disc into the shallow creek. "Answer, dammit, answer."

She came fast. "Damian? What's wrong? I can feel it." Her translucent face formed in the water. There was no graceful pooling of water in this sending. One moment she wasn't there, and the next she was.

"There's a Leviathan in Cumberland. Alan and some of the wolves are there. The military sent in tanks."

"It will destroy the tanks," Nixie said.

"No shit," I said. "We saw it."

"Get away," Nixie said. "It is beyond you."

I nodded. "I know. I know. Can you help?"

"I will send undines."

"Can you use the Ways?"

She hesitated, and then nodded.

I nodded back. If she didn't want to answer out loud, it was probably for a damn good reason.

"Now go, Damian. Go!"

"I love you," I said.

"I love you too."

I ripped the disc out of the water and the connection vanished. I was back in the car a moment later. "The witches are coming. Get us the hell out of here, Sam."

"Call Frank," Sam said. "Call him now. You tell him to get the coven together and stay with Bubbles and Peanut." Her voice was shaking. "You get Ashley over there now."

Frank's line was already ringing.

Sam punched it.

CHAPTER TWENTY-NINE

W E MADE IT to Hagerstown in thirty minutes. I wasn't sure how Sam kept the SUV on the road on that curvy-ass highway at those speeds. I was damn thankful for her super-human reflexes.

I stepped out of the SUV. "Nice driving."

"Thanks," Sam said. She opened Zola's door. Foster sat on Sam's shoulder.

I grabbed the bags out of the backseat. Sam grabbed two suitcases out of the far back and set them on their wheels before we walked toward the hotel entrance. Zola followed behind us, her cane cracking against the asphalt. The roar of the highway still echoed in the distance, but the bugs slamming themselves into the exterior lights were louder.

The door slid open and I saw a diminutive man sitting behind the counter. The light glinted off his balding head and gave his skin a deeply tanned appearance as he moved to turn the page of a thin book. Reading glasses perched on his nose.

"You are welcome to stay," the elderly man said without looking up. "I will warn you it's a full house. You'll be sleeping on a piss poor excuse for a mattress. On the floor."

"We appreciate any hospitality," Zola said.

"You fight for Gywnn Ap Nudd, yes?" he asked, looking up over the rim of his glasses.

Zola nodded.

"I would have you know, this may be neutral territory, but I still have the right to refuse shelter to any wolf, or woman."

Zola's lips tightened into a thin line.

I snarled and took a few steps forward, slamming my arm onto the counter and letting the hooked line of scars flash in the light. "I fight for the commoners. I fight for the Fae. And I fight for *you*. I am *River Pack*."

He leaned down and sniffed my arm. His eyes flashed up to meet mine. They were a blinding golden sunburst. "Vesik."

I nodded.

He shifted and power exploded across my aura. My jaw slackened as the small man became an enormous golden werewolf. The wolf-man extended his paw. I angled my head up and looked him in the eye. He was at least eight feet tall. His lips peeled back and the expression was somewhere between a grin and a snarl.

"I welcome you as a brother."

I smiled and slapped my arm into the werewolf's enormous grasp. "I was a bit concerned you were going to eat my grandmother."

The wolf laughed. It was deep, and throaty, and somewhat terrifying. "My name is Wahya. Hohnihohkaiyohos has told me much of his time with you."

"Hugh?" I said.

The werewolf nodded. "Yes. An old enemy who has become an old friend. Come, I will show you to your room."

The wolf delicately took a keycard in his claws and popped open a small room. There was one small bed and a rollaway.

"This is a fantastic room," I said. "I thought you were overcrowded?"

"It is my room. I will not be sleeping anymore tonight. The eve of battle has never led to rest for my old claws."

"Thank you," I said.

The wolf nodded. "Rest well. Tomorrow we ride into blood, and death."

I watched the golden monster walk gracefully down the hall. I wondered if he was planning on shifting back, or if he was just going to scare the shit out of people for a while.

"That was a huge fucking werewolf," Sam said. "I thought they stayed close to their human size, no?"

"Apparently not," Zola said.

"He's ancient," Foster said. We all piled into the room and let the door close. "Possibly older than Hugh."

"And how old is Hugh?" Sam asked.

"Old," Zola said. "Very, very old."

Sam's phone beeped and she slid it out of her pocket. She stared at the screen and frowned.

"Who is it?" I asked as I dropped the bags beside the television.

"Vik. He says Happy and the water witches fixed Cumberland."

"Fixed my ass," Zola said. "They probably leveled the damn city."

"Vicky?" I asked.

Sam shook her head. "Doesn't say." Her thumbs blurred as she typed a response. Her phone beeped again. "She wasn't there that he saw. He says the military is there in force now. Our people left once the Leviathan retreated."

"Retreated?" Foster said. "Why would a Leviathan retreat?

They aren't that smart."

"Let's try to sleep," Zola said. "Be thankful we heard from our friends. We'll see them soon enough." She leaned her cane against the wall and hopped onto the rollaway bed.

Sam stared at Zola and then glanced at me. "Split the bed?"

"It'll be just like camping," I said.

"Only you won't scream like a little bitch when I drop a garter snake on you," Sam said.

"I may scream like a little bitch," I said as I kicked off my shoes, "but …" My aura flashed out and wrapped around Sam's arm. The flash of knowing was subtle, I knew most things about my sister already, but the new mini-film of Frank lovin' I could have done without. I pulled my hand back, and Sam's arm followed.

Foster and Zola started laughing.

"Demon, don't. Dammit."

I gave a little flick of my wrist and Sam slapped herself in the face.

"You are so dead."

I grinned at my sister. She narrowed her eyes at me, and then she leapt. She crossed the room in a heartbeat, but I was faster. Both my hands shot up, formed into half claws. My aura surrounded her, and suspended her.

She blinked and let her arms fall. "Dammit, that is so cheating."

I let go and she bounced off the bed once. She was laughing the whole time.

"Sleep, children," Zola said. She pulled a sheet up over her cloak. "Or Ah won't make you pancakes in the morning."

Sam and I both smiled. Zola had always made us pancakes

when Sam came to visit in Coldwater. Back when Sam was human, and shit was a lot less complicated.

"Pancakes," Foster said. "Let's dream of pancakes. I like pancakes." He curled up on a double stack of napkins and pulled a hand towel up as a blanket. "And maple syrup." He yawned and stretched.

Sam slipped into her pajamas before coming back to the bed. They were strikingly similar to Ashley's Paul Frank pajamas. I changed into a slightly too big Death's Door t-shirt. Frank had a few of them made up for some holiday sale. They'd actually gone over pretty well.

I shook my head, wondering why I was thinking about such nonsense. I reached up and killed the light. The room was pitch black and quiet.

Sleep did not come easily.

✦　✦　✦

I AWOKE TO the sound of heated whispering. The light leaking through the edge of the drapes surprised me. We were well into the morning, at the least. I glanced at the small desk in the corner. Zola was leaning over Foster, pointing at something beneath him.

I crawled out of bed, careful not to wake Sam up. In a few steps, I could see they were looking at a map.

"Gettysburg?" I asked.

"Yes," Zola said quietly. "Ah've been thinking about the best entry point. Ah think we should go through the heart of the old city." Her finger traced a route.

Foster crossed his arms and shook his head. "I'm not convinced. Ezekiel won't expect us to come from the north."

"It doesn't matter," I said.

Foster and Zola both looked up at me.

"He knows we're coming. It doesn't matter where we come from. Short of popping out of one of Glenn's vortexes, he's going to know we're there."

Zola leaned back and gave a slow nod. "You may be right. Still, the city will lend us more cover."

"Shouldn't we try to stay away from the city?" Sam asked.

We all turned to look at her.

"Sorry," I said. "Didn't mean to wake you up."

"It's fine," Sam said. "I don't need as much sleep as the others."

"Ah don't think we need to worry about staying clear of the city," Zola asked. "If any of the city survives, it will be a good day."

Zola's words hung in the air. She was right, and we all knew it. We'd seen what Ezekiel was capable of. Or maybe we hadn't. That was an even more unnerving thought.

"The city will provide more cover," Zola said.

"True," Foster said. "There is more than one nexus in the area. It may do even more to conceal us than the physical city."

Sam started flipping through her phone.

"Vik?" I asked.

She nodded. "Happy and Vicky are traveling with the Nashville Pack, and Hugh. The Watchers are already there. It just says 'Anubis dies in the world below.' "

"Edgar," Zola said. She pinched the bridge of her nose. "Edgar is moving in from the north."

My phone vibrated. "The Brigade lives for the light," I said. "The dead live for the night."

"I know that one," Foster said. "It's twofold. The vampires will move in from the west, but not until night. The Irish Brigade from the east."

"Then we strike from the city," Zola said.

"We don't know where he'll be," I said.

"Ah know exactly where he'll be, boy," Zola said. "Come, let's get breakfast. We're going to need the energy."

✦   ✦   ✦

I DIDN'T EXPECT the awed looks mixed with sheer hatred as we wandered past the dining hall and into the kitchen. I heard the whispers of "Vesik, Addanaya, vampire sister."

A man in the booth closest to the kitchen stood up and walked up to Sam. He wore a torn, stained tank top. "You are not welcome here, dead one."

"Don't," I said. The man barely spared me a glance. All of his attention was on Sam.

He put his arm around her shoulder as she turned away. "Look at me when I'm talking to you, you dead bitch."

I started to do a very bad thing, but Foster beat me to it. He exploded off Sam's shoulder, sending a shower of glistening fairy dust out into the dining hall. He wrapped a hand up in the werewolf's shirt and walked the wide-eyed wolf backwards until the wolf's back slammed into a pillar. A thin webwork of cracks crawled up the drywall.

"You touch my friend again," Foster said as he drew his sword, "and I will eat my Fruit Loops out of your skull."

There was an older, gray-haired wolf in the back. I heard him whisper the words, "Demon Sword." The room fell silent. I heard a faint clicking noise that grew louder. Wahya appeared at the front of the dining hall.

"You insult us by your actions, Jon," he said. "If we did not need the cannon fodder for today, I would kill you myself." The wolf's lips pulled back in a smile that made the werewolf cringe beneath Foster's grasp.

Foster let him go, and Jon scurried back to a booth at the far side of the hall.

"Do not threaten our allies," Wahya said. "The peace between our peoples has been long in coming. If that is not motivation enough, I would invite you to remember the fairy could kill you all before you could shift."

As he turned away from the enraptured audience, Wahya winked at us. He knew Foster couldn't kill all the wolves that fast. The others didn't need to know that though.

"Pancakes," Foster said. "I just want some damn pancakes. And Fruit Loops," he added with a glance toward Jon.

I sneezed and shook my head.

"Did you forget your allergy pills?" Zola asked.

"No," I said. "That was just a crap ton of fairy dust."

Sam grabbed Foster's wrist and dragged him into the self-serve kitchen. His wings brushed the ceiling, but he didn't seem to mind. His gaze was focused on the back of Sam's head.

"Breathe, bug," Sam said.

Foster cracked a small smile.

"Save it for the true threat, my friend," Wahya said. He joined us in the small kitchen area.

Foster nodded and sheathed his sword. "How late is it?"

I glanced up at the clock beside the buffet. "Noon," I said.

"Ezekiel was spotted in Orrtanna," Wahya said. "The wolves are restless. I will try to remove those who may distract you." His claws clicked on the floor as he headed back into the dining hall. He spoke quietly, but several wolves immediately stood and walked toward the front doors.

I watched them go, and then turned my attention back to Sam when she started talking.

"Look at this thing, Foster. It's like a printer, for pancakes."

Foster leaned down and squinted at a large, rectangular box that had "Hands-Free Pancakes" written across the side. "Push here," he said as he clicked a button. Sam slid a plate underneath the edge of the machine.

"You have got to be kidding," Foster said. A steaming pancake rolled out of the edge of the machine and slapped down onto the plate. "That is mankind's greatest invention."

I watched, somewhat awed, as the fairy swiped a line of butter and syrup down the middle of the pancake, rolled the whole thing up into a cigar shape, and destroyed it in one bite.

Zola raised her eyebrows.

"It's good," Foster said. He chewed and swallowed and hit the button again.

"You shrink, and I'll swat you faster than Damian," Sam said.

Foster grinned and stuck his face down by the conveyor belt, watching the pancake march toward its doom.

Sam pulled the clear refrigerator door open. "What?" She pulled out a small translucent bag and held it up. "They have blood."

"I'm guessing Wahya cleared the commoners out of here," I said.

"You think?" Zola asked, biting off the words. "Now move. Ah need my coffee." She shoved me out of the way and filled a cereal-bowl-sized mug to the brim.

We eventually made it into the dining hall. Most of the wolves ignored us, a few seemed to revere us, and two gestured for us to join them.

"Welcome," a man said as I slid into the booth across from him.

Sam sat down beside him, and he didn't so much as flinch. I liked him already.

"I am called Gosha." He spoke slowly, almost methodically. His eyes were kind in his tanned face, round and welcoming. A small dream catcher hung from his neck. "This is Misun."

I froze and slowly raised my eyes.

The smaller man, Misun, nodded. His complexion was lighter than Gosha, but his features were similar. A long braid trailed down across each of his shoulders. He looked more wary of us than anything. I followed his gaze to Foster, demolishing another pancake. I'd probably be wary of him too.

"We've met," Misun said.

"Aha, yeah." I'd told Misun he looked like a tabby cat when he was shifted at my initiation. Hugh loved to give me hell about that. "So … Misun. Is that Sioux?"

"Yes," he said in a voice that was not as deep as I expected. "I am surprised you would know, given your penchant for cats."

"He is friends with Hugh," Gosha said.

"Umm, actually I was guessing," I said.

Gosha blinked, and then his lips curled up in a large smile.

Misun's right hand ran down the length of one braid. "Well, it was a good guess. Although if you must guess, always go with Navajo or Cherokee."

Gosha nodded. "More of them. Although we are none of those tribes."

"You're from the elder tribes," Zola said. "Like Hugh."

Gosha and Misun both nodded.

"Do you mind?" Sam asked as she held her blood bag up.

"Not at all, young one," Gosha said. "We once fought the dark-touched at the side of Camazotz. I assure you, his eating habits were far more disturbing."

"The old dogs are telling stories again," someone said from across the room.

"Ah've met Camazotz," Zola said. She turned toward the voice. "Pray you never become the focus of his wrath."

The wolf fell silent.

"We've told them the old stories," Misun said. "They pay them no heed."

"Some fools won't believe what they haven't seen," Zola said. "They'll die quickly if they're not ready."

"Wahya has trained many of them," Gosha said. "He does not tell the old stories, but he trains the wolves to fight dark-touched."

Foster nodded as he sucked down another pancake. "That's good, because the dark-touched are going to return if we win."

"And if we lose?" Misun asked.

"Well, we won't really have to worry about it then," Foster said.

Gosha laughed without humor. "You speak the truth, but it is laced with fury. Do not lose your focus in the coming fight."

"I know," Foster said.

"Most of the world has not seen the gods battle," Misun said. "They will be stunned, and they will be vulnerable. Do not hesitate to put them down."

Gosha slid his glass of water toward the center of the table and frowned.

Misun eyed him briefly. "I know you don't like ambushing the enemy, but we are outmatched."

Gosha nodded. "Yes, we are. We should prepare. Gather the wolves."

Sam stood up so Gosha and Misun could slide out of the booth.

"It was good to meet you all," Gosha said. "Even the one who called Misun a tabby cat."

I felt a blush crawl over my face. I still felt kind of bad about that.

"We will stand beside you on the field," Gosha said, "no matter the cost."

We traded grips. Misun's eyes trailed along my pack mark. I held the arm out so he could see it better.

"A pack with a necromancer," he said. "Perhaps it is time for the world to change."

He clasped my shoulder, squeezed, and walked out of the hall with Gosha. Neither of them looked back.

CHAPTER THIRTY

A TERRIBLE PALL comes before the storm of battle. I watched the trees flicker by, absently aware of the green mountains in the distance, as Sam drove us toward Gettysburg. I worried for my friends as the SUV bounced over an uneven stretch of asphalt. I worried for my family. I worried for the commoners all around us.

Sam took the exit off Highway Fifteen onto Emmitsburg Road, and a wave of unease slithered down my spine.

"Stay straight," Zola said. "Turn left when you hit Baltimore Street."

"What is that?" I asked, gritting my teeth. I already knew the answer. I just didn't want to know.

"We're close," Zola said. "Gods we're close." She began rubbing her arms.

Foster's hand flexed around the hilt of his sword. He was still seven feet tall, crammed into the back seat. There was a look of sheer focus on his face as he stared out the window. "So many," he said.

A weight pulled on my aura, like we'd driven into spider web that was trying to drag us down. I cursed and slammed my hands onto the dashboard.

"What?" Sam asked. "What is it?"

"The dead." I squeezed my eyes shut for a moment. "There

242

are … it's just … fuck."

"It will be better past the ridge," Zola said, the strain obvious in her voice.

I turned my head slowly to the right and my eyes widened. There was a field of bright souls. A thousand times more dense than Fort Davidson. At a glance, I could see two gravemakers wandering the field. Their rough-hewn forms moved slowly, gracefully. The pale souls didn't move as the monstrosities walked among them, and through them.

"Pickett's Charge," Zola said. "Many men died."

"Look at them." I said, realizing Zola still had her head down.

I heard a sharp intake of breath from the back seat. "Cemetery Ridge. Ah didn't … Ah don't remember it being so many."

Foster frowned as he watched the scene pass us by. "Here the darkness dwells. The follies of men give rise to darkness beyond measure. Only war survives."

His words ate through the buzz of the dead all around me. It was a dark saying, but it was undeniable, looking across that field.

The SUV sped forward, and we pulled away from Cemetery Ridge.

The voices whispered, and I held my left hand up to my ear.

"Do you hear that?" I asked.

"Yes," Zola said. "Something has disturbed the cemeteries. They are restless."

"It's not just the dead from the battle," I said. "There are … so many."

"Focus, Damian," Zola said. Her voice sounded normal and relaxed. "You can keep them out. Lock down your aura."

I nodded and took a deep breath as the town began to rise around us. Old brick structures were interspersed with modern strip malls on our left. The restless dead were strewn across the cemeteries on our right. I turned away from the vision. A thousand motionless eyes staring at me was beyond unnerving.

The endless march of the dead faded as motels and wooden homes of Gettysburg replaced the brick buildings. Sam swerved left at the next intersection. We ended up heading north on Baltimore Street.

"Oh my God," Sam said.

"Do not slow down," Zola said. "Quickly, Samantha. Get us through this.

"It begins," Foster said. His eyes tracked the carnage outside.

A wall of creatures and men and werewolves slaughtered each other in a small park off to our right. Some kind of enormous *thing* flattened everything around it, one tree-like arm raised above its head. When it fell, wolves died in an explosion of gore.

"What is that?" I asked.

"It's a troll from the Burning Lands," Foster said, his voice grim.

"We have to help them," Sam said.

"No," Zola said. "That creature is about to die."

I frowned and looked back as we sped past. A gravemaker wrapped its rusted, bark-like flesh around the troll's leg. The last thing I saw was the troll falling to the earth. I had little doubt it would be dead soon after.

"Three bloody gravemakers already," I said. "How long until sunset?"

"An hour," Foster said. "We won't have much help from the vampires until then."

"Take us north of the city," Zola said. "We need to find Ezekiel and Edgar. The men fighting the troll are Fae."

Foster nodded. "The King is already here."

The SUV bounced when we hit the bottom of a gentle incline at high speed. "Fucking hell, those are commoners!" I watched a pack of wisp-thin Fae fall on the bystanders. "Are they … are they *eating* them?"

"Yes," Foster said. He leaned toward the driver's side windows. "Hern's troops. He's mad. He's unleashed the Unseelie Court."

"That's what those are?" I stared at the emaciated forms. He threw a man into the gutter with strength belying his size. I saw a row of long, sharp teeth flash within the gray face before he began killing again.

"We have to help them."

"No," Zola said. "They are lost. Focus on our goal." She kept her eyes on the road ahead, not looking to the scenes of horror unfolding across the quiet town of Gettysburg.

Another time, I would have said the old city reminded me of Saint Charles, noble old structures standing tall through the centuries. But now? The scene before me was an utter nightmare.

"Was the Unseelie Court in Faerie with us?" I asked.

"At the Royal Court?" Foster said. "No, they are not welcome. Hern has long allied himself with the Unseelie lords and ladies."

"Waiting for this moment," Zola said.

Sam jerked the wheel and swerved around a body in the

road. I don't think it mattered. There were too many missing parts for any creature to have survived.

The buildings around us became gorgeous brick structures as we sped deeper into the city. It was a beautiful backdrop to a horrific scene. The pale stone library was dark and silent, bodies strewn across its steps. Werewolves and Fae formed small pockets of violence as they hurdled across the handrails on the steps. They fought as only creatures with no fear of death can fight. No hesitation. No second guessing. Vicious. Merciless. Terrifying. Their snarls and battle cries pierced the SUV and followed us down the street.

The town square was a roundabout. Meticulous landscaping graced a center island surrounded by inspired architecture. Damaged and destroyed vehicles clogged the road. Cars and vans were crushed and overturned. A bus burned, two bodies fallen at the edge of the emergency exit, charred beyond recognition.

"Over the circle," I said.

Sam nodded and plowed through a bed of flowers, kicking up dirt and grass and foliage. She narrowly missed a metal signpost as we bounced out the other side. The SUV protested as we sped over the railroad tracks a short way down the next hill. The unmoving traffic of abandoned cars and debris lightened. I could see another car speeding away in the distance. At least someone had gotten away.

The buildings grew further apart. We were all silent as we passed the last few brick structures and left the city behind for a series of open fields. In the distance, far to the east, I could see another of the trolls.

"Stay right up there," Zola said. "Table Rock."

Sam said nothing as she pulled the wheel and steered onto the new road. Homes blipped by. For a short time, it looked like any town suburbia, then the rolling fields overwhelmed our view once more.

Trees began to crowd the road up ahead.

"There, Sam," Zola said. "Pull off the road." She pointed to a thick copse of trees. We'll walk from there."

None of us even asked why. Sam maneuvered the car so it was hidden from the road. Probably a smart move. Something like a thunderclap exploded in the distance. It trailed off and crackled before finally fading away.

Zola closed her eyes and stared at the ground.

"You okay?" I swung my own legs out of the SUV. I set them on the grass, and my body burned. I ground my teeth so hard I was afraid they would shatter. "What. Is. That?"

"Hell," Zola said, exhaling sharply. "It is hell."

The voices grew louder around us as my aura burned. I closed my eyes and took a deep breath, closing my necromancy off beneath a deeper layer of my aura.

"I can't talk to Happy in this mess, can I?"

"No, you have to open your aura to locate him. You would go mad, boy. It's worse than Ah expected." She frowned.

I slung a bandolier, filled with speed loaders for the pepperbox, over my shoulder. Combined with the speed loaders laced into my vest, there was a lot of ammo to go around. The backpack followed, and I carried my staff in my left hand.

Foster unsheathed his sword as soon as he stepped out of the car. Another crack of thunder sounded in the distance. He pointed to the northeast and said, "There."

We all followed his lead. He stayed on the outside of the

woods, tracing the edge off to our right. The sun was sinking, turning the sky into a rolling, blood-red cloudbank that reflected across Foster's blade.

The sun couldn't set fast enough, as far as I was concerned.

The trees gave way to another field that climbed a hill to our east. We continued north. Sam stayed at my side and Zola trailed behind us. I thought I'd be fast enough to throw a shield around her, if it really came to it.

Grass reached the top of my ankles as we followed a sparse line of trees toward another section of woods. A well-defined crop flanked our left. I thought it might be soybeans, but I wasn't really sure.

Another thunderclap echoed around us. This time I could see a thin, blinding lance of power strike down from the sky.

"Edgar," Zola said. "Move. They're at Witmer Farm. Ah know it."

Foster picked up the pace until we were jogging. We crossed through another small field of grass and straight through a line of trees. Foster slowed to a stop as we stepped out the other side of the woods.

"Nudd be damned," Foster said. He let his sword hang loosely at his side as the four of us gaped at the scene unfolding before us.

CHAPTER THIRTY-ONE

I'D NEVER SEEN anything like what the Watchers were fighting. The creature stood twenty feet tall. Its red, cracked flesh looked like chunks of stone had been glued onto a bulky skeleton. Fire streamed from the eye sockets in its bony skull, and burst through its flesh when it moved, as if the fire itself propelled it into motion.

The dead roared all around us. Every step the creature took seemed to ignite something in the dead. I tried to focus, tried to step toward the thing … attack it … something … but I could barely keep myself upright.

The creature made contact with one of the Watchers, and the young woman screamed as her clothes ignited and her body took to the air. I didn't know if anyone could survive a hit like that. She was still screaming as she arced through the air in our general direction.

"No," Foster said. "No." He moved fast.

Zola raised her cane. *"Minas Ventusatto."* A blast of air slammed into the young woman and knocked most of the flames away.

Foster grunted as he caught her. Her face was burned and blistered. Her left arm hung limply at her side, swollen and purple and ruined. Foster laid his hands to either side of her head. *"Socius Sanation."* A flash of power turned the field around them white, and silenced the dead around us.

That was … odd.

The Watcher gasped beneath Foster's spell as her face slowly pulled itself back together and her arm began to look more like an arm. Then she screamed as Foster's power spiked and everything in her body snapped back into place.

"Who …" she said in a shaky voice. "Who are you?"

"Eddie didn't tell you?" I said after a deep breath. "We're the backup."

She stared at me wide-eyed. "Vesik." She glanced at Zola. "Addanaya. He was right about you all along."

I looked back to the battle. Edgar made several gestures and the men and women around him moved with blinding speed. Two were caught up in a single sweep of the monster's arm.

"Edgar said it's after an artifact. At the farm." The young woman closed her eyes and then pushed herself away from Foster. "I have to help."

"It's after the bloodstone," Zola said. "It *has* to be. We cannot let that happen. Don't engage that … thing. Sam, how fast can you move?"

She blurred into motion and nodded. "Pretty fast. Not as fast as I'd like. Sun needs to go down more."

"Demon of the Abyss," Foster said, his voice rising as he stepped toward the fighting. "That should not be here. The Seals aren't broken. It can't be here!"

"The Unseelie Court brought it," the Watcher said.

Foster's face turned murderous. Something crashed through the woods behind us. Two wisp-thin Fae stepped out.

"They're here!" the Fae on the right said.

Foster screamed and lunged at the Unseelie Fae. They

didn't so much as get a shield up before his strike removed their heads. He picked up one head by its hair and threw it back into the woods. The other he stomped on until it exploded. "More mercy than you deserve." The nearest ley lines siphoned the flesh away from the bodies.

Even without their heads, the Fae screamed.

"Foster, help the wounded," Zola said. "Sam. There is a cross behind the barn. Take Damian with you and find it. Ah'll help Foster. Now go!"

I didn't get a word in before Sam picked me up and started running flat out.

I could briefly make out Edgar. I thought I heard him say, "Go," as he pointed toward the red barn across the road.

Sam passed the battle, skirting around the western edge and a low cinder block wall. A red brick two-story farmhouse was on our left. I made out a white balcony before I blinked and it was gone. Sam curved to the right and slid to a stop behind the red barn.

An emaciated gray Fae, much like those Edgar was facing in the other field, looked up at us from the hole he was digging. He raised his hand. I grabbed the rune on my staff to call a shield. A bolt of power as dark as the sun is bright leapt from his hand and swarmed over my shield. Slowly, it began to eat through the barrier.

"Are you fucking kidding me?" I said as Sam set me down. "Jump when I say jump."

Sam nodded.

"Now!" I released the shield and we both dove to either side. The dark power dissolving the shield fell to the earth and sizzled.

The Fae grinned at me with knife-like teeth. I grinned back and aimed my pepperbox at his head. He collapsed when the bullet tore through his brains.

"Where's the cross?" Sam asked.

I pulled a knee up and pushed myself onto my feet. "I don't know." I looked around, surveying the ground where the Fae had been digging. There were several holes already.

My eyes trailed up to the back of the barn, and then across the other, smaller buildings in the area. My gaze snapped back to a pile of old stone.

"Shit." I pointed to one of the stones. Part of a Celtic cross was etched into a broken piece.

"Guessing that's not where it's always been," Sam said.

"Yeah." A massive crack of thunder shook the ground. "I'm going to see if I can sense it."

"Necromancy?" Sam asked. "Zola said not to do that."

"I know," I said. "I don't see a real choice. Watch my ass."

"I'd rather not," Sam said flatly.

I laughed softly.

"Be careful."

I nodded and unlocked my aura. The flood of voices took my breath away. It felt like the entire world was talking at once, their voices shaking my head to pieces. I fell to one knee and gritted my teeth.

It looked like Sam was saying something, but I couldn't hear her. I couldn't hear anything. I pushed my aura out, seeking the darkness within the bloodstone. Ghosts flickered into being around me. Some roamed the grounds freely. Others stared at me, their gray forms unmoving. Souls peered back from their lost eyes.

My aura continued crawling through the wreck of what I now realized had been a battlefield in its own right. Small, yes, but terror and blood were in the earth all around me, except for one small area of relative calm. My head snapped up and I stared over my left shoulder.

"The house. The cornerstone," I said. "It's inside of it." Sam ran over to the home as I locked down my aura once more. I stood up on shaky legs and walked over to stand behind her.

The sun was almost gone now, and a small section of the stone came away easily under Sam's increased strength.

She peered into the hole in the cornerstone. "It's hollow. It's here." Her arm fit in up to her elbow. She pulled back a small packet of what I imagine must have been wool at some point in time. It crumbled as she unwrapped it.

In the fading light, the small stone looked black, with a band of blood-red color running through it. Sam shivered and handed it to me.

I slid it into a small pocket on the side of my vest and snapped it closed. "Come on," I said. Let's get back to the others.

As soon as we cleared the edge of the farmhouse, I could see Zola dragging an injured Watcher back to Foster. The fairy's sword was sheathed and he was entirely focused on healing.

The towering creature took a quick step and slammed its foot into the ground, sending a shockwave of fire out in a circle all around it. The Watchers leapt and shielded and avoided the worst of the blast. Zola raised a shield around the makeshift infirmary as the fire swept past them, igniting the drier grass all around us.

The creature turned away from us, and Sam and I took our

chance to run to Zola and Foster.

Edgar kept his eyes on the creature while he brushed the flames off his charred suit.

The thing opened its palm and thrust its arm toward Edgar. A focused beam of fire leapt from its hand. Edgar barely got a shield up.

"Enough!" Edgar raised his arms to either side and floated away from the burning earth.

The monster's eyes followed Edgar before it stepped toward him.

"That is enough." An explosion erupted around Edgar, engulfing him in flames as bright as the sun. I squinted and my jaw dropped open as I realized it wasn't flame. It was a solar art and, as it faded, Edgar was already streaking across the sky. The scream on his lips curdled my blood. The armor adorning his body was formed of golden fire, and it took little imagination to understand why he'd been worshipped as a god.

He flew forward with his right arm pulled back. The monster tried to move, but Edgar's fist connected with the thing's face. Edgar's entire body followed his fist through the monster's head in an eruption of flesh and bone and something like magma.

Edgar impacted the ground behind his target. He clenched both hands into fists at his waist as he stood up.

The massive body fell slowly at first, and picked up speed before it smashed into the roadway. Its fiery lifeblood continued pouring from its neck as the rest of the flesh dimmed.

Edgar jogged over to us. His calm, superior demeanor was cracked and broken. "Ezekiel sent that thing here for the bloodstone. He's heading into the city."

I tapped the pouch on my vest. "We got it."

"Good," Edgar said. "You didn't see Ezekiel?"

"No," Zola said. "But there are many dead in the city. The Fae and wolves are already engaged."

Edgar nodded. "Hern has lost his goddamned mind. Bringing the Unseelie cavalry into this realm …" He shook his head.

Five men and women laid on the ground beside Foster. "I've done all I can," the fairy said. "I think they'll live."

"Thank you," Edgar said.

The brown-haired Watcher Foster and Zola had saved earlier walked up beside Edgar. "It's dead."

"Good," Edgar said. "Thank you, Stacia."

Stacia turned to Foster and Zola. "Thank you both."

"I'm sorry I couldn't save more," Foster said.

"There is always a cost in war," Edgar said. "I only hope we can pay the price. The vampires will be here soon, but they have no clue what's waiting for them. This isn't the battle we were expecting. Stay close to the Old Man and look for an opportunity to strike Ezekiel. Our allies are unprepared for this. Assist where you can."

"I'll call Vik," Sam said.

Edgar nodded.

"Cara and Aideen are with the Pit," Zola said.

"They won't be caught off guard with these creatures, then?" Edgar asked.

"No," Foster said. "They'll know what to do, and what to run from."

"Hugh will be with the wolves," Edgar said. "He's seen far worse than this."

"No one has seen worse than this," Stacia said. She rubbed

her forehead and it smeared soot across it. "We failed."

Edgar looked at her, and then looked away. "Ezekiel is more disciplined than we remember, Addanaya. He makes for the ridge."

Zola sighed. "It is a dark place."

"Will you be able to function there?" Edgar asked.

Zola nodded. "Not at our best, but yes. The Old Man will be powerful there." She turned to me with a small frown. "We must go back to Cemetery Ridge."

CHAPTER THIRTY-TWO

S AM BACKED THE car out of the woods and we headed toward the city. It didn't take long before the old buildings rose up on either side of us once more. Foster was small again and sleeping on the dashboard. The mass healing had really taken it out of him.

"We won't avoid using arts in this fight," Zola said. "Don't lose yourself in the noise."

"Noise," I said. "That's a nice way of talking about the shit that will burn the brain out of your head."

She laughed quietly. "There is much power to be had here."

I nodded. In front of us, I could see a line of wolves. They had all shifted, and stood in their slightly hunched wolf-man forms. A building burned beside them, releasing a light shower of embers into their midst. A few wolves batted at their fur as the embers landed.

Zola pointed to the left. "Park there."

Sam pulled into some kind of U-shaped bus station as she said, "Are they ours?"

"Ah think so."

"Foster," I tapped the dashboard. "Wake up."

"Awake," he said. "I'm awake."

Sam held open a pocket on her vest. "Hop in, bug."

Foster climbed in. His wings and head stuck out of her

pocket.

My eyes trailed across a pale brown wolf. "Looks like Caroline."

A huge, dark brown figure turned toward us. Something large, gray, and metal glinted in the firelight. As we got closer, past the railroad tracks, I could see it was a harp, hanging beneath what looked like a cloud on a heavy chain around his neck. Something clicked in my head, and I recognized the pattern from the green flag of the Irish Brigade, one of Caroline's.

"Peace," Caroline said as she placed a paw on the large wolf's arm. "Damian, is Carter with you?"

I shook my head. "If he's here, I can't tell. There's too much noise."

I caught Zola's smirk out of the corner of my eye.

"Damian!"

I thought I recognized the half-growl half-shout. There was no fear in his voice. It almost sounded like he was glad to see us. I scanned the ranks of wolves until I found movement.

A black wolf pushed his way between two smaller wolves and took two graceful leaps to land beside me.

"Haka," I said. I extended my arm.

He slapped his clawed arm into my own and gave me a wolfish grin. I heard a flurry of whispers start up and then die down as Caroline glared at her wolves. She stepped toward us and joined Haka.

Another smaller form jostled through the line, cursing as he went. I grinned when I saw him lift a chocolate bar and take half of it down in one bite.

"Dell, is the Old Man here?" I asked.

He shook his head. "No, but I'm going to kick his ass when he gets here. This is bloody awful."

"This one," Caroline said with a nod towards Dell, "this one likes to complain."

"I told you I'd get better with chocolate," Dell said under his breath. "I'm hardly complaining at all." An ember landed on his arm and he resumed cursing.

"Have you seen Ezekiel?" I asked.

"Yes," Caroline said. "He was heading south."

Zola nodded. "Edgar believes he'll return to Cemetery Ridge."

"Fucking hell," Dell said. "That's where the Old Man was going to go first. I think he was planning on persuading some gravemakers to help."

"We'd better go that way," I said.

Caroline shook her head. "Hern's forces have already infiltrated the city. We were able to flank the eastern line, but they are firmly ensconced to the west and south. I'm taking my wolves north. We'll try to outflank them again."

"We saw some of the fighting," I said. "I'm sorry we couldn't stop."

Caroline nodded. "We all have our priorities. I harbor no ill will for that."

"Show her," Haka said.

"What?" I asked.

"Show her the bloodstone in your pocket."

I blinked and stared at the wolf. "How did you know?"

"Is that what's making me nauseous?" Dell asked before he crumpled a candy wrapper and then bit into another chocolate bar.

I unbuttoned the pouch and pulled out the dark stone. The wolves behind Caroline recoiled. Caroline's face fell flat. If she'd been in her human form, I'd have guessed she'd be frowning.

"Put it away, please," she said.

I did.

"You cannot let that fall into Ezekiel's hands. We have enough problems."

"No shit," I said.

"Thank you for showing me," Caroline said. "It will help convince my other wolves you are not like the necromancers of old." She made two sharp, short barking sounds, which were echoed by the werewolves behind her. "Be careful. I'm afraid we've only seen part of what we face here," she said as she walked past us.

"We're staying with them," Haka said. "Dad says the water witches will be here tonight."

"Really?" I said.

He nodded. "Probably with Glenn." He waved and Dell nodded as they trailed after the Irish Brigade.

"So, should we go back for the car?" I asked.

"No," Zola said. "We go on foot from here. A car will be too obvious. Too likely to call attention. Ah want to use stealth as much as we're able." She started forward and we followed.

We finished climbing the hill that led back to the roundabout. The burning building was behind us now. Zola didn't think it would spread since it was contained within the collapsed brick frame.

Sam whimpered as we walked into the carnage that had been the town square. Her hands leapt to her mouth.

I closed my eyes and rubbed my forehead. "God dammit."

"We can't save them all," Zola said. "It's not your fault."

"But we drove right by them," Sam said while she stared at the bodies, as if she was trying to commit every detail to memory. Her voice trailed off. "We drove right by."

The dead were strewn across the street, mixed with blood and viscera and all manner of body parts. Dead banks of fur lay piled beside bodies that had been werewolves. Bits of scaled armor and weapons lay scattered along the ground where the Fae had fallen and been absorbed by the ley lines.

I stared at the face of a young wolf. She looked like she was seventeen or eighteen at the most. Her right arm was missing and her pale face stared at the stars above in sheer shock. Half her chest was burned away. A charred breast hung awkwardly from the other side.

"He dies," I said as I tore a red cape off the empty armor remnants a Fae. "Ezekiel dies." I knelt beside the mutilated girl and carefully wrapped the red cape around her. I gently tried to close her eyes, but flesh just flaked away on the burned side of her face. I tucked the edge of the cape beneath her head.

When I looked up, Foster was awake and standing on Sam's shoulder. "What happened here?" he asked.

"Ezekiel's troops met the Irish Brigade." There was far more vacant armor strewn across the field than dead wolves, but that spoke nothing of the murdered commoners. The control on my aura slipped and voices exploded across my mind as I stood up. Screams and curses of a battle long done tore through my head.

I embraced it.

"Don't," Zola said. She grabbed my arm. "Not yet."

I slowly ratcheted my control back in place and met her

eyes.

A barely contained rage lit her eyes, and her wrinkled cheeks flexed as she ground her teeth together.

Sam pulled on my other arm and it got us moving again. We stayed in the shadows of the old buildings as we left the carnage behind.

"That cape was from the Burning Lands," Foster said. "That was not an Unseelie from Faerie."

"Apparently they die just fine," I said, unable to keep from biting off the words.

"They die hard," Foster said. "They are skilled in war. Some of those commoners were zombies."

"What?" I said. I hadn't paid much attention outside of the girl. She'd been so young. My hands curled into fists again.

"At least fifteen were zombies," Foster said. "I could smell it."

"Dell must have taken them down," Zola said.

"Explains the chocolate," I said.

A small group of screaming people ran down the street ahead of us and to the left.

"Commoners," Foster said.

"Come on," I said. I broke into a flat run.

Sam was faster than all of us. The thing that was chasing the commoners rounded the corner. It wore a black cloak with a braided belt tied at its waist. I only took another second to register that it was a necromancer, but they didn't have a chance.

Sam's scream cut off as her fangs found their target. The hood flew back from the violence of the impact. A shocked face met the yellow glow of a streetlight. The man didn't have a throat left to cry out. Sam wrapped her legs around the man's chest, crushing out what little life remained. She rode his body to the ground. When he stopped twitching, she ripped his head off to the sounds of crackling gristle.

I stared at my sister as she started walking back to us. Blood ran down her chin and was splattered across her face.

"He's dead," she said.

"Thank you, Captain Obvious," I said.

She grinned. Her bloody fangs were still low in her mouth and she looked like a walking nightmare.

"You uh, got a little something right there," I said as I rubbed at my chin.

She wiped her face on her shirt, smearing away most of the blood.

"We can't let the Old Man face Ezekiel alone," Zola said. She led us forward again.

As the screams of the commoners Sam had helped faded, I heard more people screaming off to our left. The sounds of battle and explosions and magic lit up the sky two blocks over.

"We must make the ridge," Zola said. "Trust our friends to take some of the burden."

"She's right," Foster said. "None of this matters if Ezekiel wins."

"We go through the cemetery," Zola said. "It will be harder for Ezekiel to recognize us among the dead."

I shivered at the thought of running through that field of ghosts and gravemakers. Zola was right, though. Anything that kept us off Ezekiel's radar until we were ready was a very good thing.

I tried to keep telling myself that as we cut through a parking lot, hurdled a low wrought iron fence, and crashed headlong into the cemetery.

CHAPTER THIRTY-THREE

I T FELT LIKE running through honey. Cold honey that wanted to eat your brains. The dead auras dragged at us and I couldn't even close down my Sight. The ghosts were disturbingly solid, as though something was dragging them closer to our own realm. It didn't take long before I realized some of the ghosts were battlefield remnants. Lost souls left to watch over the slaughter grounds.

"Keep moving," Zola said. She weaved between the headstones.

I did that, focusing on Zola's swinging braids as she led us through a half circle of tombstones. Sam stayed at my side, pulling me forward when the worst of the voices threatened to overwhelm me. A statue caught my gaze from the corner of my left eye. I glanced at it and saw a soldier comforting another solider, laid out across a stone dais. Carved below them were the words

FRIEND TO FRIEND

A Brotherhood Undivided

"Almost there," Foster said. We continued to put one foot in front of the other, rushing through the graveyard as fast as we could.

I could see the fence that marked the other side of the cemetery. We crossed it without pausing, scurrying over the vacant street and onto the opposite sidewalk. The buildings were lower here. There were fewer shadows to hide in. The floodlights by a hotel pool cast harsh light over the grounds. We moved through quickly, leaving the lights behind when we came to a parking lot further down the street.

Bodies lay still and silent among the crushed light posts.

Zola led us across the lot into a thick stand of trees before she slowed down. She spoke quietly. "Catch your breath. Ah do not know what is waiting for us on the other side."

Ghostly cannons flickered into view as we moved forward. Soldiers stood beside them with plungers and worms, waiting to fire on an enemy that would never come.

I slowed as we crested the rise. Ezekiel stood in that field of souls. The cracked, rusted flesh of the gravemakers milled around him. A few came close, and then trailed away from Ezekiel. There were at least a dozen on the field.

I stared at the pale form beside him. Their voices rose as they began to shout at each other. Nixie's long hair and glistening armor awed and terrified me at once. We moved as silently as we could, taking up a post behind a low line of stones. Our position was dangerously exposed, but we could finally hear.

" … you?" Ezekiel said. "You could be my ally if we dethrone the Queen. I will leave you and my son to live in peace. All you need do is leave this city to the Leviathan."

"There isn't enough water here to summon a Leviathan," Nixie said.

"Will you leave Ward to die? The lakes are deeper than you

think." His voice was dead, and somewhere, some horrified part of my brain knew he wasn't lying. "It is already done. I have no quarrel with the witches. You can die last, for all it matters."

Nixie backed away slowly. "You have changed, Anubis. You are not the noble god you once were."

She turned and ran to the southeast.

I cringed as something summoned an unthinkable amount of power. A terrible smile curled Ezekiel's papery flesh. "At last," he said. "Come, meet your maker."

I couldn't see who he was talking to at first, and then I could just make out another form further down the hill. Wooden fences ran across the field in a lightning bolt pattern. The newcomer didn't even pause. He simply walked through them and they fell apart.

A gravemaker was unwise enough to approach the shadow, and the shadow absorbed it. Small pieces at first, tinkling away like black snow until the core of the form suddenly vanished. An explosion of power tore across the field after that, flattening the grass and shaking the tree branches.

"It is time to end this, Ezekiel."

I stared. I knew that voice, but the Old Man's flesh was too dark. His arms covered in a gravemaker's chaff. He was already on the verge of losing it. I cursed and looked at Zola.

"Damian, take Sam and Foster and go after Nixie," Zola said. "You can do more good with the Leviathan right now. This is not yet our fight."

I didn't hesitate. Zola knew more about war than I did. She knew more about the Old Man than I did. I trusted her gut.

"Sam, let's go," I whispered.

We followed the path to the southeast that Nixie had taken. It wasn't long before we were back in the woods, hidden on all sides, but unable to see where we were going. I tripped and cursed as my shoulder slammed into a tree.

"Oh, screw this," I said. *"Minas Illuminadda."* A sphere of pale light began to glow above the palm of my hand. I popped it gently into the air and it glided along in front of us.

"That's a new one," Sam said.

"It's the same one I used to blind you with. I'm just better now." I flashed her a smile, but caught motion out of the corner of my eye.

Briefly, it looked as though one of the battlefield ghosts began to move. As soon as I looked at it, it seemed to still.

"Did you see that?" I asked.

"It moved," Foster said. "What the hell?"

"Worry about it later," Sam said with a hiss. "Let's get out of here."

Navigating the woods was much easier with the light, and it wasn't long before we came out the other side. It was a wide field, and a modern structure was off to our right.

"It's not at the lake," Foster said. "Holy shit, it's not at the lake."

I started to ask him what he was talking about, but then I saw one of the massive tentacles swing above the tree line. Flashes of power and shouts came through from the opposite woods in muted tones.

I broke into a run. Nixie was in that mess somewhere. Foster took off into the air and streaked toward the scene of the battle. "Go!" I said to Sam.

She nodded and took off far faster than I could follow. It

was no more than two minutes before I stumbled out the other side of the woods into a decent clearing. A low stone wall, just foot-high and made of piled rocks, cut the field in two. Trees had sparsely populated the grass, but now most of them were shattered and strewn about like toothpicks. I stared at the scene before me as I let my illumination spell fade.

Ward stood half-naked in the moonlight. His body was etched in ink and one of the wards on his left arm glowed. There were more wards carved into his flesh than I could even believe existed.

Aeros was wrapped up in one of the monster's tentacles. I could see a nebulous ball of dust and fur trying to chew through the tentacle to release him. Jasper was making screeching sounds as he expanded and contracted. Aeros's feet dug furrows into the earth as the Leviathan tried to drag him down the hill.

"Help Nixie," Aeros said as Foster hacked at the tentacle beside Jasper.

Foster nodded, crouched, and launched himself into the air.

Nixie stood back-to-back with Sam, who had managed to pin one of the huge limbs to the ground by impaling it with dozens of tree branches. Nixie methodically sliced through it with a blade that glistened with black blood in the dim light.

Foster's sword joined Nixie's a moment later. Their combined strikes sent sprays of black blood across the field.

A flurry of tentacles struck out at Foster and Nixie, leveling what few trees remained standing. The pair deftly avoided each strike and returned to hack at the tentacle once more. The Leviathan's gigantic black eye pivoted in its taut gray flesh.

A trail of broken trees led away from the Leviathan, likely

ending at a lake. I ran toward Sam and Nixie.

"Jasper!" Ward said. "Move!"

The rabid ball of fur flowed away from the tentacle it had been gnawing at.

Ward laid his right palm across the upper left edge of his chest. The ley lines around us bent and flowed into him as the wards beneath his fingers glowed. As he pulled his hand away, thin streamers of bright blue power formed tracers from his fingers. In one violent motion, he struck at the air with the back of his hand. The field turned to daylight as four massive beams of power shot across the field and into the wound Jasper had opened.

The Leviathan roared, and it was as though a mountain screamed. So deep and so loud that the very earth shook around us. The Leviathan shifted its beak toward Ward. It lunged at him with surprising speed, but he easily dodged to the side. Black blood oozed from the wounds he'd punched through the Leviathan's tentacle.

"Can't you hit the body with that?" I shouted toward Ward.

"No! Too thick!" he shouted and dodged the beak. He touched another ward on his forearm. An electric blue blade ignited in his hand, so dense I would have thought it was a ley line. In the same motion he used to avoid the beak, he slammed the blade through the open wound. The last of the flesh gave way and the tree-sized tentacle fell to the earth and writhed.

"Ward!" I said, but I was too slow.

Another tentacle twisted above the Leviathan at an impossible angle and smacked Ward across the field. There was a flash of power before the man smashed into the tree line.

Jasper began chewing once more at the tentacle Aeros was

battling. The Old God had caused great trauma to the appendage, flattening it in some spots, but it still held on.

I let the staff fall from my left hand as I picked up the focus with my right. The staff would slow me down too much. Foster, Nixie, and Sam seemed to have their side under control, so I ran to help free Aeros.

I forced an aural blade through the focus as I dodged a flailing tentacle. I felt the breeze through my hair as I raised the deep-red blade and struck beside Jasper. He chittered and used his teeth to pull the wound open wider. I got the message.

I brought the blade down directly into the wound, and nothing happened. It just *stopped.*

Aeros grunted and flattened another piece of the tentacle wrapped around his chest. "You'll need a soulsword."

"Fuck," I said a moment before I unlocked the hold I'd been keeping on my aura. A world of voices exploded around me. I gasped and rammed a soulart through the focus. A golden glow wrapped around the red blade and I shouted as I brought it down into the wound. For a split second, there was resistance, and then the sword carved a gory path through the tentacle.

"Yes!" Aeros said.

I let the soulsword expire, and locked down my aura again, stumbling at the sudden silence. I backed away as the Old God began to swing the tentacle around his head at a dizzying pace. He brought it down on the Leviathan's eye.

I expected some damage, or an exploded eye, or something, but the Leviathan just blinked at us, and then pivoted its eye back to the others. The other tentacles reached up for our friends. For my sister.

"Sam!" I screamed her name, and the moment stretched

infinitely long.

She'd torn one of the smaller tentacles away, but she couldn't avoid the one that whipped around to grab her from behind.

Jasper's chitters deepened. He didn't just move. He changed. His entire body thinned into a reflective pool and then exploded. At once, his form swelled into a round reptilian ball and two muscular, scaly legs tore into the earth beneath him with their claws. Jasper launched into the air a moment before an enormous spiked tail swung from his elongating body. A slender neck shot toward the Leviathan's head.

"Oh my fuck," I said as Jasper's long snout opened and closed over the beast's face.

The claws on his hind legs tore away the tentacle that had Sam in its grasp and the gigantic clawed wings launched him into the air, all four of his legs dragging the Leviathan with him.

I watched, speechless, as the reaper carried away the Leviathan. It looked like he carried a dull moon dripping with mud. Jasper's wings stalled, and I stared as he rotated once, pulling the Leviathan up over his own body, before whipping it into the ground.

The roar that came from the winged beast dwarfed the muted cry of the Leviathan. I put my hands over my ears and turned my head toward Sam. Nixie and Foster were still staring at the sky.

Sam was staring at me, unwrapping the last of the tentacle from her waist. I could see her shaking, and her tears glistened in the moonlight.

We both turned back to the beast in the sky. Jasper's neck pulled back as his wings kept him hovering above the impact crater. When his head shot forward, his jaws opened wide, and a rolling stream of flame exploded from his mouth. Jasper roared again as embers and ash rose into the air.

The beast turned on his wings and glided down to land a dozen feet away. His wings folded back against his body as he stepped toward me. He paused and cocked his head to one side. His eyes were still the same featureless black orbs, set below a mane formed from metallic gray horns. He blinked, and reptilian flesh closed over his eyes before revealing the dark orbs once more.

I held my hand out to the beast. It knocked my hand to the side with a cold snout as big as my head. Jasper butted my chest with his nose and huffed before he fell into himself, leaving behind the small, round ball of fluff I'd known so long ago.

I registered the sniffle before I realized Sam had crossed the distance to us. She was crying as she scooped Jasper up. Jasper resumed his excited chittering and flowed around Sam's neck. The sound was almost a purr.

Ward hopped over a severed tentacle. "What. The. Fuck." He pulled a leather jerkin over his bare flesh. "How did Jasper pick up a Leviathan?"

"That was a dragon," I said. "I just saw a dragon flambé a god damned Leviathan."

"Reaper," Foster said, whipping his sword at the ground to remove the Leviathan's blood.

Aeros picked up a severed tentacle and tossed it deeper into the woods.

"Reaper," I said, trying to wrap my mind around what I'd just witnessed. "Jasper's a dragon." I took two steps toward Foster and stared at him. "You didn't tell me Jasper was a fucking dragon. A dragon!"

"He's a reaper," Foster said. "Dragons aren't real."

I narrowed my eyes at the fairy. "That's a technicality."

"He does look like a dragon," Nixie said. "We used to call the fire lizards of the Burning Lands dragons."

Foster sheathed his sword. "Fine. He's a dragon. Now you all sound like Mike with his damned dragon scales. Can we talk about this later?"

Sam ran her fingers through Jasper's fur. "The bug has a point."

I nodded and stepped closer to Sam. I pointed at Jasper and said, "You keep her safe. She is not lunch."

The fur ball exploded into a series of shrieking chitters.

"You insulted him," Nixie said, sliding around beside me.

"Yes," Aeros said. "He says he would never eat dead things."

"Aww," Sam said. "That's so sweet."

"Gods, you people are nuts," Ward said. "Hugh warned me, I just didn't understand."

"You're a hell of a fighter," I said.

"I've had a long time to practice."

"Pleasantries later," Aeros said. His joints ground and shifted so he could look back through the western woods. "Something is happening."

A flood of power washed over us and I squinted. My vision changed as if something had placed a wavy glass sheet between me and the rest of the world. "What was that?"

"Nothing good," Foster said. "Let's go."

CHAPTER THIRTY-FOUR

"I WILL MEET you at the ridge," Aeros said. "Whatever is happening, it is happening there." He sank into the ground. A pool of golden light shimmered for a moment, and then vanished.

Sam blurred into motion as Foster leapt into the air and glided over the trees. Ward followed Sam's trail, and he was almost as fast as she was.

"*Minas Illuminadda,*" I said, popping a ball of light up for Nixie and I to jog behind. "I didn't know you were here." We followed the light into the woods.

"I tried to tell you," she said. "Something is strange with the ley lines here. I couldn't send a message through the discs."

"Call me next time."

"Phones don't work in Faerie," she said, unable to keep a hint of amusement from her voice.

"Oh, right." I hopped over a large fallen tree. Another massive fluctuation in the ley lines distorted my vision. I picked up the pace as soon as my vision cleared.

"Hurry," Nixie said. Her armor caught the light and created tiny rainbows of color across its dark surface that I couldn't see from a distance. Scales overlapped each other, leaving only her fingertips exposed.

We reached the first clearing. A figure with armor much

like Nixie's stood at the edge of the field. Alexandra's long black hair was tied in a tight braid that barely moved when she turned to look at us. She motioned us to come closer.

"Damian, I need to—"

"Go," I said.

She leaned over and kissed me fiercely before taking off at an impossibly fast run. I blinked as she appeared by Alexandra a moment later. I focused on the far side of the field. I could see Sam and Foster huddling at the tree line and I wondered why they'd stopped. I crossed the field at a fast run, made easier by the even terrain.

"What is it?" I asked.

Sam pointed deeper into the woods. "I can see them too." One of the battlefield ghosts was moving slowly. Its arm was rising, a Springfield rifle propped against its shoulder.

"What the hell," I said.

"We don't know," Foster said.

"Let's just get past them." I saw two more ghosts starting to move.

The spirits began to move in earnest as we forced our way back through the trees. A distant thunder grew without the flash of lightning. I heard the screams then, the battle cries, before the thundering gunshots drowned out the world. Wisps of gray slowly curled and strayed around the trees and underbrush before more shapes formed. More ghosts rose from the mists.

The first shot that fired from one of the ghostly rifles scared the hell out of me. We dove into some heavier underbrush and stared.

I could see men running now as smoke and gunpowder

filled the air. The gray sheen of the ghosts faded, replaced by vivid color. I stared half in horror, half in fascination as a cannon shot exploded in mid-air, sending tiny balls of death ripping through a small Confederate line. Blood and viscera erupted from their bodies, cutting off war cries and screams alike. The sound of enormous bees, zipping through the air and running into things with earsplitting cracks, filled the air.

I shifted, glanced at Foster and Sam, and then ran for the edge of the woods.

Something tugged on my shirt and my arm felt like it had been stung by a huge wasp. I glanced down to find my sleeve was pierced and smoking. It took another moment to realize I'd been grazed by a bullet as blood trickled from the wound.

"Get down!" I said, my voice breaking into a scream as I called a shield.

Sam and Foster slid in beside me. Jasper was still wrapped around Sam's neck. The reaper stared silently out across the battlefield.

"What the fuck is happening?" Sam was practically screaming into my ear over the constant explosions and screams.

"It's too much power," Foster said. "They're pulling so much power it's collapsing our timeline."

"What?" I said. "That's not fucking possible."

"Look around you!" he said, gesturing to the charging ghosts. "Those aren't ghosts any longer." He picked up a rock and threw it at the nearest soldier. It didn't pass through his head. It bounced off and the man looked around before crouching behind a pile of fence posts.

"Gettysburg," I said. The horror of what Foster's words meant began to sink in.

"Why?" Sam asked.

"It's the worst thing that happened here," Foster said. "It's the strongest memory running through the land. The Old Man and Ezekiel don't care about the collateral damage. Their power is uniting different points in history."

"We have to stop this," I said.

"Out of our league," Foster said.

A pile of boulders moved in the distance. "Aeros," I said before I glanced back to Sam and Foster. "Get back to Zola. I'm going for Aeros. He'll know where Vicky and Happy are. We need them."

Sam nodded.

"Keep her safe," I said to Jasper as they started to run. Sam didn't even give me a nasty look.

I angled away from Sam and Foster. "Aeros!"

The god swung around between me and an approaching line of rebels. He looked different. The stone of his face was smoother. The scars where Gurges had cut his arm open were gone.

I took a step back as I realized he was not the Aeros I knew.

"This is not your time, boy. What are you doing here?"

"Happy and Vicky. I need to find Happy and Vicky."

Stone ground as he turned to look over his shoulder. "I will not know them for many more years." He turned his attention back to me. "The ocean of time was not meant to bend like this."

A series of high-pitched whines sounded as bullets ricocheted off the god's back.

A cluster of people ran at us from the far edge of the field. As they closed the distance, I could tell most of them were black. They wore rags and some still had manacles fastened around their ankles, broken chains dangling behind them. I felt sick to my stomach. A woman ran at the front. Her braided hair passed her shoulders.

They were almost halfway across the field when three cavalrymen broke from the sparse line of trees behind them. One of the men pulled out a pistol and shot into the retreating group. One form went down. I heard screams go up as one of the figures turned and faced the cavalry. Light flashed from their hands and half the rider's body disappeared into a misty cloud of blood.

The man—I was sure he was a man now, as I could see a beard—picked up the small body and slung it over his shoulder. The group continued running.

Someone further down the line shouted orders. Smoke and fire erupted along the clearing, causing the Confederates to take cover at the other side of the field.

The cavalry stayed in pursuit. They were going to reach the group before they made it to cover. A younger child struggled to keep up with the group. No one saw what was happening. I couldn't watch it. I ran onto the field with a shield held out in front of me.

A flicker of recognition crawled across my brain as I came closer to the men and women running at me. Metal charms were woven into the young woman's braids. I raised my pepperbox.

"Get down!" I screamed it as loud as I could, trying to project my voice over the thunder of the battlefield. "Down!"

The entire line dove near my feet. One cavalryman's eyes widened before the shot took him in the chest. The other was already on me before his comrade hit the ground. The focus came into my hand smoothly. The blade flashed out and took the head from his horse in an explosion of gore. He had a split second of terror before the blade cut him cleanly in two. His upper torso was still grasping a gun, so I followed it to the ground with two shots from the pepperbox.

I could feel the blood covering the right side of my face. It wasn't mine. It didn't matter now.

"Move!" I said to the group as they regained their feet. I jogged beside them, keeping a shield held high as the rebels began firing again. Small cracks and pings and explosions of electric blue light lit the air beside us as my shield stopped a dozen rounds. It wasn't long before we made it to the tree line and the relative safety of Aeros's bulk as he finished dispatching another cavalryman.

I turned to look at the group. My eyes passed children and young women and a man who had to be over sixty. My gaze fell on the bearded man. He embraced one of the black women like she was the only thing that existed in the world, as though no bullet or sword could ever touch them. She turned to me and met my eyes.

"Thank you, son. Ah don't think we would have—"

My jaw dropped open and a shiver ran down my spine. "Zola?"

Reality shimmered, and the battle that should not have been in our time vanished.

"Zola?" I said in a tiny whisper.

"It was," said a booming voice from beside me. I looked up to find Aeros. He was in exactly the same position as he had been in the past, only now he bore the scars from Gurges and the tiny pits and fractures I was used to seeing.

I couldn't stifle another shiver that ran down my limbs. "You … remember?"

"I do," Aeros said. "You saved many lives that day."

"But it was today."

"Time is a strange bedfellow."

Something sizzled in the distance. "Happy … Vicky. I need to find Happy and Vicky." I turned my head back towards the ridge, where the battle must have been escalating between the Old Man and Ezekiel. "What happened?"

"I do not know. Come, let us return." Aeros sank into the ground. I was sure he would beat me there, even as I broke into a jog.

CHAPTER THIRTY-FIVE

I STAYED LOW, tracking Ezekiel and the Old Man as best I could from the thinnest of shadows. The ghosts around us were frozen in time once more, but they were all sharp and far more vivid than one would expect.

Ezekiel deflected a blast from the Old Man that could have leveled a city block. "You always were the Fae's lapdog,"

The Old Man laughed, his eyes locked onto Ezekiel. "I will not be denied my vengeance."

"You?" Ezekiel said. "How do you hope to stand against the power of Anubis? I control more power than your feeble form could ever contain."

I thought I may be able to find an opening, some way to help. The power those two necromancers wielded became more insane by the minute, and I didn't think I'd be able to so much as make a scratch from a distance.

The Old Man circled and glared at Ezekiel. "There are some things you do not know, *father*. I threw the ice queen into the depths of hell!"

"She was weak," Ezekiel said, inhaling deeply and raising his head toward the heavens. "My will is done, Leviticus."

"I won't let you destroy an entire city," the Old Man said. He raised his hand and curled it into a fist. An inky darkness rose from the ground beneath him and covered his arm. "Not like Philip. Not like Pilot Knob."

Ezekiel laughed. It was slow and dead. He enunciated every sound of his laughter until his mouth opened wide and he laughed in earnest. If I can call that stuttering, maniacal screech, laughter. "Pinkerton? He never had the stomach for that."

I strained to hear what Ezekiel was saying. What the hell did he mean Pilot Knob hadn't been Philip?

"*I* destroyed Pilot Knob," Ezekiel said. "A small favor to remove that miserable town. Demons can be so very useful, do you not agree?"

"It's time you met your death, Ezekiel."

"Unlikely." Ezekiel extended both his arms out in front of his body, palms facing each other. Gravemakers started rising out of the ground around him. The slow, oozing mass of rusted bark and inky blackness rose around Ezekiel, clothing his entire body in death.

Once more the ghosts around the battlefield moved. This time I saw the artillery crews reloading shells and repositioning the cannons. Pale horses jerked at their reins and danced at the edge of the field.

"Old tricks," the Old Man said, and the roar he released … it wasn't human. The muscles in his arms bulged and tore as the tendons of his neck raged against his skin. The chaff of a gravemaker crawled out from within his own body, lacerating flesh and cascading down the Old Man's body. The rusted bark covering his arms dripped blood.

Ezekiel took a hesitant step backwards. The battlefield roared to life. The sharp report of a rifle was quickly followed by a hundred more.

"You killed my wife." The Old Man flexed his arm and ley line energy lanced into his palm. A cannon fired nearby, and the earsplitting report faded as the projectile whistled through the air. The ghosts closest to the Old Man took on a vivid color as the timelines were brought crashing together once more. "You raped my daughter." He paced toward Ezekiel's blackened form. "And my son … *my son!*" In that moment, the power of a gravemaker was forever seared into my vision.

The Old Man blazed across the battlefield. Soulswords as bright as the sun lit from either of his hands. As he closed on Ezekiel, he began to turn in an impossible dance of power and light. The blades carved furrows into the field. They elongated and flicked forward like whips before they vanished into the earth, sending dirt and rocks into the air.

Ezekiel backed away quickly, and I stared in awe and horror as a mass of gravemaker flesh crawled up his neck and over his face. It settled into a distinct form. A form I recognized as that bastard turned his head to the side. The face of a jackal was brought to brilliant life as Ezekiel parried the Old Man's first strike.

I could finally see why ancient illustrations of Anubis always bore the jackal's head. Black eyes shone from either side of the long face, and Ezekiel moved as fast as the Old Man. Another parry met with a quick thrust that the Old Man barely avoided.

Ezekiel turned as the Old Man struck again with a lightning bolt of force that sent dirt and debris thirty feet into the air.

After a time, my brain registered the line of shadows forming halfway down either side of the ridge. They stared up at Anubis and the Old Man as the two dueled beneath the bright moonlight.

More of Gettysburg began rising around us. Cannons thundered, men screamed, and the dead fell everywhere.

Anubis struck quickly, feinting with an off-balance lunge that shifted impossibly fast into a sweeping arc.

The Old Man met the attack and grunted as electric blue sparks exploded into the air around them.

Ezekiel didn't even sound winded when he spoke, and his voice was deeper through the mask he wore. "Do you understand, Leviticus? You cannot defeat me. No matter how much rage you summon. No matter how much injustice you face. I will always win." His arms shifted forward and the Old Man shouted as a flash of power sent him sailing ten feet backwards.

His feet struck first, digging deep divots in the earth as he buried his gravemaker-clad arms in the dirt before him. "So be it. You've brought this end upon yourself." The inky black substance of a gravemaker flowed over the Old Man's face, sealing off the rest of his body. I watched in horror as dead, milk-white eyes opened to stare at Anubis.

The Old Man flashed forward, his soulswords meeting Anubis's defense in a blinding explosion of sparks and lightning. The sound was a burst of electronic static, amplified a thousand times.

One of the gravemakers screamed, and I could no longer tell who it was. Four soulswords met between the blackened forms. Golden lightning exploded between them, igniting the dry grass at their feet.

The battle around us was in full force. I could see Confederate troops aligning near the base of the hill. Madness, I thought to myself as I realized they were going to charge the artillery stationed all around us. I could smell the gunpowder and the burning field. Smoke began rising from the grass.

The ghosts didn't seem to register the fight between Anubis and the Old Man, but I saw them trip and stumble over the shadows on either side of the ridge. It slowly dawned on me that they couldn't see the Fae.

Part of me wondered why the Fae weren't doing anything. They were simply watching the titanic clash of father and son as the Old Man tried to wipe out Ezekiel. Part of me wondered why *I* was only staring at the fight in slack-jawed astonishment, when a thousand words of warning came crashing back to me. *They are beyond you.*

A cannon fired nearby, and the blast vibrated my entire body. I looked up and cringed when I realized it hadn't been a cannon shot. An entire artillery unit had been wiped out by a misfire. A split, broken cannon laid in a pit of dead men. One soldier was howling in pain, holding his midsection and screaming for help. The screaming stopped a moment later.

The Old Man glanced at the carnage, and Ezekiel didn't miss his chance. He ran the Old Man through to the hilt. I heard someone scream "No!" and watched helplessly as the Old Man fell to the side, clutching the wound in his stomach.

There was a scream above us, and it was fury incarnate. A bolt of bright orange sunlight streaked across the pale, moonlit night. I stared in awe as Edgar connected with Anubis's head, slamming the god into the dirt. Earth and grass billowed out around Edgar as he landed, the force of the impact forming a small crater. The look on Edgar's face was pure rage. He was settled into a three-point stance, one hand up in the air as he snarled at Anubis. His fiery armor glistened as he launched himself into the air once more.

Ezekiel was already back on his feet. "Ra," he said. "So predictable."

Edgar streaked toward the jackal's head. Ezekiel sidestepped him and brought his arm down in a vicious strike. The blow connected across Edgar's shoulders and smashed him into the earth. Edgar slid through the dirt and rock on his face, his armor illuminating the blood and flesh as it was torn away from his exposed features.

I stared as he came to a stop, unmoving in the shadows.

"Amun Ra," Ezekiel said. He stalked toward the downed Watcher. "Pathetic little god."

The scream that sounded behind Ezekiel was beyond rage. My eyes followed that unholy noise back to the Old Man. He was on his feet once more, only his bulk was greater, and he looked to be as tall as Aeros, or more. The chaff of gravemakers flowed into him without end as he grew into a fifteen-foot giant.

"Fool." Ezekiel changed course and stalked toward the Old Man. "I will end you." Ezekiel's bulk grew to match the Old Man's in an instant, and I wondered how many gravemakers truly walked the battlefield. I could still see more in the distance, wandering among the skirmishers further down the field.

My attention snapped back to the giants as they met in the center of the ridge, their hands locked at each other's necks. The explosion of power tore at my aura until it felt like I was on fire, and then it increased exponentially.

The landscape changed around us. Where I expected trees, fields now stood. Men gave us odd looks as they jogged by, readying their guns for the impending charge. I stared as a stray shot took one of the Fae in the back of the head. Half of his face vanished into a chunky mist and he fell to the earth as his body began to dissolve.

"Stay down!" I screamed at my allies, although I knew those standing opposed to us would hear it too.

Some did take cover. Several called shields on the opposite side of the ridge, assuming the fire was only coming from behind them. I watched more of the line fall to the ancient rifle shots. I doubted the Confederates could actually see the Fae. They were simply in the path that led up to the Union forces.

Cannon fire exploded among the shouts and orders of officers and their regiments. The acrid scent of burning powder filled the air with a nearly blinding smoke. The Old Man and Anubis disengaged, and the world fell back into silence.

The landscape returned to what it had been as the massive forms circled each other. The Old Man squared off, facing Anubis as the jackal-headed god took a position to the east.

"Stronger than I thought," Anubis said, "but you still cannot win."

The Old Man released a primal scream as his dead, milk-white eyes widened. He pushed forward with his shoulders and his hands followed the motion. A bright, golden glow formed between his palms. It grew more and more intense until it looked like the sun a moment later. A beam of light launched from the Old Man's hands.

In the time it had taken him to gather the power, Ezekiel had done the same. The collision of those incantations turned the world white in a blinding flash of violence. As my vision returned, I could see the two gravemakers were locked in a stalemate. The power swelled and rolled between them, casting violent explosions of lightning and fire. Some of that stray power lanced through the nearby lines, annihilating friend and foe alike.

It's what the Fae had been waiting for. The line of Unseelie came streaming across the ridge.

Someone slid in beside me. I glanced to my left and found Ward huddled down. "The water witches are holding back a small force of Fae near the Pennsylvania Monument. Samantha and Foster are with them."

I knew where the monument was, but I couldn't see it, crouched down where we were.

"I'll knock out the front line," Ward said. "Follow the hole through and do not hesitate to kill everything."

"Why not attack Ezekiel?" I asked. Ward was powerful, damned powerful.

Ward shook his head. "They are beyond us, Damian. That damned gravemaker armor they've taken on can't be hurt by anything I can do."

Briefly, I wondered about the Splendorum Mortem. But how would I even get close enough to try it without getting annihilated myself? "Where's Zola?" I asked.

"With the witches."

"Good."

"Ready?" he asked.

I nodded as the nearest Fae came into focus in the light.

CHAPTER THIRTY-SIX

WARD STOOD, TOUCHING one of the many patterns across his chest. Streamers of light followed his fingers until he snapped them forward. Thick white beams of power dissolved the front line of the attack and carved a path to the opposite side of the ridge.

Something rustled in the trees behind us. I glanced back for a moment, and then turned away as my brain tried to process what I'd seen. A squadron of fairies flew overhead, but half or more were riding atop owls.

Ward focused on our left flank, closer to the gravemakers, and I began firing into the approaching line on our right. The pepperbox shot flame and death into our enemies while I kept a shield up with my left arm. One of the Fae made it past Ward and lunged at me. I backhanded the Fae with my shield. He stumbled, and Ward's next attack created a gaping hole where our enemy's chest should have been.

My shield deflected an incoming incantation in a shower of blue sparks. I swung my arm around and the shield curved around my fist. I caught another Fae with a vicious jab. I wasn't left handed, but the Old Man's training had already paid off in spades. Ward casually flicked his fingers and removed the attacker's head.

The ley lines began to absorb bodies and less defined piles

of gore. Flashes of green light and streamers of energy shot off in random directions as the ley lines tore the fairies to pieces. Between that and the mass of energy coming from the Old Man and Anubis, the entire battle was cast into an eerie, shifting light.

Ward and I cut a bloody path to the top of the ridge, and then our attack slowed. We looked out over the fields at the living nightmare of Fae warfare. I slammed a speed loader home as I watched a wall of werewolves sprinting to the west. They were met by an equal number of armored Fae. Even from our vantage point, we could hear their roars and snarls.

Beyond that carnage of dying screams and airborne limbs, the vampires swarmed. I couldn't tell what they were fighting, but the speed of the exchange suggested more vampires. Aeros fought beside them. He threw a sweeping haymaker into one of the trolls from the Burning Lands. The collision echoed from the top of the ridge as the troll literally came off his feet and crashed down onto his allies. More trolls stormed in from the west. Their speed was terrifying for such huge beasts.

It didn't seem real, looking at that mass of flesh undulating in a constant, murderous dance.

"Focus," Ward said. "Keep your head on a swivel. I am not explaining your death to your master or your sister or your witch."

I smiled without looking at Ward. "They do have a reputation."

"You don't know the half of it," he said. "Now move!"

There was no cover as we started down the hill. The woods faded behind us. A sea of men, women, and ghosts spread out before us.

The violence swallowed us whole, and part of me reveled in it. As fast as I could pull the trigger, I dropped six necromancers. A small circle of zombies collapsed to the earth, and the werewolves closest to us swarmed through the opening.

A part of me wanted to run screaming from the thunder of paws and growls as an entire company of werewolves roared, and clawed, and chewed until there was nothing left of the opposing company of Fae. No success comes without a price on the battlefield. When the wolves moved deeper into the fray, I could see a dozen of them dead on the ground, slowly changing back to human. A light breeze caught the piles of fur, sending small drifts of the stuff across the field. Fae metal pierced the wolves' heads and hearts, and some of them had been blasted to pieces by violent incantations.

A massive arc of lightning shot toward us from the northeast.

"Fuck!" Ward screamed as he tried to backpedal. The glow of whatever incantation he'd been working faded as he scrambled for a different ward.

I leapt in front of him and slammed my staff into the ground, grabbing the rune that would summon a circle shield. The shield flashed blue-white as it rose and the lightning seared my vision before the thunder threatened to deafen me.

I let the shield fade.

"Damn good staff," Ward said.

I tossed it to him and he caught it as it slapped against his palm.

"I'm guessing you already know the wards," I said.

He laughed but didn't answer.

"That blast came from the monument," I said. "My friends

are there. Stay close."

This time, I led Ward. The thought of whatever fired that lightning strike getting its shots in at Sam sent my adrenaline into overdrive. I ran hard toward the back line of wolves.

The werewolves had turned back the first wave of Unseelie, but the next wave was already moving in. I didn't recognize any of the bulky wolf-man forms engaging the Fae in beside us, but my mind was focused on making it to Sam.

The white stone dome of the Pennsylvania Monument loomed ever closer. My Sight was wide open and I almost stumbled as I saw the hideous mass of red and black swelling and twisting at its peak.

"What the fuck?" I said, not expecting an answer.

Ward grabbed an incoming sword strike with his bare hands as the line of wolves broke in front of us. Shock flooded the Fae's gray face when Ward snapped the blade in two. Ward brought the broken blade up over his head and slammed it home through the Fae's helmet.

"Cannons," he said, stepping over his slain enemy. "They melted down battlefield cannons and cast that thing from them."

I fired six quick shots with the pepperbox, sending three more Fae to be sucked into the ley lines. I slid a speedloader out of the bandolier and slammed it home.

"Fucking hell," Ward said. "I hope you're ready."

I followed Ward's gaze and stopped. I hadn't even noticed that the Unseelie we'd been fighting didn't have wings. A line of winged faeries came in from the west, led by two giant trolls. The fairies were as big as Foster, and clad in gleaming midnight armor, more like Nixie's than the golden armor of the Seelie

Court.

"Run!" Ward said. "Make for the monument!"

We smashed through the nearest line of the smaller Fae. It stalled their flanking maneuver against the wolves as we crossed deep into their lines. We easily picked off the front line, turning their flanking strategy against them. They surrounded us a moment later. I holstered the pepperbox and drew the focus.

A glance over my shoulder showed one of the larger fairies closing on us fast. His wings were like Foster's, black and gray and loosely patterned like an Atlas moth's. He raised his arm to strike. I planted my right foot and altered course in a heartbeat. The fairy didn't have a chance to react as the blood-red aural blade shot from the focus. I whipped the blade upward in a sweeping arc, removing the upper half of his body as I snarled. Blood sprayed across the Fae behind him and the nearest wolves went insane. I didn't know why until I saw the new fairies had been chewing through the wolves like puppies. Their dead were strewn across the field in pieces.

My victory over one of the newcomers drew the attention of the rest. The wolves hadn't missed a beat. In the center of the line I could see a golden wolf. His snout was covered in blood. He held a fairy's armored head in the claws of his left hand. He didn't drop it until it started fading into the ley lines. By that time, he downed the next fairy and tore at the back of its head.

"Wahya," I said, turning away as a murderous grin crawled over my face. Ward had gotten away from me. He had one of the winged Fae in front of him, and a troll closing on him from behind. The troll's fist rose into the air. Ward didn't have a chance. "Ward!"

His head turned slightly and he frowned as he realized what was coming.

It happened so fast. I sent my hand into the air and the gravemakers came to me. The earth exploded a foot behind Ward. A Hand of Anubis rose into the air. The troll didn't even try to stop. Its body slammed into the mass of corroded flesh.

The fingers bulged and grew, gaining enough length to close over the troll's shoulders. I laughed as power filled every fiber of my being. I curled my fingers into a fist against the resistance of the gravemakers, and the Hand of Anubis snapped closed. There was a grotesque pop before blood and viscera oozed between the bark-like fingers.

I released it, enraptured at the way the mushy torso held the arms together, before I turned to the line of Fae. Weak, pathetic, Fae. They ran from me, shouting warnings to the other Fae. They weren't worthy of my attention. The trolls though ... so many trolls.

The Hand of Anubis slowly filtered back into the earth, and I screamed, spreading my fingers and raising my arms, bringing hell out of the earth. I didn't need the Hand of Anubis. All I needed was target and a mass of gravemakers. Here, I had both. Obelisk-like spears of gravemaker flesh rocketed out of the ground, rending the ground and drawing in more gravemakers as they went. The more I absorbed into the art, the more were drawn into it.

The spears struck ten trolls at once, not so much piercing their hearts as blasting gory holes through their chests. The creatures went down in heaps and I laughed. I wanted more. I wanted to end them all.

"The fuck was that?" Ward asked as we marched toward the

dome. It was close now … there was something I was supposed to do there. Something with Ward, but what did that matter?

We rounded the corner, and I froze when I saw Sam and Zola. They stared at me like they didn't know me, like I might be a threat, and it cut me to the bone. I let go of the power. Slowly, almost painfully, it slid back into the earth, leaving trolls to collapse all across the battlefield.

"Damian?" Sam said.

I nodded. "I'm … I'm here."

There were four or five dead trolls piled up on that side of the monument. They formed a rudimentary wall to the south, and two fairies cloaked in golden armor stood atop the corpses. I wondered why the trolls weren't disappearing, but at the same time I didn't really care.

"Keep yourself locked down," Zola said. "That was too close."

Sam stood beside her. Blood coated my sister, and much of it wasn't evaporating into the ley lines. I wanted to stay with her. I worried about her, though I knew she could damn well take care of herself. I didn't see Jasper anywhere. A man stood beside them. His arms were crisscrossed with dozens of cuts. He held a wicked looking dagger in his right hand and nodded to me. His face looked carved from old stone, and it took me a moment to recognize his blood coated, balding head.

"Cornelius?" I asked.

"Damian," he said as he held his arms out.

One of the fairies dropped down from the dead troll, landing beside its huge, open mouth. Aideen leaned over Cornelius's hands and then began healing each arm. "I can close the wounds, but you've lost a lot of blood."

"I can lose more." He grimaced beneath her power. "Ward?"

"Odd times, Cornelius," Ward said.

"You have long had a gift for understatement."

My eyes swept up to the other fairy on top of the trolls. Beneath the blood and viscera staining his wings, I could make out Foster's sharp features. He pointed to the southwest. "At least a dozen more trolls. Something else is moving in the woods with them. I can't see it clearly. Looks big."

"More knights?" Sam asked, hopping up beside the fairy.

Foster shook his head before he casually beheaded one of the smaller Fae who'd made the terrible decision to play king of the hill. Between the gaps in the corpses I could see a small pack of Unseelie Fae retreating.

"Where's Jasper?" I asked, projecting my voice so Sam could hear me over the chaos around us.

"He went out with Happy and Vicky. They're surveying the western front."

I nodded. Seemed like a good idea.

"It was you," Zola said.

I turned to meet her gaze and she was staring at me. "You saved us."

"Aeros told you?" I asked. I wondered if we'd permanently broken time or some such thing, but I wasn't too worried about it considered the thunder of the battle still raging nearby.

"Do you understand?" Zola asked. "You saved us all. Alan, Philip, everyone."

I frowned and then I realized what she was saying. "The boy."

"Yes." She nodded. "Philip went back for Alan when he was

shot."

Something screamed above us and I turned to find one of the winged Fae, one of the knights, leaping toward us from the dome. Aeros swung his torso in a near half circle. His fist connected with the Fae's armor, which collapsed with a horrific crunch.

The attacker's inertia completely reversed, and he flew backwards into the monument. Blood splattered against the pale stone and the fairy fell to the earth dead. I didn't watch as the ley lines absorbed him and the corpse began screaming.

"Talk later," I said to Zola.

She squeezed my arm and nodded.

"The Court will come behind the knights," Aeros said. "It will not be long before we know who our true enemies are in Faerie."

"Vampires!" Foster roared from the top of the trolls. They were on us in moments.

Cornelius slashed his own arms open and the blood began to drip. The first two vampires closed on him. The voice that echoed from Cornelius's mouth was not his own. It was like the roar of a bear, distorted and amplified a dozen times.

The air shook around him. A sickly red light shot from his hands and pierced both of his attackers. They fell to the ground unmoving, but Cornelius fell to his knees too. The man was killing himself bit by bit, every time he attacked. Part of me admired the blood mage, and another part thought he was completely fucking nuts.

"Damian, left!" I didn't stop to think about Foster's words. I just turned to the left, raised my pepperbox, and unloaded six barrels into a vampire's surprised face. Half his head was gone, but his body was still twitching on the ground.

Something golden and impossibly fast ripped the remnants of the downed vampire's head off. I reached for a speedloader, but another vampire was already closing behind the first.

The vampire leapt.

My aura flared as my necromancy flashed forward and caught him in mid-air.

Benedict Anderson. I knew him like he was a brother, and I screamed at the darkness flowing from his soul. He tortured the neighbor's dog when he was four. He stabbed a babysitter with scissors when he was ten. His first murder was at seventeen when he ran down a pedestrian and never looked back. By thirty he found his calling as a gun for hire. He met his fate at forty-five when he was contracted to kill a vampire lord named Vassili. Now his mission was to wipe out Zola Adannaya and Samantha—

I lost my fucking mind. I saw the orders come down from Vassili. He'd ordered us killed. That mother fucker had played us from day one. My scream was beyond rage. The vampire's body came apart at the cellular level. The rain of gore was enough to stop the rest of his men in their tracks. Foster and Aideen quickly reduced three of them to portable piles of dead flesh.

"It's Vassili!" I screamed. I could hear the betrayal in my own voice. "He sent them to kill us!"

"Fucking hell," Ward spat. "Why can you never trust the god damned vampires?" I turned to find a group of Unseelie Fae swarming over the troll wall.

I needed to reload the pepperbox. I was still shaking from using my necromancy, never mind the revelation I'd just borne witness to. Even with a speedloader, the Fae would be able to kill me before I could reload.

"Damian, we're here."

I didn't have to see Carter to know his voice. I stepped back, set my right foot, and waited. The closest Fae came at me like a striking snake. He pulled his arm back and swung his sword with abandon.

I stepped into the attack. A small shield flashed up around my left arm as I deflected the sword in a crackle of electric blue power. The Fae's eyes went wide as my hand came up beneath his chin.

"Modus Ignatto!"

The ley lines burned through my aura as a small volcano of flame bathed the area in an orange glow. The Fae's helmet was so much slag as his body fell to the ground.

I clenched my left hand into a fist as I pulled as much power as I could into the pack marks on my left forearm. It flowed into the Ghost Pack effortlessly. Golden werewolves flashed into existence all across the battlefield. There were shouts from both lines as confusion took hold. The Ghost Pack wasn't confused at all. They routed the Unseelie forces with a terrible precision.

"Caroline and the Irish Brigade are coming," Carter said. He eyed the carnage around us. "They were tied up with the Pit."

I nodded. If the wolves and the vampires were on their way, it wouldn't take them long to join the battle. "Do they know about the ghosts?"

"Yes," Carter said. "Caroline lost a wolf to a point blank cannon shot. There … there wasn't much left."

"What did you say about Vassili?" Sam asked. Her voice was quiet in the thunder of the fighting.

"He set us up," I said. "Those vampires were sent here to kill us. To kill Zola, me, and you."

Zola spewed a string of curses that almost made me blush, but I knew exactly how she felt. Sam just looked sad, and it broke my heart. Sam pulled a phone out of her breast pocket and her fingers blurred across the screen.

She looked up and met my eyes. "I just told Frank. He'll tell the others."

I nodded.

"Foster," Zola said. "Can you take Cornelius behind the lines?"

"Fine ... I'm fine," Cornelius said, but he swayed on his knees.

"Come on," Aideen said. "If we both carry him it will be faster." There was no more talk as the two fairies picked up Cornelius and hauled ass down the western line. I watched them go, surprised at how much of an opening there was in the battlefield.

"We've broken their entire western line." Carter was filled with a golden light as he stepped through the dead trolls. "We need to tighten the noose. Bring the vampires around behind their lines."

Sam climbed back up onto the trolls to keep watch. Aeros's gaze watched our backs.

Ward rubbed his left shoulder. "Can we trust any of the vampires?"

"I don't know," I said, and then I thought back to everything I'd been through with some of them. I counted them among my friends, and even my family. "Yes, I trust Vik, and Dominic."

Zola nodded in agreement. "Ah can always check their motives. A little touch of necromancy is the best truth serum."

"Vassili," Aeros said. "I am disappointed. I truly thought he'd come to support Camazotz."

"All he's going to support now is a funeral pyre," I said.

"More vampires," Sam said, her voice flat.

"Anyone we know?" I asked, and the fact I had to ask it made me sick.

"No, but they're … fast. They're almost here. Get a shield up!"

Sam leapt backwards off the trolls and I caught her as Zola finished dragging her cane in a wide circle.

"*Orbis Tego!*" Zola said. The glassy dome snapped into existence as the first vampires leapt completely over the troll wall. They smashed themselves against the dome of force, breaking their bodies. The dome shimmered as more and more vampires joined them.

I stared at the mass, and my Sight showed me absolute horror.

"They're all zombies," I whispered. "They're all zombies!"

The pile grew. Aeros hammered away as many as he could, sending blood and pieces in every imaginable direction, but he wasn't fast enough. Electric blue lightning flew away from the shield as it decayed. In my own terror, I sent my aura flashing out across the battlefield, and I screamed one, desperate, word.

"Happy!"

The shield fell.

The bear materialized, and hell came with him.

CHAPTER THIRTY-SEVEN

HAPPY HIT THE collapsing wall of vampiric zombies like a wrecking ball. Vicky rode through the portal behind him. Her hair trailed out behind her, and soulswords blazed from both her hands. She tucked herself into a ball and spun. The resulting carnage as those unstoppable swords struck through the vampires was beyond words. Entrails and organs and limbs flashed through the air in a thunderstorm of blood. Vicky unfolded and slid to a graceful stop, her soulswords at the ready against a rain of gore.

The avalanche of vampires was diverted, but we were still surrounded. Zola fired off a ten-foot wall of flame that took out the northeastern line of zombies. Ward was on his knees, frantically carving something into the open wood on my staff. I stepped in front of him and bashed one of the vampires away with a lucky strike from a small shield. I could see Foster and Aideen rushing back to us, but something else saw them coming too. Four of the zombies peeled off and streaked toward the fairies.

Carter locked in with one of the vampiric zombies. The thing struck over and over as Carter snarled and bit and clawed.

I recognized Sam's scream in the blur of motion around us. I couldn't see her, and it scared the hell out of me. Happy bounded into the fray, and his jaws made short work of one of the zombies. There were still twenty or more left. They were distracted by the bear and Vicky and Sam.

Aeros was covered in the damn things. They pummeled and kicked and clawed at his rocky form and I only hoped they couldn't hurt him.

Ward stood and grabbed the end of my staff like a baseball bat. Electric blue fire ran through the intricate inlays of Magrasnetto as he planted his foot and swung at the nearest vampire. There was a grunt, and then the zombie collapsed to the ground, unmoving.

Sam screamed again, and this time I could see her through the carnage. She limped toward me, her left arm motionless at her side. Two of the vampiric zombies closed in on her, and I was too far away to do anything.

Everything was happening too fast. I could barely track the vampiric zombies attacking me, much less the swarm attacking everyone else.

Vicky rammed a soulsword through the head of my closest assailant and then set her back against me. "Zola's hurt, Sam too."

"Zola?" I said.

Vicky nodded. "Carter is with her. Jasper is coming," and then she leapt back into the fray.

I drew the focus and added my own soulsword into our defenses. I slammed another vampire to the ground and removed its head, but another clipped my ankle from behind. I went down hard. I didn't need to look to know it was shattered.

"Damian!"

Foster's voice pierced the screams and snarls of my allies.

Blood sprayed across my face as the zombie's head bounced across the ground in front of me. I screamed as Aideen's healing spell came from nowhere and knit the bone.

I charged forward, carving a bloody path to Sam. One of the vampiric zombies was above her on the troll wall. It leapt, and I watched helplessly as it reached out for my sister. Nothing I had could hit it without killing Sam. I couldn't touch it with my necromancy because its aura was buried beneath its skin. I screamed Sam's name as time slowed to a hideous crawl.

Sam threw herself to the side. I didn't think she'd gotten out of range.

Jasper hit the vampiric zombie so hard it blew apart the troll corpse behind it as he drove them both into the ground. The dragon's roar was deafening. His spiked tail whipped forward and impaled two more vampiric zombies before it swung back around and turned them to mush on top of another zombie. In the same motion, his jaws snapped forward, splitting a stunned Fae in two.

I ran to Sam and scooped her up, running as fast as I could through the opening Jasper had created. My ankle hurt like hell, but I knew my brain just wasn't registering the fact it was already healed. Zola was on the ground, dragging herself up against the monument as Carter eviscerated a vampire beside her.

"Put me down," Sam said, irritation plain in her voice. "I just need a minute."

I set Sam down beside Zola.

"You okay?" I asked, and my voice sounded muffled to my own ears.

"Ah'll live," Zola said. "For now."

Happy had a head in his mouth and dropped it at my feet, panting.

"Thank you," I said. "Watch over them?"

The bear chortled and began pacing between Sam and Zola.

"Jasper," Sam said, flexing her broken arm. "I thought I was dead."

"You are dead." I ruffled her hair and turned back to the battle.

Foster and Aideen danced through the field of death, a ballet of blood and blades. The flow of vampiric zombies seemed to have slowed and they went down effortlessly. Ward struck at the stragglers as Foster and Aideen engaged the front.

Foster leapt into the air, and as his attacker's eyes tracked him, Aideen removed the vampire's upper torso in one brutal strike. Foster laughed as viscera poured out of their foe, and he came down on another zombie, splitting its crown with his sword and lodging the weapon firmly in its gut.

The earth shook as Aeros fell backwards and collapsed onto the bloody field. My heart skipped a beat until the Old God began to drag himself up again. He smacked his fist against his chest and vampiric zombies exploded with the impact. He was still overwhelmed.

Jasper oozed over the remnants of the troll wall, his limbs moving in a blur as he closed on Aeros. His neck flexed, and his jaws opened wide. A tremendous blue cone of fire engulfed Aeros. The vampires fell away into so much ash. Aeros rose to a knee and nodded at Jasper. The dragon made two quick leaps back to Sam before he stood sentinel.

There was only one vampire left alive at the end.

"You're not a zombie." I looked at his shattered legs as I

slammed a speed loader into the pepperbox. "This won't kill you, but it's going to hurt like a bitch." I shot him in the gut, started to ask him a question, and then shot him again for good measure. "Do you work for Vassili?"

What? The voice seemed to come from inside my head even as it vibrated the air around me.

I looked to my left and found Happy staring at me. I nodded once. "We were betrayed."

"You'll kill me either way," the vampire said.

I sighed and fell onto the bullet wounds with my knee.

The vampire screamed.

"There's something you need to understand, my fanged friend. You see that vampire?" I pointed at Sam. "That's my sister you just tried to kill. So you can tell me what I want to know …" I leaned close enough he could have bitten me. "Or I will feed you to that dragon in little bitty pieces. Starting with your toes."

"In the middle of war?" the vampire scoffed at me and then winced when I shifted.

I pulled him up slightly by the collar of his black silk shirt. I smiled, called a shield around my right hand, and punched him as hard as I could. His nose flattened and ruptured and he screamed again.

"Yes!" he said in a wet, nasally cry. "Vassili gave the orders to kill you after Devon failed."

"Devon?" So many little, terrible pieces began falling into place in my mind.

Zola shook her head. "To kill who?" she asked. "Say it."

The vampire shook beneath me. "Vassili gave the orders to kill Zola and the Vesiks! Is that what you wanted to hear?"

"It's not what Ah *wanted* to hear," Zola said. "But it's why Ah have to do this."

She reached out and wrapped the vampire in her necromancy. A deep frown crawled over her face before rage took its place. Golden light flared through the dark wave of necromancy, and the vampire's soul was torn away. His body fell limp beneath me.

"Carter," Zola said. "If you would be so kind?"

Carter's claws flashed out and the vampire's soul fell into ribbons.

Zola began picking up the pieces with a soulart.

"What are you doing?" I asked.

"Sending a message," she said. "Aeros, where is the Pit?"

He closed his eyes and then turned to point. "They move in the west, but they are headed south."

Zola nodded. "Joining up with the Unseelie." She tied the strips of yellow soul in her hands, quickly overlapping the edges until they resembled a Celtic knot.

"Zola," Ward said. "Are you sure?"

"A man has declared war on us, Ward. Ah'm only letting him know Ah accept." Zola's hands suddenly turned palms-up. The tight-knit ball soared through the sky. A thin trail of ley line energy led back to Zola's hand. When the light was over the southwestern trees, she lit the fuse.

Electric blue power shot across the sky, and the yellow knot detonated. An image of the dead vampire appeared in the sky, larger than the moon. His voice drowned out the battle.

"Vassili gave the orders to kill Zola and the Vesiks! Is that what you wanted to hear?" The voice repeated itself three times before it began to fade. The vampire's soul expired doing Zola's will.

"Oh my," Aeros said, a smile fracturing his face. "I do not believe that is how Vassili believed the evening would go." Aeros turned and looked at Sam. "You have many friends within the Pit, Samantha. They are broken. Our allies are coming."

A deep, resounding note echoed in the distance. We all looked up and to the southwest as another note played. It was like the timpani of a forgotten god vibrating from the depths of the earth. The tempo increased as a fine mist rolled out of the woods. It was white and stayed low to the ground, oozing forward in a steady rise and fall to the beat of the drums.

Ghosts and magic seemed to surge with every beat that sounded across the field. Voices of ten thousand souls threatened to overwhelm us all as the line marched forward.

"Concentrate," Zola said. "You have done well to block them out in this battle. Do not let down your guard yet."

I took a deep breath and blocked out as much as I could.

A single shadow followed the mist. Antlers that ended in wicked black points gleamed in the dim light atop Hern's bulky form. He carried a bow in one hand, and a massive axe strapped to his back. His armor was made from mail as black as his antlers, accented with silver details so fine I couldn't make them out at a distance.

I watched him draw an arrow from his quiver as a hundred more shadows eased their way through the mists behind him. Our enemy was many, and I knew the tides had turned for the worse.

The trolls stopped milling around the woods and began heading in our general direction.

"Carter," Aeros said, his voice deep enough to compete with the basso pounding of the drums. "Go to the wolves. The Irish Brigade comes from the northwest."

"Maggie is with them," Carter said."

Aeros nodded. "Vicky, Happy, with me. Sam, take Jasper and get behind the lines. Watch the back of our line. Everyone else return to Leviticus. We cannot let the Fae interfere. If Leviticus loses control, everything here will die."

I nodded at the Old God. I trusted his judgment more than my own at that point.

The blur that leapt over the remnants of the troll wall caused me to flinch. A heavy cape snapped in the wind behind it, and the vampire's feet squelched as it impacted the blood-soaked earth.

CHAPTER THIRTY-EIGHT

"Zola," Vik said. "Thank God." His face was a mass of blood. A wound tore through his right shoulder, but he didn't even seem to notice. He reached out to Sam and hugged her briefly. "You are all okay?"

"For now," I said. Three more shadows flew over and around the wall to join us.

"I couldn't kill him," Dominic snarled as he punched his fist into his palm. "Fucking bastard got away."

A wisp-thin vampire looked even smaller beside Dominic. I hadn't seen him in years. He'd become a recluse after Alexi died. "Jonathan?"

He nodded to me. "Alexi, rest his soul … Alexi loved Sam like a sister. Vassili will die for this."

Sam put her arms around the smaller vampire. More shadows swarmed our small gathering. Some faces I recognized, but there were several I didn't.

"Vesik?" the nearest vampire said. I couldn't place his accent. His skin seemed darker than the other vampires' and his nose was a bit broader.

I nodded to him.

"I am Cizin."

"Cizin?" Zola asked. "You're with Camazotz."

The vampire laughed. "You ruined my surprise. Camazotz

310

sent me to watch Vassili long ago. Only recently did he order me into the Pit."

"Ah doubt he had to order you to do much of anything."

Cizin smiled.

Lightning as black as the Abyss I'd walked with Gaia struck the earth and caused Hern to stumble backwards out in the field. Shards of charred earth burst into the air and a gray mist trailed up from a figure cloaked in darkness.

Glenn did not speak. He moved.

Hern loosed an arrow faster than I could follow. Glenn slid to the left, and the shaft passed him harmlessly, embedding itself in the stone of the monument not twenty feet from my head.

The battle blurred into motion from there.

Cheers erupted behind us. I turned to find the line of were-wolves going into a frenzy as they pushed toward Glenn. The wolves had killed the majority of the Unseelie's front line, but several still fought as the werewolves charged forward. Their massive arms reached out and crushed the Fae as fast as their claws could rip out their innards. The sudden charge caught the Fae off guard.

Aeros turned his attention from the enemy to the vampires. "Vik, how damaged was the Irish Brigade?"

"They had some casualties," Vik said.

"Reinforce them." Even when the Old God spoke softly, the earth beneath our feet vibrated with it. "We need to strengthen our western flank."

"Consider it done," Vik said.

Several knights took to the air and flowed toward Glenn. Black mist rose from his shoulders, and the knights recoiled as

Glenn's helmet solidified. The white streak across his faceplate was a stark contrast to the darker depths of his armored form, and it marked him for what he was. He drew a sword, and the light around him vanished into its pitch-black blade.

Glenn butchered three knights in two quick sweeps of his arm. I cursed as the swords and armor of his foes shattered like glass beneath the enchanted blade. The cheers of the Fae were joined by the howls of the wolves. Our entire line reunited behind Glenn.

The Unseelie Fae crossing the field behind Hern began to move faster.

"Remember the plan," Aeros said. "Move!"

We scattered like roaches.

Ward joined us as we passed the opposite edge of the monument. I blinked as I realized he hadn't been with us when the vampires showed up.

"Too many powers," Ward said. "I prefer not to be surrounded by powers I don't know."

"Smart," Zola said.

Our line pushed forward again. It felt surreal, charging behind the line in relative safety, while our allies engaged the front. Every fiber of my being wanted to kill something, or run in the other direction, but the line insulated us. Almost all of the Unseelie's front was dead. Empty armor and broken weapons littered the battlefield. For every vacant suit of armor, it seemed there was at least one dead wolf. Bodies were bent and broken and disfigured.

Foster ran beside me. The steady rhythm of his golden chainmail ringing as it rose and fell was reassuring. The glaze of blood and gore covering his entire body was not. "Look at them," Foster said.

I followed his gaze and almost stumbled when I saw the battle between Ezekiel and the Old Man. Incantations flashed between them that could level a city if executed poorly. Every moment seemed to increase the pace and severity of their attacks. I wondered why until I noticed the slow forward movement of the battlefield's gravemakers. They walked into the conflict and were sucked up into a vortex of power. Something about the rising gravemakers seemed off. They looked small, and I could view them with my Sight without feeling like the power would sear my eyes from their sockets.

To my sight, the battle looked like two suns in a state of flux, expanding and crashing into each other while blue plasma crawled across their surfaces before falling away and starting anew.

Someone yelled "Trolls!" as we reached the northern part of the line. A roar followed, and Jasper's form disappeared over the hill. Something else screamed, and pieces of a massive troll flew over the tree line. Half its body was almost ash.

The earth roiled in front of us. Tiny bits of iron and earth and rust rose from the field like ink through water. They slithered and built upon each bit that came before them. I unfocused my Sight as much as I could. The power was too much to look upon directly. The legs solidified first, ending in feet like tree stumps. The body snapped out from there, torso, arms, and head.

Its fingers began to twitch as thin, inky tendrils of darkness rose from the shadows beneath the gravemaker. One finger jumped and then relaxed before another random finger did the same. The gravemaker's skin solidified into a grotesque surface like fleshy bark with deep cracks and crevices. A thousand cracks echoed around us like cartilage breaking as the gravemaker straightened and raised its face.

Gravemakers had deceptively fast attacks, and this was no different. It struck out and caught the jerkin around Ward's waist. He tore the garment off and let the gravemaker have it.

"Look out!" Foster said.

The wolf hadn't heard him. It backed up too close to the gravemaker as it battled one of the Fae knights. The gravemaker's hand settled over the wolf's skull and squeezed. I almost gagged as brain and bone erupted from the wolf's face.

Horror etched itself across the knight's features. He retreated, one of limp wing trailing behind him as he ran back into the enemy lines.

"Run!" Zola said.

The gravemaker caught her cloak and she choked as it slammed her to the ground.

I didn't think. I reacted. The Splendorum Mortem came into my hand. Its cold metal blade warmed in my palm and then ignited. A dark power lit from its cutting edge, extending no more than a foot. I jammed the Splendorum Mortem through the gravemaker's jaw, and into what should have been its brain.

Dead white eyes shifted from Zola to me. I ripped the dagger out through its face and the gravemaker lurched backwards as Zola's cloak fell from its hand. I watched in fascination and horror as fragments of iron and rust filled the wound and the face knit itself back together.

"Fuck me," Ward said, shock plain in his voice. "Run!"

This thing, this gravemaker, was every bit the monster Zola

had told us about as children. The Splendorum Mortem had the power to slay a god, and this creature simply rebuilt itself around the wound.

We ran.

"Get to the other side of the Old Man," Zola said between ragged breaths as we sprinted. "It may get absorbed."

I angled back to the east, staying just south of the battle raging between Ezekiel and the Old Man. It was the first look I'd gotten at the Old Man since the battle had escalated.

"It's not going to be absorbed," I said.

"What do you mean?" Zola asked as she turned to me. "We don't know that yet."

I pointed to the circle of shadows around the battle. The power slamming against my senses was sucking in the poorly formed gravemakers, but a line of at least fifteen freely circled Ezekiel and the Old Man.

"I don't understand," I said. "What about the gravemakers I destroyed at Stones River?"

"You cannot destroy them," Ward said. "Scatter them to the four winds, and eventually their damned pieces will find one another."

I stumbled as we made our way closer to the fight. Stone and dirt had been pulled and blasted from the ground, scarring the earth all around us. Some of the larger rocks had settled over the field like headstones, splayed at random angles like an ancient cemetery fallen into disrepair.

A thick beam of yellow light riddled with black energy swelled in Ezekiel's left hand as his right held the Old Man's attack at bay. He pushed it into the conflagration between them and the fiery exchange reached mammoth proportions. I couldn't see any possible way either combatant could see the other. There was so much power pouring into the deadly light it felt as though my own aura was going to be torn away. The ghosts around us began to move once more.

"Knights!" Zola shouted as something crackled and detonated behind me.

I turned in time to see smoke rising from one of the ghost cannons. Charred wings fluttered to the ground, their owner a smear of gore across the field. I crossed my arms, drawing the pepperbox and the focus simultaneously. We were no longer insulated by our lines. The chaos of the battle loomed ever closer.

At that point, I'd decided to stop taking chances. I channeled a soulsword the instant the blade's path would be clear of Ward. It was there, just outside the circle of gravemakers, that we started to realize how much of the Court stood against Gwynn ap Nudd.

They came from the woods, barely shadows in the cover of trees until they broke from cover. Clad in black armor like Glenn's, but medallions hung around each of their necks. A smaller Fae, fast on his feet, closed on us first. I saw the antlers set into the Celtic knot on his medallion as he leapt at me.

Bits of his brain went in the opposite direction of his body as I pulled the second trigger on my pepperbox. I awkwardly slid a speed loader home while maintaining a soulsword.

Something roared in the north, drowning out the howl of power between the two giant gravemakers. I glanced over my left shoulder. Jasper's wings whipped through the air as he carried one of the trolls skyward before slamming it down closer to the eastern woods. He'd keep Sam safe. I had no doubt.

Some of the Fae slowed as Ward made quick work of our next assailant. I caught a glimpse of Zola to the south. Far beyond her, Aeros ripped into the trolls, a panda barking at his heels and a whirlwind of golden death that could only be Vicky's soulswords beside him.

I recognized faces, but I did not know their names. Beautiful, graceful creatures slinked along beside hunched, crudely armored Fae that could have passed for boulders.

"We treat," said a pale, slender man.

"We fight," Ward said in response.

"Join Hern's ascension," the pale man said, his hand sliding slowly through the thin covering of white hair that hung to his shoulders. "There is no need for more death."

"He's stalling!" Zola yelled from the south.

I started to move forward, but Ward threw his hand out to stop me as a black vortex opened on the far side of Ezekiel. It robbed what little natural light was left in the area before it snapped out of existence. I could only catch glimpses of the figure, as my attention was continually forced back to the pale Fae and the potential foes to either side of him. The new arrival looked like Hern, but short one antler.

"You must *not!*" I followed that desperate cry back to a man I'd never expected to hear desperation from. Gwynn ap Nudd's breastplate was damaged, and dark liquid ran down his torso. "The Fae must remain hidden. Some cannot protect themselves!"

"You should have killed me along with my Queen." Hern pulled his arm back and snarled as he threw something into the mass of power fluxing between Ezekiel and the Old Man.

"No!" Glenn flashed forward. He was fifty feet away, and then he was there, reaching out for the spiraling stones. I wondered why one looked like a seeing stone and the other a soulstone. Glenn's fingertips just missed them. The stones vanished into a swell of electric blue power.

I wasn't sure what the stones meant, but I was sure it wasn't good.

CHAPTER THIRTY-NINE

THERE WAS A noise like a snapping arc of electricity. Something sucked sound away from the entire battlefield. Glenn threw himself violently to one side.

It was as if every horn in all the world sounded at once. My body shook with it. Every living creature in the field ran, or screamed, or covered their ears. Light came next. Only it wasn't light. It was death on a scale the world had never seen. Unleashed by a Fae. Unleashed upon humanity.

Ezekiel's body, with its jackal-like head, disappeared in the blast. A cone of power erupted from there, cutting a swath through the battlefield. It annihilated trees and wolves and Fae and earth in an ever-expanding field of destruction. Gravemakers and ghosts and souls vanished into that light, a light that brought nothing but shadows and darkness in its wake.

Glenn slid beneath that force. He screamed as he raised his arms around the light. The beam narrowed, as if focusing. He reduced the width of the beam's reach, but I had no idea how much he'd helped.

Slowly, far too slowly, the light began to fade.

The Old Man lay sprawled out on his back in a crater, the inky blackness of the gravemakers slowly seeping into the earth around him as his body became his own once more. A similar sight waited at the other end of the pit, but Ezekiel's body was burned and flayed and barely recognizable.

Most of the fighting had stopped across the battlefield. Fae and wolves and vampires and gods stood equally confused. Glenn rose to his knees. His hands smoked as his helmet evaporated into the ether. Blood dripped down his face.

"We rise!" Hern's voice thundered through the silence. "You lost your way in this world, Gwynn ap Nudd. We return to our rightful place! The commoners will be fodder once more." His voice slowed, and grew in volume. "Let them gaze upon Falias and kneel!"

"You are a fool," Glenn said, his voice cracking. "You've brought war upon the world."

Awestruck and horrorstruck Fae wandered into the field of destruction, their battle forgotten. Scorched, blackened earth spread out at our feet. Fires stretched into the distance, fire I had no doubt extended to the horizon.

A high-pitched whine filled the silence when Nixie came running up beside the crater.

"The blast!" Nixie was screaming, but I could barely hear her words. I wondered how I'd heard Glenn so well. I wondered where Nixie had come from, but my brain still managed to make out "Tsunami" and "Europe."

"Go!" I said, my own voice rising to a scream. "Stop it!"

She smashed her lips against my own an instant before she became translucent and streaked toward the lakes with Alexandra.

Some of the Fae took up Hern's cry. They reformed their lines, and I just stared at them in disbelief. Our own lines reformed, and I couldn't understand the insanity.

Others ran from the battlefield. I saw the pale Fae, and it

looked like tears ran down his face as he vanished into a small copse of trees. Many more escalated their efforts, cheering for the death of the commoners and the rise of the Fae that Hern so promised.

They started to push our line back. My stomach dropped as I realized the line might break. Aeros vanished into the ground, and I felt relieved when he reappeared beside us. Vicky and Happy followed suit. The little ghost maneuvered around behind us to guard our northwestern flank.

"We cannot stand up to this," Aeros said. "Hern has rallied his troops. They've seen Glenn injured. They think victory is all but—" He stopped speaking and his head swiveled to the west. "All is not lost."

The pack marks on my left arm began to burn.

"Carter," I said, my voice cracked. "Maggie." My heart rose as the largest pack of werewolves I'd ever seen came roaring out of the western woods. The Ghost Pack led the Irish Brigade, and the vampires came with them. Three bloody forms were mixed in with the Ghost Pack, and I smiled as I recognized Hugh and Alan. The third wolf was Caroline. She bounded from her legs to her arms, seeming to glide through air.

Their claws rent the earth as their roars tore the air.

Behind the line of werewolves ran three figures. Cara, Mike the Demon, and a little ghost that matched their pace, Mike's little necromancer. Mike the Demon leapt into the air as the wolves in front of him crashed into the enemy lines. Trolls reached down to grab the wolves.

The Smith's Hammer exploded in Mike's hands and came down in an arc, crushing the first troll's head. Mike hit the troll's chest with his feet and vaulted off the falling body, rolling as he hit the ground. The next troll's legs shattered as the fiery war hammer struck.

The wolves flowed forward through the gap in the lines. Anything that didn't run, died, until some new horror came at us from behind.

"Get them off me!" The child's scream cut to my bones.

I knew Vicky's scream. I never wanted her to suffer again, and I turned to the east, ready to kill. Souls flowed over her, drowning her in a golden yellow light.

I stumbled toward the girl. "Hold on, Vicky!"

Flames poured from the earth beyond her, no longer the blaze of a simple fire. I didn't have to see past that hell to know anything in the path of the blast was gone. People, cars, homes, cities. The souls of the dead rushed back toward the power that had stolen their life. Only the power was gone. It was just us now. The night skies brightened with a crushing wave of golden light. So many. My god, there were so many.

I reached out toward Vicky. I could tear the souls off her, I knew it. I knew how. I cried out to her as she fell to her knees, and my cry became a primal scream. My aura lashed out, bonded to my own soul.

The world around me decayed into a churning mass of screaming, golden, death.

I HEAR THEM all as I pull them away from Vicky. A mother laying her kids to sleep, a grandfather anxious to see his grandchildren the next day, a doctor delivering sad news to a desperate parent, a child excited about finishing his new book, an elderly woman angered about a failed car repair, a teenager celebrating a gaming victory, a college graduation that ... that will never happen. Hern. Hern will die for this. I reach out to them. To protect them. Soothe them. Love them.

And I am consumed.

I CLUTCHED MY chest as one hundred searing points of pain lanced through my heart chakra. It grew into the scream of a thousand, ten thousand, and my world went white with a million burning souls crying out for help. Help I could not give.

Some functioning part of my brain saw Zola fall to the ground before my vision was completely lost. She was screaming, clawing at her skull. *What had they done?* I wondered as my face fell to the charred earth.

✦　✦　✦

"DAMIAN!" I HEARD the voice first. The little girl's voice. We'd saved her. No, we hadn't. We'd been too late. "Damian!"

My eyes fluttered slightly, and something smacked my cheek hard enough to bruise.

My eyes shot open. Vicky and Sam were crouched over me.

"Damian," Sam said as her voice cracked. "I thought you were dead."

A bloody, battered fairy stood above me in shadow. He reached his hand down and pulled me to my feet. "Ezekiel is still alive."

I stared at Foster. His face looked carved from stone.

Sam crushed me in a hug.

Vicky pushed up beside her and wrapped her arms around me. "You saved me from the angry lights."

The battle around us was no more. Wolves and Fae and gods only stared to the east.

Golden souls flickered through the sky like fireflies. It was beautiful, and it was terrifying. Beyond those lights stood the ruins of architecture never seen by a mortal's eye. I'd only seen it in paintings.

The ruins of Falias stood upon our world.

I started walking back toward the crater where Ezekiel and the Old Man had fought. I could see Leviticus on the other side of the churned earth. Aeros stood beside him. Blood coated the Old Man's entire body. I thought it was probably from the gravemaker art he'd used to cover himself in those damned creatures.

The gravemakers around us had left. I didn't know why, and I didn't know where they'd gone, but I didn't particularly care at that point in time. I squeezed Vicky and stepped away from her.

I slid down the embankment and stared at Ezekiel's broken form. I frowned slightly. I wasn't used to seeing such a powerful creature so utterly defeated. The Splendorum Mortem slid easily from its hidden sheath.

Ezekiel whispered something, but I couldn't hear him.

I knelt beside the immortal and waited.

"This was not my intention."

I laughed without humor.

I thought his eye was trying to blink, but most of the skin was gone from that side of his face.

"You only wanted to kill the world," I said. "You're as mad as Philip was."

"I am a Seal," he choked out.

"What could ever do more damage than you've done here?" another voice asked as a helmet fell to the earth beside me.

I looked up to find Edgar staring down at Ezekiel. Something like pity crossed his bruised and bloodied face.

"Don't you want to know why?" Ezekiel asked, charred flesh flaking away as his jaw moved.

"No."

The Splendorum Mortem slid easily through Ezekiel's skull.

The immortal's right eye widened, and then his body went still.

I heard Edgar take a deep breath, and his armor scraped together as he crossed his arms.

I stood up and put my hand on Edgar's shoulder. He nodded, and we both turned to climb out of the pit.

CHAPTER FORTY

"SO, NO BIG explosion or fireworks when a Seal breaks?" I asked.

Edgar laughed quietly. "In the Abyss, perhaps, but not here. The Seal keeping the dark-touched at bay has fallen. They will return to this world with a vengeance."

I sighed and held my hand to my forehead. Thousands of voices tried to speak to me at once, and I had to focus to fight them back. I started to say something else, but Gwynn ap Nudd's voice drew my attention.

"Hern," Glenn stared wide-eyed at the ruins before us and his voice broke into a growl. "What have you done?"

"I have done what you would not." Hern let the blade of his axe settle over his shoulder. "I have brought Faerie to the world above."

Some of the Fae began to square off once more. Others shied away from the tension rising between their leaders. Gwynn Ap Nudd stood in the center on one side. Hern stood opposite.

"You are marked traitor," Glenn said. "The sentence is death."

Hern gave one, sharp shake of his head. "It is you who has betrayed the Fae. You thought to lock us away and forget about your own people. We will rule this world as we were meant to."

"Fool! Anyone in Falias is now lost to the Abyss. Have we not lost enough lives to this pointless war? Your soldiers are leaving the field. Without them you cannot hope to defeat us all. You will die for this, Hern, but I have seen enough death today. Leave."

Hern took a hesitant step backwards. His remaining forces looked at each other, and as soon as Hern had that single moment of hesitation, their lines broke.

I sighed and cursed in relief as the Unseelie Fae trickled away from the battlefield. A few headed into the ruins of Falias. A few vanished. Very few stayed at Hern's side.

"Leave," Glenn said, and his voice deepened and grew in that one syllable. It echoed off the hills around us and returned louder than it had started.

Hern turned slowly, and then marched deliberately away from our line.

Something made a keening cry beside me and I turned to find Vicky curled up on the ground, trembling. I scooped her up and held her as her arms wrapped around my neck. "They aren't dead, Damian."

"What?" I asked. I ran my hand over her head.

She pulled her face away from my shoulder and looked at me. "I pulled them through the Abyss. I could feel them. They're in our world now."

Glenn's focus changed from Hern to Vicky. "That's not possible."

At the same time as he spoke, a door creaked open on an impossibly thin, broken spiral tower. A Fae with large black eyes in a pale face stuck his head out. He gestured back inside the building as a smaller Fae, a child I thought, tried to look out the door beside him.

Both figures vanished back into the building.

"Gods," Glenn said. He looked back to Vicky. "Thank you, child. It is good to have some small joy today." He looked back to me before a fairy grabbed him from behind and spun him around.

Cara stood there, her armor bloodied and cracked. "Are you okay?" she asked, looking Glenn over. Her eyes paused at the wound in his chest.

"Shallow," he said. "I am fine."

I raised my eyebrows as Cara grabbed either side of Glenn's head, leaned forward, and kissed him. It was not a chaste kiss. It was full of passion, and I had to fight not to let my jaw hang open. Cara was one of the most faithful people I knew, which meant …

"That's your *husband?*" I said, unable to keep a squeak out of my voice. Cara. Glenn's wife? Foster. His right hand man? I had a sinking feeling our living arrangements had nothing to do with chance.

"Certainly explains some things," Zola said, tamping her cane on the scorched earth.

"Quiet you," Cara said, pulling away from Glenn. "Falias is truly here then?"

Glenn nodded.

"Do we know how much of it?"

Glenn sighed and looked to the east. "All of it."

Cara's bloody hand massaged her forehead, leaving a streak of red behind as she frowned.

"Falias is a huge city," Glenn said. "Its ruins will stretch from here through the coast."

I thought I was going to puke. "You mean, everything from here to there is …"

"Destroyed," Glenn said, closing his eyes at the word. "I fear some of your cities have been replaced by our own."

"All those people," I said. "What happened to them?"

Glenn met my eyes as Vicky buried her head in my shoulder again. "You already know."

Distantly, it felt like thousands of voices screamed in my mind. As fast as they'd started, the sounds faded to a whisper and then to silence. I shook my head and stared at the ruins of Falias. Lost souls still flickered and glided through the air between the towers and smaller stone structures.

Aideen sat beside Foster. I wasn't sure when she'd joined us, but the condition of my mind made it easy to miss things.

"So much death," Aideen said, crossing her hands between her bloodied knees.

Cara pulled the younger fairy up to her feet.

Aideen raised her eyes to Cara briefly, but then her gaze locked onto Foster. The moonlight warped in his dented armor and his torn golden mail. A smear of crusted, dried blood hid whatever damage his right leg had sustained, and one of his wings hung limp, nearly torn off. Foster's mouth tightened into a line, and his forehead creased. I watched as he slowly lined up his sword with the sheath at his side and slammed it home.

The metal rang through the quiet night as his eyes lifted to Gwynn ap Nudd.

"You could have prevented this, King." Foster's voice was so full of venom I almost took a step backwards. "Do not lead us into the Abyss. We won't go quietly."

He held his arm out to Aideen. They walked together, arm

in arm, into the ruins of Falias.

Gwynn ap Nudd watched them leave in silence.

✦   ✦   ✦

MOST OF THE battlefield emptied after Hern's departure. Only a few of us remained.

I crossed my arms as a silent darkness overtook the crater once more. "I can't believe Glenn left."

"There will be more fighting in Faerie," Cara said. She inspected the results of her healing on the Old Man's wounds. "Now we know what Hern is capable of. Glenn must protect Faerie."

"The world is changed," Aeros said, settling himself on the edge of the crater beside Vicky and Happy. "Hern destroyed a seeing stone in the battle between you and Anubis."

"Christ," the Old Man said. He ran a shaky hand through his hair. Blood still covered his body, a terrifying effect when combined with his scars.

"You understand what that means?" Zola asked.

The Old Man nodded. We all stared into the crater as the conversation continued.

"What's it mean?" Sam asked as she walked up behind us with Vik. Jasper sat on her shoulder, just an innocuous little fur ball.

"A moment, please."

I turned to see who spoke. I couldn't help but smile as Hugh and Alan walked up to us. Wahya and Haka were with them, talking animatedly with Carter and Maggie.

"Hugh," I said.

He extended his arm to exchange grips. Recent scars and

blood were obvious across his entire forearm. I slammed my arm into his, and then did the same with Alan.

"Good to see you alive," Alan said. "I had my doubts I'd be seeing anyone alive after this."

"I know," I said. I couldn't help but stare at him, the boy that Philip had rescued so very long ago.

"What?" Alan asked.

"Nothing," I said, shaking my head.

I raised my eyebrows when Maggie hugged me.

"You did great, Damian."

"I didn't do much."

She frowned at me and then looked at Hugh.

The wolf shook his head slightly. I wondered why, but there was more to worry about at that moment. Carter gave me a brief nod, and Haka waved, but both kept talking to Wahya. The golden werewolf was smiling.

Vik and Dominic stood beside Edgar on the opposite edge of the crater when I turned back.

"Vassili is gone," Vik said.

"At least we know who our enemy is," I said.

"Our enemies are many."

I nodded.

"I am sorry, Zola," Hugh said. "Please continue." He projected his voice enough to silence the conversations around the crater.

"The world of the Fae is no longer hidden," Zola said. Her voice was quiet, but the meaning behind her words struck like lightning. "Humanity will not come to us with open arms."

"Not when their first encounter with Faerie cost millions of lives," Edgar said.

"Millions?" I said quietly. I had no words.

Edgar nodded slowly. "Millions."

"They will come for us," Zola said. "Some of us can hide, as we seem normal."

Sam snorted.

"Or normal enough, Samantha," Zola said with a small smile. "Others, like some Fae. They are different, and Ah think we all know how well humanity deals with things that are different."

"They go to war," Edgar said.

Foster and Aideen slowly walked out of the golden glow of Falias. She leaned on his arm, and I could see his damaged wing had been repaired.

The reality of Zola's words hit me at that moment. The entire world had been affected by the seeing stone. Every commoner on earth would be able to see the Fae. See Foster and Aideen walking through the wrecked city. See Aeros sitting on the edge of a crater. They would see everyone.

"But Foster's wings," I said.

"We can hide our wings," Cara said. "It was not so long ago Faerie was not entirely hidden from the world. We have not forgotten how to hide."

I stared at Foster, and Foster stared back. Even if you couldn't see his wings, his face would stand out. How could you hide the angular features and sharp ears? He was seven feet tall when he wasn't small, and now people could see him when he was small too. They could always see him.

My eyes trailed back to Zola. Her eyes locked onto mine.

"You begin to understand, boy. The world is changed."

"What now?" I asked.

"For now," Zola said, "we go home. Hard times lie in wait for the world. We must be prepared to help."

CHAPTER FORTY-ONE

I BLINKED AS I stood at the saloon-style doors in the middle of the Double D. Two men in military fatigues paid rapt attention to the man speaking to them. One of them even took notes.

Frank's silver hair was cut short, almost military, and the light casting part of his face in shadow made me realize he'd lost even more weight than I'd thought. He pointed to the north, and I heard him say werewolves.

I pushed through the doors, Bubbles and Peanut trotting along behind me.

The man taking notes nodded. "The locals said this was the place to go."

"We'll help where we can," Frank said.

Bubbles let out a quiet growl. Both the men took half a step back when they saw the bristly green cu siths.

"What *are* those?" the younger, bearded man said.

"They're harmless," Frank said. He paused, and reevaluated his statement. "They're usually harmless."

I walked closer to the trio. "Hello." Bubbles stayed at my heel while Peanut bumped up against Frank.

"Evening," the older man said. I glanced at his uniform. He didn't have any rank or identification.

"Who are you?" I asked, cutting right through the bullshit.

"If I had to guess," Frank said, "my money is on Rangers."

The two men stared blankly at Frank.

"Special recon," Frank said, raising one of his bushy eyebrows. "Sent to find out if we're a threat or a potential ally?"

"I'm not saying you're right," the bearded man said, "and I'm not saying you're wrong, but what in the hell gives you that idea?"

"I was an Army brat," Frank said. "My father was stationed at Hunter for a few years."

"Ranger?" the bearded man asked.

Frank shook his head. "Major in the Air Force."

The two men looked at each other, and the older man nodded before he spoke. "We're recon," he said. He didn't elaborate further, and Frank didn't push him.

"The sign out front," the bearded man said. "It's rather conspicuous."

"It didn't used to be," I said. "Before the whole world was … gifted with Sight, commoners couldn't read it."

"Handy," the man said.

Bubbles crept forward, sniffing as she went. Her tail popped up and down as she bumped her nose against the bearded man's hand. He reached out slowly, and started scratching her behind the ears.

"That's a huge dog."

I almost started to explain what Bubbles actually was, but I just said "Yeah."

"So that video really was real?" he asked Frank.

"Yes."

"I appreciate you being so open with us."

Foster walked up from the back at his full seven-foot height, wings extended. The two men didn't even flinch, so I was pretty sure they'd already met the fairy.

"Your message has been sent," he said. "It will take some time, but it will arrive."

"We appreciate your assistance, and I will be sure our allies are aware of it. Take care of yourselves. Strange days lie ahead."

"You don't know the half of it," I said under my breath as they walked through the front door. I turned to Foster. "What was the message?"

"Seems the military wants to meet Gwynn ap Nudd," Foster said, his eyes following the two rangers as they walked past the front of the store. "I can't imagine that being a good idea."

"What did Cara say?" I figured she'd be the one taking the message back to Faerie if anyone was going to.

"She's going to talk to Glenn," Foster said. "Aideen went with her."

"Humanity just had a blindfold torn off its eyes," Frank said. He turned to look at me. "They're going to be trigger happy. This could get bad, very, very fast."

"It's already bad," I said.

Frank nodded in agreement.

"What did you have to tell them?" Foster asked.

"Not too much," Frank said. "I just confirmed what they'd already seen on the video. They were happy to hear the blood mage was dead." He frowned slightly. "I didn't tell them who Ashley is. They seemed keenly interested in her."

I stared at Frank. I was so used to his bumbling, nice guy persona, I sometimes forgot he'd been a damned arms dealer. One does not last long as an arms dealer by being stupid.

"What about the Pit?" Frank asked.

"Taken care of."

"They found Vassili?"

I pursed my lips. "Allow me to rephrase. Partially taken care of."

Foster laughed. Peanut hopped around in a circle and bumped up against the fairy. "They raised Vik to be the new Lord," he said as he scratched Peanut's ruff.

"Good," Frank said. "Vik will be great for them."

Foster and I both nodded.

"I just want Sam to be safe," Frank said, keeping his eyes toward the front of the shop.

"We'll make damn sure of that," I said.

Bubbles growled beside me. I smiled at the cu sith and scratched her ears. I frowned as her tongue shot up over her head and wrapped itself around my wrist when I tried to stop petting her.

✦ ✦ ✦

I PAUSED WHEN I reached my '32 Ford. A patrol of National Guardsmen crossed the street nearby. They'd become a common sight since returning from Gettysburg. One of the men at the front raised his hand in greeting, and I waved. They'd all been cordial enough since being deployed, but I worried what their presence meant for the future.

I took a deep breath, closed the door, and my car rumbled to life. I wanted to see a bear about a girl, and it wasn't long before I pulled off at Hampton and crossed over into Forest Park.

I left the SUV in a questionably legal parking spot and stared at the birdcage. There was a man there, talking to Vicky.

"Damian!" Vicky said when she saw me approaching. She ran up and hugged my ribs half to death.

I realized the man was Mike the Demon when he turned around.

Vicky leaned against my side while Mike walked closer. He held out his hand and we traded grips.

"You did well," he said.

I shook my head. "We failed. That was disastrous."

You are wrong, Happy said. The bear faded into view, trundling away from the birdcage.

Mike watched, unmoved as the bear became the man.

"You are wrong," Shiawase said. "There is still a world to fight for. We lost millions, yes, but do not forget the billions we saved."

"The bear's right," Mike said. "Ezekiel had the power to reshape the world as he wanted it."

"You knew he wasn't a bear?" I asked, completely changing the subject.

Vicky giggled and Mike laughed. A small ghost flickered into being beside Mike.

"I may have spoiled the surprise," the little necromancer said.

"Apparently she has known for over a century," Mike said. "It just 'wasn't important.' " He raised an eyebrow.

"What brings you here?" Shiawase asked, turning to me.

I shrugged. "Just driving. Saw the exit and thought I'd stop."

Vicky pulled on my arm. "You just wanted to see us."

I flashed her a smile and squeezed her shoulders. "You know it, kiddo. And ... I talked to Glenn about the Burning

Lands."

"Really?" Mike asked as he crossed his frighteningly muscular arms. "This just *happened* to come up?"

"Yep," I said. "I hear it's a good hunting season for devils."

"Damian," Mike said as he glanced at Vicky. His eyes
snapped back to me. "Do you mean?"

"Yes, I do," I said. "Interested?"

Shiawase chuckled and Mike smiled.

"Crazy as ever." Mike knuckled his eyes. "Let's talk about
that later."

"A wise idea," Shiawase said. "Do not doubt that we are
with you, but for now, let us enjoy our company."

I stayed for a while, talking to the bear, the ghost, the demon, and the child I would do anything to save from becoming
the Destroyer.

✦   ✦   ✦

EVEN WALKING ACROSS my own street, I saw another small
patrol of guardsmen standing around what looked to be a
personnel carrier.

I sighed and slid down a short embankment before splashing into the shallows of the Missouri River. I ran my thumb
over the blue obsidian disc in my hand, sat it beneath the water,
and waited. The river began to bubble a minute later, and
Nixie's face rose up through the dark waters.

"Damian," she said, the smile on her face a welcome sight.

"I saw the news," I said. "They're calling you heroes."

Nixie nodded. "It is … odd. Some good has come of this.
Several more undines have deserted the Queen."

"Why?" I asked.

"The Queen wanted the tsunami to make landfall, to kill as many commoners as it could."

"I've seen the photos with the tsunami. It was beautiful, Nix."

"It was," she said. "There are few beautiful things in the world that are not capable of great destruction."

I dragged my fingers from my nose to my chin as I blew out a breath. "How are your people?"

"I am safe, Damian. The Queen is not so dimwitted as to attack us now."

"Am I that obvious?"

She laughed, and a genuine smile crossed her translucent face. "Always."

"What are you doing tonight?" I asked.

"Planning for a new fortress," Nixie said. "Alexandra has an idea to build a stronghold in the Burning Lands."

I raised my eyebrows.

Nixie nodded. "It is insane, but it does have merit."

"Any dinner plans?"

"No. Why would you ask?"

"Well, Frank's watching the shop. Foster's watching the cu siths. Ashley is lording over some huge gathering of every coven from here to Canada. Sam's—"

"Damian!"

"Yeah?"

"Why would you ask?"

"Oh, that." I smiled and bent down to pick up the blue obsidian disc.

"What are you doing?"

I reached over my shoulder and pulled the hand of glory

out of my backpack.

"Damian?"

"I'll be there in five." I winked at Nixie as I intertwined my fingers with Gaia's and stepped into the Abyss.

Note from Eric R. Asher

Thank you for spending time with the misfits! I'm blown away by the fantastic reader response to this series, and am so grateful to you all. The next book of Damian's misadventures is called Destroyer Rising, and it's available now.

If you'd like an email when each new book releases, sign up for my mailing list (www.ericrasher.com). Emails only go out about once per month and your information is closely guarded by hungry cu siths.

Also, follow me on BookBub (bookbub.com/authors/eric-r-asher), and you'll always get an email for special sales.

Thanks for reading!
Eric

Please enjoy the following excerpt from

Destroyer Rising

The Vesik Series, book #5

By Eric R. Asher

It's been three years since we failed Vicky, the child once known as Elizabeth Gray. Three years she's lived as something not quite alive, but far from dead. Her path grows darker, even as she spreads light and hope through a tortured world. The Destroyer has come to claim her, and I can't fail her again. I won't. Elizabeth's fate lies in the Burning Lands, and we will storm the gates.

I T WAS THE nightmares. That was the worst part of having a million screaming voices inside my head, because they weren't really nightmares. They were the dreams and hopes of a million lost souls. They took over what little sleep I could get, replacing my thoughts with their own. Every night filled me with visions of lives and homes and cities that no longer existed, annihilated in Hern's gambit. I could not escape them.

I left another dreamscape behind as my eyes flew open. The pounding in my chest wasn't my own fear, not really; it was the fear of a father's final moments as he watched a blinding light swallow his family before the world went white.

"You okay?"

I glanced up at the perilously stacked old books on the table beside me. Foster sat on top of them, his brow furrowed and his black and white Atlas moth wings slowly flexing behind him.

"Yeah."

"It's been weeks," he said. "I thought it would get better by now."

"You didn't tell me Cara was married to Glenn, Foster."

The fairy looked away.

"And don't tell me he couldn't have stopped it." I narrowed my eyes. "What did you expect me to do? Just forget it happened? Just forget how half the people I trust with my life conveniently forgot to mention their relation to Glenn?"

"I meant the nightmares," Foster said, shifting on his perch, "not the rise of Falias."

I grimaced and leaned forward, rubbing my eyes with the palms of my hands.

"Have you found anything in the older texts?" he asked.

"No. I've been trying to find a way to free Vicky before … you know."

"You might need to help yourself before you can help her. How can you think clearly if you have a thousand voices in your head at once, and no sleep?"

I reached out and dragged the Black Book across the oak coffee table. It was an old tome, dripping with forbidden things and rituals I wished I could un-see, but it also seemed the most likely place to find out more about Vicky's fate. Foster was right, I wasn't going to be sleeping any more, so I might as well get more research done.

"I talked to Sam," Foster said. "They still haven't found Vassili. There were traces of him in Phoenix, but the trail went cold."

I stared at the book.

"You can't hide up here forever," Foster said. "Mom will be pissed if you don't get over it soon."

"Yeah, right."

I looked up when the air moved beside me, and I watched Foster glide down the aisle of books and vanish into the stairwell. He was still my friend, goddammit. I just needed some proof he wasn't waiting to ambush me with something even more dangerous than Cara had: Gwynn Ap Nudd, the Fae King, husband to one of my grandfather-clock-dwelling fairies. Foster was her son, and he hadn't told me.

I ground my teeth and turned the page of the Black Book. The text on the tanned parchment wavered for a moment before coming back into focus. Several pages were like that, and each fell after a passage about the Burning Lands. Every time it felt like I was getting closer, a pale symbol marked one of those pages. Koda thought it could be an old code, and possibly a map to a dark thing known as the Book that Bleeds. That was months past, though, and none of us had found mention of it. Not in the vampires' archives, not in my collection, not anywhere. Something was hidden inside that tome, and if it could help Vicky, I had to figure out what.

Destroyer Rising

The Vesik Series, book #5

Available now!

Also by Eric R. Asher

Keep track of Eric's new releases by receiving an email on release day. It's fast and easy to sign up for Eric's mailing list, and you'll also get an ebook copy of the subscriber exclusive anthology, *Whispers of War*.

Go here to get started: www.ericrasher.com

The Steamborn Trilogy:

Steamborn

Steamforged

Steamsworn

The Vesik Series:

(Recommended for Ages 17+)

Days Gone Bad

Wolves and the River of Stone

Winter's Demon

This Broken World

Destroyer Rising

Rattle the Bones

Witch Queen's War – coming fall 2017*

*Want to receive an email on the day this book releases? Sign up for Eric's mailing list.

www.ericrasher.com

Mason Dixon – Monster Hunter:

Episode One

Episode Two – coming summer 2017*

*Want to receive an email on the day this book releases? Sign up for Eric's mailing list.

About the Author

Eric is a former bookseller, cellist, and comic seller currently living in Saint Louis, Missouri. A lifelong enthusiast of books, music, toys, and games, he discovered a love for the written word after being dragged to the library by his parents at a young age. When he is not writing, you can usually find him reading, gaming, or buried beneath a small avalanche of Transformers. For more about Eric, see: www.ericrasher.com

Enjoy this book? You can make a big difference.

Reviews are the most powerful tools I have when it comes to getting attention for my books. I don't have a huge marketing budget like some New York publishers, but I have something even better.

A committed and loyal bunch of readers.

Honest reviews help bring my books to the attention of other readers.

If you've enjoyed this book, I would be very grateful if you could take a minute to leave a review on the platform of your choice. It can be as short as you like. Thank you for spending time with Damian and the misfits.

Connect with Eric R. Asher Online:

Twitter: @ericrasher

Instagram: @ericrasher

Facebook: EricRAsher

www.ericrasher.com

eric@ericrasher.com

Made in the USA
Monee, IL
05 October 2022

15312485R00208